Praise for *Intere*

"Eloquent, pinpoint prose . . . Lee's writing speaks from the intellect but knows intimately the ways of the heart."

—*O, The Oprah Magazine*

"Accomplished . . . all [stories] are distinguished by lucid sensual language."

—*San Francisco Chronicle*

"Refreshing and amusing . . . these interesting women are both jaded and triumphant, wearily accustomed not only to defeat, but to prevailing as well."

—*Newsday*

"Andrea Lee spins savvy stories from around the globe."

—*More*

"Ms. Lee's prose is as clear-headed as her characters, who make great leaps between oceans and men only to 'ponder the wonderful seductiveness of action, of clean defiant acts; and the tedium of consequences.'"

—*The Economist*

"The stories are full of tension . . . [they] provide instant and sophisticated gratification."

—*Publishers Weekly*

"Lee is at her best detailing encounters between brash New World women and sophisticated Old World men, but she is also good at probing complicated relationships between women. . . . Lee is a polished writer."

—*Library Journal*

"Each droll, masterfully crafted, electrifyingly perceptive, and wryly cosmopolitan and epicurean story deftly decodes the tricky dynamics of sexual, racial, and cultural trespass."

—*Booklist*

"A collective voice of very independent, self-defining, and interesting women who may be 'far from their own culture, but not out of their depths.' Their voice and their stories make this a book not to be missed."

—*The Bloomsbury Review*

"Lee easily enthralls with the smallest description or observation, and her knowledge of this lifestyle is intoxicatingly thorough. . . . Lee's pinpoint accuracy for the right word and perfect tone bring a universal truth to these stories."

—*Kirkus Reviews*

Also by Andrea Lee

INTERESTING WOMEN

Stories

Andrea Lee

SCRIBNER
New York   London   Toronto   Sydney   New Delhi

Scribner
An Imprint of Simon & Schuster, Inc.
1230 Avenue of the Americas
New York, NY 10020

This Scribner trade paperback edition January 2022

SCRIBNER and design are registered trademarks of The Gale Group, Inc., used under license by Simon & Schuster, Inc., the publisher of this work.

For information about special discounts for bulk purchases, please contact Simon & Schuster Special Sales at 1-866-506-1949 or business@simonandschuster.com.

The Simon & Schuster Speakers Bureau can bring authors to your live event. For more information or to book an event, contact the Simon & Schuster Speakers Bureau at 1-866-248-3049 or visit our website at www.simonspeakers.com.

Manufactured in the United States of America

1   3   5   7   9   10   8   6   4   2

Library of Congress Control Number: 2001048228

ISBN 978-1-9821-7949-6
ISBN 978-1-9821-7950-2 (ebook)

Some of the stories in this work were previously published in *The New Yorker* and *Zoetrope*. "Anthropology" was originally published in *The Oxford American*.

To Alexandra,
who merits her middle name,
and to Ruggero and Charles,
i miei uomini interessanti.

Pinkerton (con franchezza):
Dovunque al mondo lo Yankee vagabondo si gode e traffica
sprezzando i rischi. Affonda l'ancora alla ventura.

—Luigi Illica, Giuseppe Giacosa, *Madama Butterfly*

Contents

The Birthday Present

A cellular phone is ringing, somewhere in Milan. Ariel knows that much. Or does she? The phone could be trilling its electronic morsel of Mozart or Bacharach in a big vulgar villa with guard dogs and closed-circuit cameras on the bosky shores of Lake Como. Or in an overpriced hotel suite in Portofino. Or why not in the Aeolian Islands, or on Ischia, or Sardinia? It's late September, and all over the Mediterranean the yachts of politicians and arms manufacturers and pan-Slavic gangsters are still snuggled side by side in the indulgent golden light of harbors where the calendars of the toiling masses mean nothing. The truth is that the phone could be ringing anywhere in the world where there are rich men.

But Ariel prefers to envision Milan, which is the city nearest the Brianza countryside, where she lives with her family in a restored farmhouse. And she tries hard to imagine the tiny phone lying on a table in an apartment not unlike the one she shared fifteen years ago in Washington with a couple of other girls who were seniors at Georgetown. The next step up from a dorm, that is—like a set for a sitcom about young professionals whose sex lives, though kinky, have an endearing adolescent gaucheness. It would be too disturbing to think that she is telephoning a bastion of contemporary Milanese luxury, like the apartments of some of her nouveau-riche

1

friends: gleaming marble, bespoke mosaics, boiserie stripped from defunct châteaux, a dispiriting sense of fresh money spread around like butter on toast.

Hmmm—and if it *were* a place like that? There would be, she supposes, professional modifications. Mirrors: that went without saying, as did a bed the size of a handball court, with a nutria cover and conveniently installed handcuffs. Perhaps a small dungeon off the dressing room? At any rate, a bathroom with Moroccan hammam fixtures and a bidet made from an antique baptismal font. Acres of closets, with garter belts and crotchless panties folded and stacked with fetishistic perfection. And boxes of specialty condoms, divided, perhaps, by design and flavor. Are they ordered by the gross? From a catalog? But now Ariel retrieves her thoughts, because someone picks up the phone.

"Pronto?" The voice is young and friendly and hasty.

"Is this Beba?" Ariel asks in her correct but heavy Italian, from which she has never attempted to erase the American accent.

"Yes," says the voice, with a merry air of haste.

"I'm a friend of Flavio Costaldo's and he told me that you and your friend—your colleague—might be interested in spending an evening with my husband. It's a birthday present."

When a marriage lingers at a certain stage—the not uncommon plateau where the two people involved have nothing to say to each other—it is sometimes still possible for them to live well together. To perform generous acts that do not, exactly, signal desperation. Flavio hadn't meant to inspire action when he suggested that Ariel give her husband, Roberto, *"una fanciulla"*—a young girl—for his fifty-fifth birthday. He'd meant only to irritate, as usual. Flavio is

Roberto's best friend, a sixty-year-old Calabrian film producer who five or six years ago gave up trying to seduce Ariel, and settled for the alternative intimacy of tormenting her subtly whenever they meet. Ariel is a tall, fresh-faced woman of thirty-seven, an officer's child who grew up on army bases around the world, and whose classic American beauty has an air of crisp serviceability that—she is well aware—is a major flaw: in airports, she is sometimes accosted by travelers who are convinced that she is there in a professional capacity. She is always patient at parties when the inevitable pedant expounds on how unsuitable it is for a tall, rather slow-moving beauty to bear the name of the most volatile of sprites. Her own opinion—resolutely unvoiced, like so many of her thoughts—is that, besides being ethereal, Shakespeare's Ariel was mainly competent and faithful. As she herself is by nature: a rarity anywhere in the world, but particularly in Italy. She is the ideal wife—second wife—for Roberto, who is an old-fashioned domestic tyrant. And she is the perfect victim for Flavio. When he made the suggestion, they were sitting in the garden of his fourth wife's sprawling modern villa in a gated community near Como, and both of their spouses were off at the other end of the terrace, looking at samples of glass brick. But Ariel threw him handily off-balance by laughing and taking up the idea. As she did so, she thought of how much affection she'd come to feel for good old Flavio since her early days in Italy, when she'd reserved for him the ritual loathing of a new wife for her husband's best friend. Nowadays she was a compassionate observer of his dawning old age and its accoutrements, the karmic doom of any superannuated playboy: tinted aviator bifocals and reptilian complexion; a rich, tyrannical wife who imposed a strict diet of fidelity and bland foods; a little brown address book full of famous pals who no longer phoned. That afternoon, Ariel for the first time had the satisfaction of watching his composure crumble when she asked him sweetly to get her the number of the best call girl in Milan.

"You're not serious," he sputtered. "Ariel, *cara*, you've known me long enough to know I was joking. You aren't—"

"Don't go into that nice-girl, bad-girl Latin thing, Flavio. It's a little dated, even for you."

"I was going to say only that you aren't an Italian wife, and there are nuances you'll never understand, even if you live here for a hundred years."

"Oh, please, spare me the anthropology," said Ariel. It was pleasant to have rattled Flavio to this extent. The idea of the *fanciulla*, to which she had agreed on a mischievous impulse unusual for her, suddenly grew more concrete. "Just get me the number."

Flavio was silent for a few minutes, his fat, sun-speckled hands wreathing his glass of *limoncello*. "You're still sleeping together?" he asked suddenly. "Is it all right?"

"Yes. And yes."

"*Allora, che diavolo stai facendo?* What the hell are you doing? He's faithful to you, you know. It's an incredible thing for such a womanizer; you know about his first marriage. With you there have been a few little lapses, but nothing important."

Ariel nodded, not even the slightest bit offended. She knew about those lapses, had long before factored them into her expectations about the perpetual foreign life she had chosen. Nothing he said, however, could distract her from her purpose.

Flavio sighed and cast his eyes heavenward. "*Va bene;* Okay. But you have to be very careful," he said, shooting a glance down the terrace at his ever-vigilant wife, with her gold sandals and anorexic body. After a minute, he added cryptically, "Well, at least you're Catholic. That's something."

So, thanks to Flavio's little brown book, Ariel is now talking to Beba. Beba—a toddler's nickname. Ex-model in her twenties. Brazilian, but not a transsexual. Tall. Dark. Works in tandem with a Russian blonde. "The two of them are so gorgeous that when you see them it's as if you have entered another sphere, a paradise where everything is simple and divine," said Flavio, waxing lyrical during the series of planning phone calls he and Ariel shared, cozy conversations that made his wife suspicious and gave him the renewed pleasure of annoying Ariel. "The real danger is that Roberto might fall in love with one of them," he remarked airily, during one of their chats. "No, probably not—he's too stingy."

In contrast, it is easy talking to Beba. "How many men?" Beba asks, as matter-of-factly as a caterer. There is a secret happiness in her voice that tempts Ariel to investigate, to talk more than she normally would. It is an impulse she struggles to control. She knows from magazine articles that, like everyone else, prostitutes simply want to get their work done without a fuss.

"Just my husband," Ariel says, feeling a calm boldness settle over her.

"And you?"

Flavio has said that Beba is a favorite among rich Milanese ladies who are fond of extracurricular romps. Like the unlisted addresses where they buy their cashmere and have their abortions, she is top-of-the-line and highly private. Flavio urged Ariel to participate and gave a knowing chuckle when she refused. The chuckle meant that, like everyone else, he thinks Ariel is a prude. She isn't—though the fact is obscured by her fatal air of efficiency, by her skill at writing out place cards, making homemade tagliatelle better than her

Italian mother-in-law, and raising bilingual daughters. But no one realizes that over the years she has also invested that efficiency in a great many amorous games with the experienced and demanding Roberto. On their honeymoon, in Bangkok, they'd spent one night with two polite teenagers selected from a numbered lineup behind a large glass window. But that was twelve years ago, and although Ariel is not clear about her motives for giving this birthday present, she sees with perfect feminine good sense that she is not meant to be onstage with a pair of young whores who look like angels.

The plan is that Ariel will make a date with Roberto for a dinner in town, and that instead of Ariel, Beba and her colleague will meet him. After dinner the three of them will go to the minuscule apartment near Corso Venezia that Flavio keeps as his sole gesture of independence from his wife. Ariel has insisted on dinner, though Flavio was against it, and Beba has told her, with a tinge of amusement, that it will cost a lot more. Most clients, she says, don't request dinner. Why Ariel should insist that her husband sit around chummily with two hookers, ordering antipasto, first and second courses, and dessert is a mystery, even to Ariel. Yet she feels that it is the proper thing to do. That's the way she wants it, and she can please herself, can't she?

As they finish making the arrangements, Ariel is embarrassed to hear herself say, "I do hope you two girls will make things very nice. My husband is a wonderful man."

And Beba, who is clearly used to talking to wives, assures her, with phenomenal patience, that she understands.

As Ariel puts down the phone, it rings again, and of course it is her mother, calling from the States. "Well, you're finally free," says her mother, who seems to be chewing something, probably a low-calorie bagel, since it is 8:00 A.M. in Bethesda. "Who on earth were you talking to for so long?"

"I was planning Roberto's birthday party," Ariel says glibly. "We're inviting some people to dinner at the golf club."

"Golf! I've never understood how you can live in Italy and be so suburban. Golf in the hills of Giotto!"

"The hills of Giotto are in Umbria, Mom. This is Lombardy, so we're allowed to play golf."

Ariel can envision her mother, unlike Beba, with perfect clarity: tiny; wiry, as if the muscles under her porcelain skin were steel guitar strings. Sitting bolt upright in her condominium kitchen, dressed in the chic, funky uniform of black jeans and cashmere T-shirt she wears to run the business she dreamed up: an improbably successful fleet of suburban messengers on Vespas, which she claims was inspired by her favorite film, *Roman Holiday*. Coffee and soy milk in front of her, quartz-and-silver earrings quivering, one glazed fingernail tapping the counter as her eyes probe the distance over land and ocean toward her only daughter.

What would she say if she knew of the previous call? Almost certainly, Ariel thinks, she would be pleased with an act indicative of the gumption she finds constitutionally lacking in her child, whose lamentable conventionality has been a byword since Ariel was small. She herself is living out a green widowhood with notable style, and dating a much younger lobbyist, whose sexual tastes she would be glad to discuss, girl to girl, with her daughter. But she is loath to shock Ariel.

With her Italian son-in-law, Ariel's mother flirts shamelessly, the established joke being that she should have got there first. It's a joke that never fails to pull a grudging smile from Roberto, and it goes over well with *his* mother, too: another glamorous widow, an intellectual from Padua who regards her daughter-in-law with the condescending solicitude one might reserve for a prize broodmare. For years, Ariel has lived in the dust stirred up by these two dynamos, and it looks as if her daughters, as they grow older—they are eight and ten—are beginning to side with their grandmothers. Not one of these females, it seems, can forgive Ariel for being herself. So Ariel keeps quiet about her new acquaintance with Beba, not from any prudishness but as a powerful amulet. The way, at fourteen, she hugged close the knowledge that she was no longer a virgin.

"Is anything the matter?" asks her mother. "Your voice sounds strange. You and Roberto aren't fighting, are you?" She sighs. "I have told you a hundred times that these spoiled Italian men are naturally promiscuous, so they need a woman who commands interest. You need to be effervescent, on your toes, a little bit slutty, too, if you'll pardon me, darling. Otherwise, they just go elsewhere."

Inspired by her own lie, Ariel actually gives a dinner at the golf club, two days before Roberto's birthday. The clubhouse is a refurbished nineteenth-century castle built by an industrialist, and the terrace where the party is held overlooks the pool and an artificial lake. Three dozen of their friends gather in the late September chill to eat a faux-rustic seasonal feast, consisting of polenta and *Fassone* beefsteaks, and the pungent yellow mushrooms called *funghi reali*, all covered with layers of shaved Alba truffles. Ariel is proud of the meal, planned with the club chef in less time than she spent talking to Beba on the phone.

Roberto is a lawyer, chief counsel for a centrist political party that is moderately honest as Italian political parties go, and his friends all have the same gloss of material success and moderate honesty. Though the group is an international one—many of the men have indulged in American wives as they have in German cars—the humor is typically bourgeois Italian. That is: gossipy, casually cruel, and—in honor of Roberto—all about sex and potency. Somebody passes around an article from *L'Espresso* which celebrates men over fifty with third and fourth wives in their twenties, and everyone glances slyly at Ariel. And Roberto's two oldest friends, Flavio and Michele, appear, bearing a large gift-wrapped box. It turns out to hold not a midget stripper, as someone guesses, but a smaller box, and a third, and a fourth and fifth, until, to cheers, Roberto unwraps a tiny package of Viagra.

Standing over fifty-five smoking candles in a huge pear-and-chocolate torte, he thanks his friends with truculent grace. Everyone laughs and claps—Roberto Furioso, as his nickname goes, is famous for his ornery disposition. He doesn't look at Ariel, who is leading the applause in her role as popular second wife and good sport. She doesn't have to look at him to feel his presence, as always, burned into her consciousness. He is a small, charismatic man with a large Greek head, thick, brush-cut black hair turning a uniform steel gray, thin lips hooking downward in an ingrained frown like those of his grandfather, a Sicilian baron. When Ariel met him, a dozen years ago, at the wedding of a distant cousin of hers outside Florence, she immediately recognized the overriding will she had always dreamed of, a force capable of conferring a shape on her own personality. He, prisoner of his desire as surely as she was, looked at this preposterously tall, absurdly placid American beauty as they danced for the third time. And blurted out—a magical phrase that fixed forever the parameters of Ariel's private mythology—"*Tu sai che ti sposerò.* You know I'm going to marry you."

Nowadays Roberto is still *furioso*, but it is at himself for getting old, and at her for witnessing it. So he bullies her, and feels quite justified in doing so. Like all second wives, Ariel was supposed to be a solution, and now she has simply enlarged the problem.

Roberto's birthday begins with blinding sunlight, announcing the brilliant fall weather that arrives when transalpine winds bundle the smog out to sea. The view from Ariel's house on the hill is suddenly endless, as if a curtain had been yanked aside. The steel blue Alps are the first thing she sees through the window at seven-thirty, when her daughters, according to family custom, burst into their parents' bedroom pushing a battered baby carriage with balloons tied to it, and presents inside. Elisa and Cristina, giggling, singing "Happy Birthday," tossing their pretty blunt-cut hair, serene in the knowledge that their irascible father, who loathes sudden awakenings, is putty in their hands. Squeals, kisses, tumbling in the bed, so that Ariel can feel how their cherished small limbs are growing polished, sleeker, more muscular with weekly horseback riding and gymnastics. Bilingual, thanks to their summers in Maryland, they are still more Italian than American; at odd detached moments in her genuinely blissful hours of maternal bustling, Ariel has noticed how, like all other young Italian girls, they exude a precocious maturity. And though they are at times suffocatingly attached to her, there has never been a question about which parent takes precedence. For their father's presents, they have clubbed together to buy from the Body Shop some soap and eye gel and face cream that are made with royal jelly. "To make you look younger, Papa," says Elisa, arriving, as usual, at the painful crux of the matter.

"Are we really going to spend the night at Nonna Silvana's?" Cristina asks Ariel.

"Yes," Ariel replies, feeling a blush rising from under her night-gown. "Yes, because Papa and I are going to dinner in the city."

The girls cheer. They love staying with their Italian grand-mother, who stuffs them with marrons glacés and Kit Kat bars and lets them try on all her Pucci outfits from the sixties.

When breakfast—a birthday breakfast, with chocolate brioche—is finished, and the girls are waiting in the car for her to take them to school, Ariel hands Roberto a small gift-wrapped package. He is on the way out the door, his jovial paternal mask back in its secret compartment. "A surprise," she says. "Don't open it before this evening." He looks it over and shakes it suspiciously. "I hope you didn't go and spend money on something else I don't need," he says. "That party—"

"Oh, you'll find a use for this," says Ariel in the seamlessly cheerful voice she has perfected over the years. Inside the package is a million lire in large bills, and the key to Flavio's apartment, as well as a gorgeous pair of silk-and-lace underpants that Ariel has purchased in a size smaller than she usually wears. There is also a note suggesting that Roberto, like a prince in a fairy tale, should search for the best fit in the company in which he finds himself. The note is witty and slightly obscene, the kind of thing Roberto likes. An elegant, wifely touch for a husband who, like all Italian men, is fussy about small things.

Dropping off the girls at the International School, Ariel runs through the usual catechism about when and where they will be

picked up, reminders about gym clothes, a note to a geography
teacher. She restrains herself from kissing them with febrile intensity, as if she were about to depart on a long journey. Instead she
watches as they disappear into a thicket of coltish legs, quilted navy
blue jackets, giggles and secrets. She waves to other mothers, Italian, American, Swiss: well-groomed women with tragic morning
expressions, looking small inside huge Land Cruisers that could
carry them, if necessary, through Lapland or across the Zambezi.

Ariel doesn't want to talk to anyone this morning, but her ram-
bunctious English friend Carinth nabs her and insists on coffee. The
two women sit in the small *pasticceria* where all the mothers buy their
pastries and chocolates, and Ariel sips barley cappuccino and listens
to Carinth go on about her cystitis. Although Ariel is deeply dis-
tracted, she is damned if she is going to let anything slip, not even to
her loyal friend with the milkmaid's complexion and the lascivious
eyes. Damned if she will turn Roberto's birthday into just another
easily retailed feminine secret. Avoiding temptation, she looks de-
fiantly around the shop at shelves of meringues, marzipan, candied
violets, chocolate chests filled with gilded chocolate cigars, glazed
almonds for weddings and first communions, birthday cakes like
Palm Beach mansions. The smell of sugar is overpowering. And,
for just a second, for the only time all day, her eyes sting with tears.

At home, there are hours to get through. First, she e-mails an
article on a Milanese packaging designer to one of the American
magazines for which she does freelance translations. Then she telephones to cancel her lesson in the neighboring village with an old
artisan who is teaching her to restore antique *papiers peints*, a craft
she loves and at which her large hands are surprisingly skillful.
Then she goes outside to talk to the garden contractors—three
illegal Romanian immigrants who are rebuilding an eroded slope

on the east side of the property. She has to haggle with them, and as she does, the leader, an outrageously handsome boy of twenty, looks her over with insolent admiration. Pretty boys don't go unnoticed by Ariel, who sometimes imagines complicated sex with strangers in uncomfortable public places. But they don't really exist for her, just as the men who flirt with her at parties don't count. Only Roberto exists, which is how it has been since that long-ago third dance, when she drew a circle between the two of them and the rest of the world. This is knowledge that she keeps even from Roberto, because she thinks that it would bore him, along with everyone else. Yet is it really so dull to want only one man, the man one already has?

After the gardeners leave, there is nothing to do—no children to pick up at school and ferry to activities; no homework to help with, no dinner to fix. The dogs are at the vet for a wash and a checkup. Unthinkable to invite Carinth or another friend for lunch; unthinkable, too, to return to work, to go shopping, to watch a video or read a book. No, there is nothing but to accept the fact that for an afternoon she has to be the loneliest woman in the world.

Around three o'clock, she gets in the car and heads along the state highway toward Lake Como, where over the years she has taken so many visiting relatives. She has a sudden desire to see the lovely decaying villas sleeping in the trees, the ten-kilometer expanse of lake stretching to the mountains like a predictable future. But as she drives from Greggio to San Giovanni Canavese, past yellowing cornfields, provincial factories, rural discotheques, and ancient village churches, she understands why she is out here. At roadside clearings strewn with refuse, she sees the usual highway prostitutes waiting for afternoon customers.

Ariel has driven past them for years, on her way to her mother-in-law's house or chauffeuring her daughters to riding lessons. Like everyone else, she has first deplored and then come to terms with the fact that the roadside girls are part of a criminal world so successful and accepted that their slavery has routines like those of factory workers: they are transported to and from their ten-hour shifts by a neat fleet of minivans. They are as much a part of the landscape as toll booths.

First, she sees a brown-haired Albanian girl who doesn't look much older than Elisa, wearing black hot pants and a loose white shirt that she lifts like an ungainly wing and flaps slowly at passing drivers. A Fiat Uno cruising in front of Ariel slows down, makes a sudden U-turn, and heads back toward the girl. A kilometer further on are two Nigerians, one dressed in an electric pink playsuit, sitting waggling her knees on an upended crate, while the other, in a pair of stilt-like platform shoes, stands chatting into a cellular phone. Both are tall, with masses of fake braids, and disconcertingly beautiful. Dark seraphim whose presence at the filthy roadside is a kind of miracle.

Ariel slows down to take a better look at the girl in pink, who offers her a noncommittal stare, with eyes opaque as coffee beans. The two-lane road is deserted, and Ariel actually stops the car for a minute, because she feels attracted by those eyes, suddenly mesmerized by something that recalls the secret she heard in Beba's voice. The secret that seemed to be happiness, but, she realizes now, was something different: a mysterious certitude that draws her like a magnet. She feels absurdly moved—out of control, in fact. As her heart pounds, she realizes that if she let herself go, she would open the car door and crawl toward that flat dark gaze. The girl in pink says something to her companion with the phone, who swivels on the three-inch soles of her shoes to look at Ariel. And Ariel puts her foot on the gas pedal. Ten kilometers down the road, she stops again and yanks out a Kleenex to wipe the film of sweat from her face. The only observation she allows herself as she drives home, recovering her composure, is the thought of how curious it is that all of them are foreigners—herself, Beba, and the girls on the road.

Six o'clock. As she walks into the house, the phone rings, and it is Flavio, who asks how the plot is progressing. Ariel can't conceal her impatience.

"Listen, do you think those girls are going to be on time?"

"As far as I know, they are always punctual," he says. "But I have to go. I'm calling from the car here in the garage, and it's starting to look suspicious."

He hangs up, but Ariel stands with the receiver in her hand, struck by the fact that besides worrying about whether dinner guests, upholsterers, babysitters, restorers of wrought iron, and electricians will arrive on schedule, she now has to concern herself with whether Beba will keep her husband waiting.

Seven-thirty. The thing now is not to answer the phone. If he thinks of her, which is unlikely, Roberto must assume that she is in the car, dressed in one of the discreetly sexy short black suits or dresses she wears for special occasions, her feet in spike heels pressing the accelerator as she speeds diligently to their eight o'clock appointment. He is still in the office, firing off the last frantic fax to Rome, pausing for a bit of ritual abuse aimed at his harassed assistant, Amedeo. Next, he will dash for a pee in his grim brown-marble bathroom: how well she can envision the last, impatient shake of his cock, which is up for an unexpected adventure tonight. He will grab a handful of the chocolates that the doctor has forbidden, and gulp down a paper cup of sugary espresso from the office machine. Then into the shiny late-model Mercedes—a monument, he calls it, with an unusual flash of self-mockery, to the male climacteric. After which, becalmed in the Milan evening traffic, he may call her. Just to make sure she is going to be on time.

Eight-fifteen. She sits at the kitchen table and eats a frugal meal: a plate of rice with cheese and olive oil, a sliced tomato, a glass of water.

The phone rings again. She hesitates, then picks it up.

It is Roberto. *"Allora, sei rimasta a casa,"* he says softly. "So you stayed home."

"Yes, of course," she replies, keeping her tone light. "It's your birthday, not mine. How do you like your present? Are they gorgeous?"

He laughs, and she feels weak with relief. "They're impressive. They're not exactly dressed for a restaurant, though. Why on earth did you think I needed to eat dinner with them? I keep hoping I won't run into anybody I know."

In the background, she hears the muted roar of an eating house, the uniform evening hubbub of voices, glasses, silver, plates.

"Where are you calling from?" Ariel asks.

"Beside the cashier's desk. I have to go. I can't be rude. I'll call you later."

"Good luck," she says. She is shocked to find a streak of malice in her tone, and still more shocked at the sense of power she feels as she puts down the phone. Leaving him trapped in a restaurant, forced to make conversation with two whores, while the other diners stare and the waiters shoot him roguish grins. Was that panic she heard in Roberto's voice? And what could that naughty Beba and her friend be wearing? Not cheap hot pants like the roadside girls, she hopes. For the price, one would expect at least Versace.

After that, there is nothing for Ariel to do but kick off her shoes and wander through her house, her bare feet unexpectedly warm on the waxed surface of the old terra-cotta tiles she spent months collecting from junkyards and wrecked villas. She locks the doors and puts on the alarm, but turns on only the hall and stairway lights. And then walks like a night watchman from room to darkened room, feeling flashes of uxorious pride at the sight of furnishings she knows as well as her own body. *Uxorious*—the incongruous word actually floats through her head as her glance passes over the flourishes of a Piedmontese Baroque cabinet in the dining room, a watchful congregation of Barbies in the girls' playroom, a chubby Athena in a Mantuan painting in the upstairs hall. When has Ariel ever moved through the house in such freedom? It is exhilarating, and slightly appalling. And she receives the strange impression that this is the real reason she has staged this birthday stunt: to be alone and in conscious possession of the solitude she has accumulated over the years. To contemplate, for as long as she likes, the darkness in her own house. At the top of the stairs she stops for a minute and then slowly begins to take off her clothes, letting them fall softly at her feet. Then, naked, she sits down on the top step, the cold stone numbing her bare backside. Her earlier loneliness has evaporated: the shadows she is studying seem to be friendly presences jostling

to keep her company. She relaxes back on her elbows, and playfully
bobs her knees, like the roadside girl on the crate.

Ten o'clock. Bedtime. What she has wanted it to be since this afternoon. A couple of melatonin, a glass of dark Danish stout whose bitter concentrated taste of hops makes her sleepy. A careful shower,
cleaning of teeth, application of face and body creams, a gray cotton
nightdress. She could, she thinks, compose a specialized etiquette
guide for women in her situation. One's goal is to exude an air of
extreme cleanliness and artless beauty. One washes and dries one's
hair, but does not apply perfume or put on any garment that could
be construed as seductive. The subtle enchantment to be cast is that
of a homespun Elysium, the appeal of Penelope after Calypso.

By ten-thirty, she is sitting up in bed with the *Herald Tribune*,
reading a history of the FBI's Most Wanted list. Every few seconds,
she attempts quite coolly to think of what Roberto is inevitably
doing by now, but she determines that it is actually impossible to do
so. Those two pages in her imagination are stuck together.

She does, however, recall the evening in Bangkok that she
and Roberto spent with the pair of massage girls. How the four of
them walked in silence to a fluorescent-lit room with a huge plastic
bathtub, and how the two terrifyingly polite, terrifyingly young
girls, slick with soapsuds, massaging her with their small plump
breasts and shaven pubes, reminded her of nothing so much as
chickens washed and trussed for the oven. And how the whole event
threatened to become a theater of disaster, until Ariel saw that she
would have to manage things. How she indicated to the girls by a
number of discreet signs that the three of them were together in
acting out a private performance for the man in the room. How the

girls understood and even seemed relieved, and how much pleasure her husband took in what, under her covert direction, they all
contrived. How she felt less like an erotic performer than a social
director setting out to save an awkward party. And how silent she
was afterward—not the silence of shocked schoolgirl sensibilities,
as Roberto, no doubt, assumed, but the silence of amazement at a
world where she always had to be a hostess.

She turns out the light and dreams that she is flying with other
people in a plane precariously tacked together from wooden crates
and old car parts. They land in the Andes, and she sees that all the
others are women and that they are naked, as she is. They are all
sizes and colors, and she is far from being the prettiest, but is not the
ugliest, either. They are there to film an educational television special, BBC or PBS, and the script says to improvise a dance, which
they all do earnestly and clumsily: Scottish reels, belly dancing,
and then Ariel suggests ring-around-the-rosy, which turns out to
be more fun than anyone had bargained for, as they all flop down,
giggling at the end. The odd thing about this dream is how completely happy it is.

She wakes to noise in the room, and Roberto climbing into bed and
embracing her. "Dutiful," she thinks, as he kisses her and reaches
for her breasts, but then she lets the thought go. He smells alarmingly clean, but it is a soap she knows. As they make love, he offers
her a series of verbal sketches from the evening he has just passed, a
bit like a child listing his new toys. What he says is not exciting, but
it is exciting to hear him trying, for her benefit, to sound scornful
and detached. And the familiar geography of his body has acquired
a passing air of mystery, simply because she knows that other

women—no matter how resolutely transient and hasty—have been examining it. For the first time in as long as she can remember, she is curious about Roberto.

"Were they really so beautiful?" she asks, when, lying in the dark, they resume coherent conversation. "Flavio said that seeing them was like entering paradise."

Roberto gives an arrogant, joyful laugh that sounds as young as a teenage boy's.

"Only for an old idiot like Flavio. They were flashy, let's put it that way. The dark one, Beba, had an amazing body, but her friend had a better face. The worst thing was having to eat with them— and in that horrendous restaurant. Whose idea was that, yours or Flavio's?" His voice grows comically aggrieved. "It was the kind of tourist place where they wheel a cart of mints and chewing gum to your table after the coffee. And those girls asked for doggie bags, can you imagine? They filled them with Chiclets!"

The two of them are lying in each other's arms, shaking with laughter as they haven't done for months, even years. And Ariel is swept for an instant by a heady sense of accomplishment. "Which of them won the underpants?" she asks.

"What? Oh, I didn't give them away. They were handmade, silk. Expensive stuff—too nice for a hooker. I kept them for you."

"But they're too small for me," protests Ariel.

"Well, exchange them. You did save the receipt, I hope." Roberto's voice, which has been affectionate, indulgent, as in their best times together, takes on a shade of its normal domineering impatience. But it is clear that he is still abundantly pleased, both with himself and with her. Yawning, he announces that he has to get some sleep, that he's out of training for this kind of marathon. That he didn't even fortify himself with his birthday Viagra. He al-

ludes to an old private joke of theirs by remarking that Ariel's present proves conclusively that his mother was right in warning him
against immoral American women; and he gives her a final kiss.
Adding a possessive, an uxorious, squeeze of her bottom. Then
he settles down and lies so still that she thinks he is already asleep.
Until, out of a long silence, he whispers, "Thank you."

In a few minutes he is snoring. But Ariel lies still and relaxed, with
her arms at her sides and her eyes wide open. She has always ra-
tioned her illusions, and has been married too long to be shocked by
the swiftness with which her carefully perverse entertainment has
dissolved into the fathomless triviality of domestic life. In a certain
way that swiftness is Ariel's triumph—a measure of the strength of
the quite ordinary bondage that, years ago, she chose for herself.
So it doesn't displease her to know that she will wake up tomorrow,
make plans to retrieve her daughters, and find that nothing has
changed.

But no, she thinks, turning on her side, something is different.
A sense of loss is creeping over her, and she realizes it is because
she misses Beba. Beba, who for two weeks has lent a penumbral
glamour to Ariel's days. Beba, who, in the best of fantasies, might
have sent a comradely message home to her through Roberto. But,
of course, there is no message, and it is clear that the party is over.
The angels have flown, leaving Ariel—good wife and faithful
spirit—awake in the dark with considerable consolations: a sleeping man, a silent house, and the knowledge that, with her usual
practicality, she has kept Beba's number.

Full Moon over Milan

It began with rubber bands. The silly sentence bobs up in Merope's mind as she sits over a plate of stewed octopus that along with everyone else's dinner will be paid for by one of the rich men at the table. Rogue phrases have been invading her brain ever since she arrived in Milan and started living in another language: she'll be in a meeting with her boss and a client, chatting away in Italian about headlines and body copy for a Sicilian wine or the latest miracle panty liner, when a few words in English will flit across the periphery of her thoughts like a film subtitle gone wild.

Her friend Clay with typical extravagance says that the phrases are distress signals from the American in her who refuses to die, but Merope has never intended to stop being American. Her grandparents came from the British Caribbean island of Montserrat, and her earliest continuous memories are of her mother and father, both teachers, wearing themselves out in New Rochelle to bestow a seamless Yankee childhood on their two ungrateful daughters. Such immigrants' gifts always come with strings attached that appear after decades, that span continents and oceans: at twenty-eight Merope can no more permanently abandon America than she could turn away from the exasperating love engraved on her parents' faces. So she is writing copy in Italy on a sort of indefinite sabbatical, an extension of her role as family grasshopper, the daughter who at college dabbled in every arcane do-it-yourself feminist Third World folklorish arts-and-crafts kind of course as her sister Maia plowed dutifully along toward Wharton; who no sooner graduated than went off to Manhattan to live for a mercifully brief spell with a crazed sculptor from whom she was lucky enough to catch nothing worse than lice.

With family and lovers Merope learned early to defend her own behavior by adopting the role of ironic spectator, an over-perceptive little girl observing unsurprised the foibles of her elders. The role suits her: she is small with large unsettling eyes and nowadays a stylish little Eton crop of slicked-back straightened hair. Milan suits her, too: after two years she is still intrigued by its tenacious eighties-style vulgarity and by the immemorial Gothic sense of doom that lies like a medieval stone wall beneath the flimsy revelry of the fashion business. The sun and communal warmth of the Mezzogiorno have never attracted her as they do her English girl-friends; she likes the northern Italian fog—it feels like Europe. She respects as well the profound indifference of the city to its visitors from other countries. From the beginning she's been smart enough to understand that the more energetically one sets oneself to master all kinds of idioms in a foreign country, the sooner one uncovers the bare, incontrovertible fact that one is foreign. The linked words that appear and flit about her brain seemingly by sheerest accident, like bats in a summer cottage, seem to Merope to be a logical response to her life in a place where most really interesting things are hidden. The phrases are playful, but like other ephemera—dreams, advertisements, slips of the tongue—if you catch and examine them, they offer oblique comment on events at hand.

This dinner, for example—three Italian men and three foreign women gathered without affection but with a lot of noisy laughter on a May evening in the outdoor half of a restaurant in the Brera district. It did in a certain way come about through rubber bands— the oversized pink ones that provide fruitful resistance to the limbs of the women in the exercise class where Merope met Clay at noon. If Merope hadn't been dripping with sweat and demoralized by the pain, she would have said no, as she has privately resolved to do whenever Clay gets that glint in her eye and starts talking about extremely interesting, extremely successful men.

The exercise class they attend is a notorious one in Milan: it is dedicated entirely to buttocks, and is even called simply "Buttocks"—"*Glutei*." Rich Milanese housewives, foreign businesswomen, and models without any hips to speak of flock to the Conture Gym to be put through their paces by a Serbian ex-gymnast named Nadia, in an atmosphere of groaning and mass agony that suggests a labor ward in a charity clinic. Merope is annoyed at herself for being insecure enough to attend—her small, lofty Caribbean backside, after all, ranks on the list of charms she sometimes allows her boyfriends to enumerate. Yet, Tuesdays and Thursdays at midday, she finds herself there, resentfully squatted on a springy green mat. Sometimes, looking around her, she draws a professional bead on those quivering international ranks of fannies: she sees them in a freeze-frame, an ad for universal feminine folly.

Her friend Clay, on the other hand, adores Ass Class, or the Butt Club, as she alternately calls it. She says that she likes her perversions to work for her. Clay is the class star, the class clown. In a glistening white Avengers-style unitard, she hoists and gyrates her legs with gusto, lets out elemental whoops of pain, swaps wisecracks in Italian with Nadia, flops about exuberantly in her bonds, tossing her sweat-soaked red hair like a captive mermaid, occasionally sending a snapped rubber band zinging across the dance floor. Merope sometimes thinks that if Clay didn't exist, it would be necessary to invent her—at least for her, Merope's, own survival on the frequent days when Milan appears through the mist as a dull provincial town.

A case in point: last Sunday, when Merope and Clay and a friend of Clay's, a Colorado blonde who works at Christie's, were taking the train over the Swiss border to Lugano to see the American Impressionist show at the Thyssen-Bornemisza, Clay got up to go to the toilet, found the toilet in their train compartment not up to her exacting standards, went down to the next car, and there suddenly found herself left behind in Italy as the train divided in two at the border. Merope and the other woman sat staring dumbly at Clay's beautiful ostrich-skin bag on the seat as their half of the train tootled merrily on into Switzerland.

However, after a few minutes, the train drew to a halt in a small suburban station not on the schedule of express stops, and as the few other people in the car began peering curiously out of the window, a clanking, clanging sound announced the arrival of another train behind them. Merope and the other girl jumped up, ran to the end platform of the car, and saw arriving a sort of yellow toy engine, the kind used for track repair, and inside, flanked by two Italian conductors wearing besotted grins, was Clay, red hair flying, waving like the Queen Mother.

Clay is busy these days ironing out the last wrinkles of a complicated divorce from a rich Milanese who manufactures something rarely thought of but essential, like tongue depressors. Then she is immediately getting married again, to a Texan, with dazzling blue eyes and a glibber tongue than an Irishman's, who won Clay by falling on his knees and proposing in front of an intensely interested crowd of well-dressed drinkers at Baretto, in Via Sant'Andrea. Maybe Texas will be big enough for her. Italy, thinks Merope, has always seemed a bit confining for her friend, like one of those tight couture jackets Clay puts on to go to the office, where for the past few years she has run a gift-buying service for Italian companies who want to shower Bulgari trinkets on crucial Japanese. Nowadays she's shutting down the business, talks about Texas real estate, about marketing Italian cellulite creams in America, about having babies.

Merope feels a predictable resentment toward the Texas Lochinvar who rode out of the West and broke up the eleven months of high times she and Clay had been enjoying as bachelorettes in Milan. Now she would have to start a real life in Milan—unlikely, this—or return home. Her weather instincts tell her that her friend's engagement means that she herself will fall in love again soon: another partner will come along in a few beats to become essential as salt, to put her through changes, perhaps definitive ones. Clay says that what she wants most in the world to see before she leaves for Houston is Merope settled with a nice man; every time they go out together, she parades an international array of prospects, as if Merope were a particularly picky executive client.

Merope isn't in the mood yet to settle down with a nice man; in fact last October, when she met Clay, she had just made a nice man move out of the apartment they'd shared for a year and a half in the Navigli district. She'd explained this to Clay in the first five minutes they'd started talking, at a party in the so-called Chinese district, near Corso Bramante. "He was awfully dear. He was Dutch: sweet in the way those northern men can be sweet. Crazy about me the way a man from one of those colonizing countries can be about a brown-skinned woman. A photographer. Never fell in love with models, *and* he cooked fantastic Indonesian food. But he was making me wicked."

Clay, shoehorned into a Chanel suit of an otherworldly pink, stuck her chin into her empty wineglass and puffed out her cheeks. Across the room she'd looked like a schoolgirl, wandering through the crowd with downcast eyes, smiling at some naughty thought of her own; up close her beautiful face was a magnet for light, might have been Jewish or not, might have been thirtyish or not, might or might not have undergone a few surgical nips and tucks. Merope had at first glance classified her, erroneously, as "Fashion"—as belonging to the flamboyant tribe of ageless nomads who follow the collections between Europe and New York as migrant workers follow the harvests.

Clay, however, was beyond Fashion. "Because he was too good," she said in a thoughtful voice, of Merope's Dutch ex-boyfriend. Her accent in English, like her face, was hard to define: a few European aspirates that slid unexpectedly into an unabashed American flattening of vowels. "No respectable woman," she added, "should have to put up with *that*."

The party was given by a friend of Merope's—a model married to an Italian journalist, who occasionally got together with some of the other black American and Caribbean models to cook barbecue. The models got raunchy and loud on these occasions, and that night hung intertwined over the beer and ribs, hooting with laughter, forming a sort of gazebo of long, beautiful brown limbs, while a bit of Fashion and a few artistic Milanese buzzed around the edges. Merope had arrived with a painter who dressed only in red and kept goats in his city garden—the type of character who through some minor law of the universe inevitably appears in the social life of a young woman who has just broken off a stable relationship. When the painter left her side and went off to flirt vampirishly with every-one else in the room, Merope started talking with Clay and instantly realized, with the sense of pure recognition one has in falling in love, or in the much rarer and more subtle process of identifying a new friend, that this was the person she had been looking for to get in trouble with in Milan.

Clay's too hastily proffered description was of a family vaguely highborn, vaguely European, vaguely American (her passport, like her pithy syntax, demonstrated the latter) and of a childhood passed in a sort of whistle-stop tour of the oddest combination of places—Madrid; Bristol, England; Gainesville, Florida. By comparison, Merope's own family seemed as stable as Plymouth Rock. She was tickled: Clay gave her a school's-out feeling after her model friends, who, for all their wild looks and the noise they made, were really just sweet, hardworking, secretly studious girls.

Over that fall and winter she and Clay, without finding out much more about each other, spent a lot of time together, chivying a string of Italian and foreign suitors and behaving like overage sorority sisters. They hardly ever went to bed with anybody, not from fear of AIDS but from sheer contrariness, and they called each other late at night after dates and giggled. They cock-teased. Merope wondered occasionally how it was possible for fully em-ployed grown women to act this way: did adolescence, like malaria, return in feverish flashbacks?

The same thought occurs to her again tonight in the restaurant gar-den, because she can feel the spring getting to her. After a cold wet April, warm weather has finally arrived, bringing wan flourishes of magnolia and sultry brown evenings heavy with industrial exhaust.

The hordes of Fashion in town for the prêt-à-porter collections have been and gone like passenger pigeons, leaving in their wake not desolation but a faint genuine scent of pleasure. Tonight there is even a full moon: coming in the taxi from work, she caught a glimpse of it, big and shockingly red as a setting sun. Moons and other heavenly personages are rare in Milan: this one vanished under the smog by the time she reached the restaurant. Now between the potted hedge and the edges of the big white umbrellas overhead she sees only the cobblestones of Piazza del Carmine, a twilit church facade, and part of a big modern sculpture that looks like a Greek torso opened for autopsy.

Across the table, Clay is looking good in black. The man to Clay's right is obviously impressed. His name is Claudio, he is a Roman who lives half the time in Milan, and he owns shoe factories out in the mists beyond Linate: a labyrinthine artisanal conglomerate whose products, baptized with the holy names of the great designers, decorate shop windows up and down Via Spiga and Via Montenapoleone. He's been making not awfully discreet pawing motions at Clay since they all met up at Baretto at eight-thirty. He is touching the huge gilt buttons of her jacket with feigned professional interest, and her hands and the tip of her nose with no excuse at all, and Clay is laughing and talking about her fiancé in Texas and brushing him off like a mosquito or maybe not even brushing him off but playing absentmindedly with him, the way a child uses a few light taps to keep a balloon dancing in the air.

The other men at the table are designed along the same lines as this Claudio, though one is Venetian and the other a true Milanese. All three are fortyish men-about-town whom Merope has been seeing at parties for the last two years: graying, tanned, with the beauty that profligate Nature bestows on Italian males northern or southern, of all levels of intelligence and social class. They are dressed in magnificent hybrid fabrics of silk and wool, and their faces hold the faintly wary expression of rich divorced men.

Like all the dinner companions Clay has provided recently, they are all impossible, for more reasons than Merope could list on a manuscript the length of the Magna Carta. Without having been out with them before, she knows from experience that soon they will begin vying with each other to pay for this dinner, will get up and pretend to visit the toilet but really go off to settle things with the headwaiter or to discover with irritation that one of the others pretending to visit the toilet has gotten there beforehand. When it has been revealed that someone has succeeded in paying, the other men will groan and laughingly take to task the beaming victor, who has managed to buy the contents of their stomachs.

The other woman at the table is Robin, the Colorado Christie's blonde from the train incident. She is pretty but borderline anorexic, with a disconcerting habit of jerking her head sharply to one side as she laughs. Clay uses her shamelessly to round out gatherings where another woman is wanted who won't be competition. Merope likes her but pities her because after five years in Italy she hasn't yet understood the mixture of playfulness and deep conservatism in Italian men and goes from one disastrous love affair to another. Just a few weeks ago, she spent a night shivering in a car in front of a house where her latest lover was dallying. Now she's looking hopefully around, as if she's eager to get burned again.

On the right side of Merope, the Venetian, Francesco, is recounting something that happened to him last month: a girl of about sixteen, a Polish immigrant who had been in the country only a few months, had bluffed her way in to see him in the offices of his knitwear business and without preamble pulled off her shirt. "She told me that she'd done a bit of lingerie modeling—you can imagine the body—but that she wasn't making enough money, and she proposed for me to keep her. Viewed with the greatest possible objectivity, *era una fica pazzesca*—she was an amazing piece of ass. She said that she didn't care about luxury, that she'd accept one room in any neighborhood, that she didn't dress couture, only Gaultier Junior, and that she rode a motorbike, so that her overhead costs would be very low. She used that expression: 'overhead costs.' "

"Well, what did you do?" demands Clay.

Francesco pauses to scrape a mussel from its shell, and then glances around the table with his shrewd, pale Venetian eyes. He seems pleased with the story and with himself. "I don't like complications, so I kept my head with extreme difficulty, made her put her shirt on, and sent her away. And lucky for her, not morally but practically, because a week ago I ran into her at the gala the Socialists gave at La Scala—covered with jewels, on the arm of old Petralzo the rug man, who must be seventy-five."

"Lucky girl," says Clay. "So she has minimum work for maximum compensation."

"It's an inspiring story," Merope says. "Even ideologically. When you think of her, born under Polish socialism, progressing to the Italian brand—"

A waiter dashes up and shows them an enormous boiled sea bass, lead-colored in the candlelight, and then runs off to bone it. Though they are all laughing, the story about the Polish girl has changed the atmosphere of the group, momentarily causing each one of them to envision the candlelit outdoor restaurant with its stylish diners as a temporary and unstable oasis of safety, an illuminated bubble poised at the murky edges of the chaos going on not far enough away to the East: the Wall toppled and strewn; teenage Germans nonchalantly resuscitating the Third Reich; international mafiosi and ex-apparatchiks making pacts in the shadow of the Kremlin; Croats slicing heads off Montenegrins; Czech whores servicing the flights between Vienna and Prague; dissolution spilling over into the once safe and prosperous fields of Western Europe in the form of refugee hordes from every tattered state on earth. Each of the men at the table thinks of certain investments and says an inward prayer. The three American women experience a brief, simultaneous thrill of empathy with that coldhearted young girl, as foreign as they are.

Subdued, they finish off two bottles of Piedmontese red wine and eat the fish with thin flat salad greens called *barba di frate*—"friar's beard." Merope chats with the man on her left, who has a posh Milanese accent with a glottal *r* that sounds as if he's constantly clearing his throat. His name is Nicolò, and he agreeably surprises her by accepting without comment the fact that she is American of African-Caribbean ancestry—most Italians feel obliged to observe that she doesn't look American, as if one could—and that she actually works in advertising rather than at one of the jobs that many otherwise intelligent people in Milan consider the only possibility for a pretty young woman with skin the color of cedarwood: runway work, or shaking her behind in television ads for tropical juice.

She tells him that at work she has set herself the private task of trying to change attitudes and images, a generally futile ambition in a small Italian agency grateful for any accounts it can attract. Italians aren't natural racists, she explains, not like Americans, but they tend to view foreigners in a series of absurd roles as set as those of the commedia dell'arte. "It's funny, really. The last campaign we did for an air conditioner, what the kids in the creative department held out for was two black models dressed as cannibals carrying the air conditioner slung on a stick. Cannibals, can you imagine? Bare breasts, strings of teeth around their necks, little grass umbrellas around the hips. The company directors loved it. I screamed and yelled."

Nicolò smiles. "They must love *you*."

"Well, I'm somewhat of a crown of thorns for them. But I provide comic relief."

She knows this Nicolò by sight; she has seen him at parties, always with a different oversized, underage beauty glued to his flank. He has even gone out with one of her friends, a lanky nineteen-year-old from Santo Domingo who is doing a lot of work for Armani this year. "Nicolò" she thinks of as a young name, impetuous, boyish, ardent, like the medieval revolutionary Cola di Rienzo, but this Nicolò is no boy. He has a head of bushy graying curls and weary, protuberant blue Lombard eyes with—surprising for a *viveur*—an expression of gentle, lugubrious sentimentality.

He is well dressed like the others, but his clothes seem slightly too big, giving him a curious orphaned air that must, thinks Merope unkindly, be the secret of his success with women. That and his money. He is the only one of the three who is not newly rich: his family has professors in it, and a famous collection of Futurist art, and people say he keeps up the textile business his great-grandfather started only to satisfy his taste for very young models. (In fact, his eyes glistened mournfully at the description of the Polish girl.) It is said that he falls in love constantly, with untidy results.

He sits and talks about a big house in the Engadin Valley where his seventy-eight-year-old mother passes the winters making nutcake, skiing, hiking, fighting with the family board of directors via phone or fax.

"She sounds fantastic," Merope says. She tells him about her father's mother, Jazelle, a school principal with a taste for Plutarch as well as for a certain type of hot yellow-pepper sauce—a tall, rigid, iron-colored woman who commanded obedience from family and pupils in a whispering deadly Montserratian voice that both awed and embarrassed her Americanized grandchildren. It's just an impulse: her family is her own private thing that she doesn't usually talk about with the people Clay trots out.

"I don't understand what you're doing in Milan," he says.

"Well, I have to see the world. This is as good a place as any, maybe better."

Nicolò taps the base of his wineglass with his fingernail. "St. Augustine was converted in a garden here. I think that that was probably the last time this city has done anyone any good."

"I wonder where the garden was," says Merope.

Nicolò laughs and says it was a child's voice that spoke to Augustine in the garden, and that he is thinking at the moment that Merope has the face of a child who knows too much. She reminds him, he says, of Velázquez's Infanta Margarita. This is a nice compliment, but spoiled by being said in a self-satisfied, overly proficient manner that makes it clear that he habitually comes up with artistic comparisons to impress his very young models. It annoys Merope. She sees that he is quite interested, and this is puzzling, since she is not at all his type.

They are interrupted from across the table by Claudio, the Roman shoemaker, who has heard them talking about the mountains. In between bouts of flirting outrageously with Clay, he starts reminiscing about a party given at Champfer in the sixties by a spendthrift cousin of Nicolò's. The cousin had wanted to tent a forest for his guests to dance in like gnomes, but this was against Swiss law, so he filled a tent with tall potted larches specially imported from Austria. At dawn the men, a black phalanx in evening dress, had descended from Corviglia on skis.

The two other men at the table chime in to exclaim nostalgically over how much time they spent in dinner jackets, their crowd of young blades, in the sixties. They were so stylish they never wore ski clothes even on ordinary days, but skied in three-piece suits, the wasp-waisted, flare-trousered sixties kind, with a high-collared shirt and a wide tie up under your chin. "We were dandies," sighs Francesco.

Clay says that they are still dandies, that it is a basic instinct of the Latin male to decorate himself. But are they still up to snuff physically, she asks in a rhetorical tone that makes Robin and Merope giggle. Tossing back her red fringe, she says she doubts it, and she commands without further ado that they show her their legs. Clay has an effect on men like a pistol held to the back of the neck: all three of them at the table—fathers of adult children and heads of companies—rise promptly from their places, considerably surprising the waiters and the other diners in the restaurant, and line up like naughty schoolboys in front of Clay, who, with a Circean smile, has swiveled in her chair to survey them. They pull up their trousers to reveal a variety of knobby, sock-covered ankles and calves. Clay keeps them standing there a second longer than necessary before pronouncing them acceptable and allowing them to file back to their dinners. "But you'll have to work on that musculature, gentlemen!" she says.

"Of course they behave this way because we're foreigners," Clay tells Merope a bit later in the ladies' room. Clay has a frequently voiced conviction that Italian men view foreign women as escape hatches, vacations from the immemorial stress of life with Italian women, who are all descendants of exigent Mediterranean earth goddesses.

"Italians are just intensified versions of men from anywhere," says Merope. "The real mystery, the riddle of the ages, is why we go to buttock class and put ourselves through severe pain for their benefit. Look at them—those bony legs!"

Merope is redoing her lips with a tint from a little pottery dish her ex-boyfriend brought her from Marrakech. Clay has left the toilet door open to talk to her and sits with her black skirt hiked up and her tights down, her chin propped on her hands and her elbows on her knees.

When Clay is washing her hands, they start talking about Claudio the shoemaker, who, as Merope accurately observes, has been making passes at Clay like a Roman café waiter with a schoolgirl on a junior year abroad. Clay, always merciful when one least expects it, declares that there is no real harm in poor Claudio, who is upset about having less money than his friends and about having had his business partner hauled off to prison last month as a result of the government bribery scandal.

"Well, if you're so sympathetic, you should cure him of that behavior," says Merope, dropping the Moroccan dish into her bag. "Why don't you act like his charm has caused you to lose your head, and grab him in front of everybody and kiss him. Stick your tongue in his mouth. That would scare the shit out of him. It might change his life. At the very least it would teach him some manners."

Clay says it isn't at all a bad idea, and when they are back at the table she actually does grab Claudio the shoemaker and give him a whammy of a kiss—a real bodice ripper, as she describes it later. She doesn't do it right away but waits until they've had dessert and small cups of black coffee, which intrude on the languid meal like jolts of pure adrenaline.

Merope sees Claudio reach out for the twentieth time and trail his fingers down Clay's cheek while he formulates yet another outrageous compliment, and she watches Clay laugh, turn to him, grab his shoulders, and give him a long, extremely kinetic kiss. They all stare, and Robin from Christie's claps her thin hands spontaneously like a child at the circus when the elephants come in. Clay lets Claudio go, and his face has blushed dark as a bruise. He is groping for an expression. The rest of them follow Robin and burst into applause, because there is nothing else to do, and people at other tables turn around to look.

"Brava, Clay! That's showing him," calls Francesco.

Clay herself is pale, but she has lost no equilibrium at all. She takes a sip of mineral water. "That was possible," she says evenly, without a smile, "only because with Claudio there could *never* be the possibility of anything more."

Shrieks of laughter, invocations of the Texas fiancé, loud protests from the men, especially from Claudio himself, who has enough of the Roman genius for saving face to cover his tracks—to court Clay still more flamboyantly, to laugh artlessly at himself. But the atmosphere, observes Merope, is momentarily murderous; at least, under the voices, through the candlelight diffused beneath the white umbrella, travels a dire reverberation like that which follows the first bite of an ax into a tree trunk. She herself feels half angry at Clay for taking her at her word, half full of unwilling admiration.

"So what do you think, precocious child?" Nicolò asks her a few minutes later, when Francesco reveals that he has paid the bill, and they all get up to leave.

"That precocious children come to bad ends," replies Merope.

The six of them take two cars to Piazza Sant'Ambrogio to visit Angela and Lucia, a pair of forty-year-old twins who design a sportswear line for Francesco. These sisters with first names like chambermaids are in fact members of an aboriginal Milanese noble family whose dark history of mailed fists and bloody political intrigues dominates medieval Lombard chronicles. The twins themselves, leftover scraps of a dynasty, are small, with masses of streaked hair and frail chirping voices like a pair of crickets; at parties they dress alike to annoy their friends. Tonight they are darting around in red and yellow bloomer suits in Lucia's apartment, which adjoins her sister's in a damp sixteenth-century palazzo with a view onto the church of Sant'Ambrogio. The two sisters boast that even during their marriages and love affairs they have rarely spent a night apart.

In the room where the guests are gathered, there are Man Ray photographs leaning against the baseboards, couches and poufs covered in sea green damask, and a carved Malaysian four-poster bed; the windows look down into a leafy wilderness starred with white blossom—the kind of courtyard Merope had at first been surprised to find behind the pitted, smog-blackened facades of Milanese palazzi.

Merope detaches herself from Nicolò, who has been hovering since they got out of the car, and goes and sits down on a wobbly pouf beside a handsome Indian designer who works with one of the twins. The designer's name is Nathaniel, and he is talking emotionally about Cole Porter to a large, round Englishman whom Merope remembers chiefly for the fact that in the summer he bounces around the city in the most beautiful white linen suits, like a colonial governor on holiday.

"My mother," continues Nathaniel, "used to sit down at the piano at sunrise with a pitcher of cold tea beside her and start in with 'Night and Day.' It's a very peculiar sensation, Cole Porter in Delhi at dawn." He passes one hand over his forehead as if to dispel an unbearable memory and then props his elbow on Merope's shoulder. "Hello, chum," he says. "You look appetizing tonight."

Merope pushes his elbow off and smiles. She likes Nathaniel, who is a friend of her boss, Maria Teresa. He asks her about work, and she tells him about the most interesting thing she is doing these days, which is a freelance project writing scripts for a video series on the fantasies of top models.

"Oho," interjects the round Englishman.

"Well, it's not as hot as it sounds. These are the kind of fantasies most women have at the age of eleven. The sex is all submerged. One of the girls, Russian, really gorgeous, dreams of being Catherine the Great—"

"I don't call that submerged," protests Nathaniel. "Think of her and the horse."

Merope tells him that the horse is a myth and that anyway the video limits itself to onion domes and fur-edged décolletage. Then she describes another video, in which the model fantasizes about being a Mafia princess, climbs out of a black Mercedes with an Uzi in her hand while the voice-over observes that she has looks to kill for.

The two men giggle, and then the Englishman asks Merope about Ivo, her Dutch ex-boyfriend. When she says that she left him almost a year ago, he leans toward her looking simultaneously lascivious and avuncular and says, "I hope you haven't gone over to the wops. My child," he goes on, "I have a definite paternal concern for your romantic future. Too many nice girls come over here and get flummoxed by the Eyetalians. Bad situation—very, as

Mr. Jingle would say. Because, all indications of myth and popular tradition to the contrary, the Italian—"

"Is the most difficult male on the planet," interjects Nathaniel, with the happy air of one climbing onto an old and beloved hobby-horse.

"That stands, though I was about to say conservative," says the Englishman. "Difficult, because with the Asian, the African male—".

"Don't forget the Indian," adds Nathaniel.

"You know where you are," says the Englishman. "And one expects behavior along primitive authoritarian lines. But the Italian has a veneer of modernity that makes him infinitely more dangerous. Underneath the flashy design is a veritable root system of archaic beliefs and primitive loyalties. In Milan it's better hidden— that's all."

Getting excited, he waves across the room at, of all people, Nicolò, possibly because he's seen him come in with Merope. "Just pick an example! One look at him and the discerning eye sees not just an overdressed example of the Riace bronzes but an apartment! Yes, behind every Milanese playboy lurks an immense, dark, rambling bourgeois apartment in the Magenta district, with garlands on the ceiling and the smell of generations of pasta in *brodo*—oh, that *brodo*!—borne to the table by generations of maidservants with mustaches.

"And the tribal life in these apartments—all-powerful mothers, linen closets, respectful tradesmen presenting yearly bills, respectful priests subtly skimming the household wealth, ceremonial annual removals to the mountains and the sea, young men and young wives slowly suffocating, gold clinking in coffers to a rhythm that says, family, family, family."

He fixes Merope with a sparkling periwinkle eye. "One grows up in one of these miniature purgatories with a sense of sin ingrained in one's cells—a sense that human compromise and human corruption are inevitable. It's the belief at the root of all the wickedness in this city—and this is a very wicked city. Wicked in a silly and not even very interesting way. An exotic American like you can't comprehend the weight of it."

Presumptuous old donkey, thinks Merope, who has been looking around and only half listening. It would be nice to get through an evening out without hearing the word *exotic*. "I have a family, too," she says, distinctly.

"It's eminently clear that you are a sheltered and highly educated flower of the New World, and that makes you more vulnerable." He points to Clay. "That's the kind of girl who gets on in Italy: hit and run."

Clay is standing across the room talking to one of the twins. Unlike anyone else, she looks better as the night wears on: her eyes and earrings gleam and she seems more voluptuous, whiter, redder, more emphatic. By her side hovers Claudio the shoemaker, who has not left her since she gave him that kiss. If he was annoyingly forward in his behavior before the event, now he is desperate.

"Yes, that intelligent young woman has had the good sense to hook up with a cattle baron and get the hell out."

"You sound jealous," says Merope.

"Oh, extremely," says the Englishman. "But it's too late for me."

"At this point we're fixtures," sighs Nathaniel.

One of the twins darts over and compliments Merope on the wonderful new shoes she has on, which are black with straps, and this somehow gets everyone talking about the British Royal Family, since Nathaniel claims to have heard on reliable authority that what the Prince of Wales really desires in his troubled marriage is straps, plenty of them, but that the Princess declines to oblige.

Clay waltzes up and plops down on the Englishman's lap, nearly knocking him over; meanwhile they start discussing a new conspiracy theory that links the Queen with the latest Mafia executions in Palermo. They go on to the fiasco of the AIDS benefit gala held the previous week at the Sforza Castle, where a freak storm fried the outdoor lights and nearly electrocuted an international crowd of celebrities. After that they argue over the significance of the appearance of a noted art critic on a late-night television sex show hosted by a beautiful hermaphrodite. Then they thoroughly dissect the latest addendum to the sensational divorce case of a publishing magnate: his wife's claim that he violated her with a zucchini and then served his friends the offending vegetable as part of a risotto.

Nicolò has come over and sat down on the arm of a couch next to Merope, and through all the laughter she feels him watching her. Under cover of everyone else's chatter, he leans over and says, "I have to fly to New York the day after tomorrow. Do you want to come with me?"

She rises and moves away from the rest of the group toward the window, and he follows her. Then she stands still and looks directly at him. "I don't think you are really interested in me," she says. "I'm not your type at all—not extraordinarily young, not tall, not beautiful at the professional level you like. And I have a personality. An attitude, though you can't possibly know what that means. So the question is why you are behaving this way: To keep your hand in? To practice for the Third World models?"

He reddens, but not as much as he should, and apologizes. He admits he's been horribly clumsy but says she's being too hard on him. The fact is that she's different from the women he usually meets, and that has thrown him off base. He should have guessed—

"I go to New York quite often for work," Merope interrupts pitilessly. "You offered me a trip like someone offers stockings to a little refugee. Offer it to that Polish girl who came into Francesco's office, the one who took off her shirt. I could see that got you excited."

He reddens some more, rubs his right eye with a nervous forefinger, but he is not, she sees, displeased; on the contrary, he is liking this intensely. What's going on, she thinks, that all the men want us to tread on them? Even the poor old Prince of Wales likes a spanking. From across the room Clay winks at her as if she knows what she's thinking, and Merope feels suddenly tired.

Francesco has helped one of the twins put together a batch of *sgropin*, the vodka-and-lemon-sherbet mixture Venetians drink after heavy meals; when Merope sits down again the others are sipping it from *spumante* glasses and continuing to chatter away at the top of their lungs, now about telepathy and magic.

Clay talks about a friend of hers in Rome who can call you up on the phone and tell you the colors of the clothes you are wearing at that moment. One of the twins describes the master wizard from Turin, Gustavo Rol, who in his heyday in the nineteen fifties would tell you to select any book from your library, turn to a page you chose, and there would be his name, written in an unearthly handwriting. Francesco tells of his uncle who, while living in a huge old villa on the Brenta, had a dream one night that an unknown woman instructed him to lock a slab of limestone into a small storage room and throw away the key. The uncle obeyed the dream, and when he and his family broke down the door a day later, they found the slab engraved with the words *"Siete tutti maledetti"*—"You are all cursed."

These dismal words don't directly end the party, yet no one manages to stay around much after they are spoken. People go off for a drink at Momus, or to watch the latest crop of models dance at the eternal model showcase, Nepentha. Some go home, since there is no shame in this in the last, frugal years of the millennium. Clay does one of her fast bunks, adroit as usual at collapsing with exhaustion when she feels bored; hissing to Merope that she'll call her later to rehash, she slips into a taxi that no one knew she had called. She leaves Claudio the shoemaker on the sidewalk with a peck on the cheek. From the corner of her eye Merope observes him standing, just standing as the taxi whisks off. He looks suddenly two-dimensional, as if his stuffing has all fallen out. "Marsyas flayed, eh?" says the Englishman, from over Merope's shoulder. "I told you she was an expert."

Nicolò offers to drive Merope home, and she says yes. Which leaves her walking toward the car at 1:00 A.M. through the ancient center of Milan with a man who doesn't attract her, whom she doesn't want to try to understand. What strange glue has them still stuck together?

Under their feet the worn paving stones are slippery with damp, and from gardens hidden behind the smog-blackened portals of the old palaces comes a breath of earth and leaves and cat pee. Occasionally they pass a doorway littered with disposable syringes, but they see no one—no addicts and no lovers. Approaching is the quietest hour of the night, the hour when the unchanging character of the city emerges from the overlay of traffic and history.

Their footsteps echo on the walls of the narrow streets with a late-night sound that Merope thinks must be peculiar to Milan, as each city in the world has its own response to night voices and footfalls. As if her scolding had pushed a button that vaporized in-hibitions, Nicolò has been talking steadily since they said good-bye to the others and he continues after they have gotten into his big leather-lined car, where the doors make a heavy prosperous sound when they slam, like a vault closing.

He talks about his estranged wife, whom he has never quite been able to divorce, about the excellence of her family, a pharmaceutical dynasty from Como, about her religion, about her well-bred pipe-stem legs below the Scottish tartan skirts she favored in the nineteen seventies, about how her problem with alcohol began. He talks about how until a certain age a man goes on searching for a woman to heal who-knows-what wound, until some afternoon one looks up from scanning a document and realizes that one has stopped search-ing and how that realization is the chief disaster one faces. He talks about his son, who is with Salomon Brothers in London, and his daughter, in her last year at Bocconi; he asks Merope how old she is.

"Twenty-eight." She says it with careless emphasis, knowing that it is too old for his tastes, that probably one of the most intense pleasures he allows himself is the moment he learns definitively how young, how dangerously young, is the girl at his side. It heightens her sense of power, not to be to his taste, and yet there is something companionable in it. Any tiredness she felt has passed: she feels beautiful and in control, sustained by her little black dress with its boned bodice as if by a sheath of magic armor.

On impulse she asks him not to take her immediately home but to drive out of town and follow the canal road toward Pavia first so they can have a look at the rice fields, which are flooded now for the spring planting. To get to the Pavese canal they cut through the neighborhood near Parco Sempione where the transvestite and transsexual whores do business. It's late for the whores, whose peak hour for exhibiting themselves on the street is midnight, but those who are not already with clients or off the job go into their routine when they see the lights of Nicolò's car. Variously they shimmy and stick out their tongues, bend over cupping their naked silicone breasts, turn their backs and wag their bare bottoms.

They are said to be the best-dressed streetwalkers in Italy, and certainly in fast glimpses they all look gorgeous, fantastically costumed in string bikinis and garter belts, stockings and high heels, with their original sex revealed only by the width of their jaws and the narrowness of their hips. All together they resemble a marooned group of Fellini extras. One of them is wrapped in a Mephistophelian red cloak that swirls over nipples daubed with phosphorescent makeup; another is wearing a tight silver Lycra jumpsuit with a cutout exposing bare buttocks that remind Merope, inevitably, of the *Glutei* class.

Nicolò slows down the car to allow the two of them a good look, and makes a weak joke about urban nocturnal transportation services. He tells Merope that the transvestites are nearly all Albanians or Brazilians, something she already knows. With Clay and other friends she has driven around to see them a number of times after dinner; only now, however, does she consider what life must be like for these flamboyant night birds, foreigners to a country, foreigners to a gender, skilled but underappreciated workers in a profession that makes them foreigners to most of the rest of the world.

She can see that Nicolò is eyeing them with the veiled expression that men adopt when with a woman companion they look at whores, and this fills her with friendly amusement. She's starting to feel slightly fond of him, in fact, old Nicolò. His overlong curls, the superb quality of the fabric of his jacket, his anguish, even his timid taste for adolescents are all, as the Englishman said, parts of a certain type of equation. It has to do not only with vast gloomy apartments with plaster garlands but also with escapes from that world—endless futile escapes with the returns built right in. Nicolò, she knows, would like her to be one of his escapes. He's not brave enough for the transvestites.

They reach the Naviglio Pavese and drive along the canal toward the periphery of the city, past the darkened restaurant zone and the moored barges full of café tables, the iron footbridges and the few clubs with lights still lit. Nicolò continues to talk: spurred by her silence, he starts improvising, gets a bit declarative. He is confessing to her that he is tired of young models and wild evenings. Even tonight, with that kiss—He has nothing against her friend Clay, who is a fascinating woman, but there is something about her—In any case, at a certain time one wants a woman one can introduce to one's children, one's mother. He personally could never involve himself seriously with a woman who—The minute he saw Merope he sensed that, though they were so different, there was a possibility—

They pass through the periphery of Milan: factories, government housing, and hapless remnants of village life swallowed by the city. Then suddenly they are among the rice fields that stretch outside of Pavia. Beside them the sober gleam of the still canal stretches into the distance, and to the right and the left of the empty two-lane road is a magical landscape of water, divided by geometric lines. It could be anywhere: South Carolina, China, Bali. And there is light on the water, because once they are beyond the city limits the moon appears. Not dramatically—as full moons sometimes bound like comic actors onto the scene—but as a woman who has paused unseen at the edge of a group of friends at a party calmly enters the conversation.

The sight of the moon dissolves the flippant self-confidence Merope caught from Clay, which carried her through dinner and the party. She looks down at her bare knees emerging like polished wood from black silk, shifts her body in the enveloping softness of the leather seat, and feels not small, as such encounters with celestial bodies are supposed to make one feel, but simply in error. Out of step.

Once, four or five years ago, on vacation in Senegal, she and her sister sneaked out of Club Med and went to a New Year's Eve dance in the town gymnasium and a local boy led her onto the floor, where a sweating, ecstatic crowd was surging in an oddly decorous rhythm of small, synchronized stops and starts; and in those beautiful African arms she'd taken one step and realized that it was wrong. And not just that the step was wrong in itself but that it led to a whole chain of wrong steps and that she—who had assumed she was the heiress of the entire continent of Africa—couldn't for the life of her catch that beat. Sitting now in this car, where she has no real desire or need to be, she experiences a similar dismay. She feels that a far-reaching mistake has been made, not now but long ago, as if she and Nicolò and Clay and the other people she knows are condemned to endless repetitions of a tiresome antique blunder to which the impassive moon continues to bear witness.

"I think it's time to go back now," she says, breaking into whatever Nicolò is confessing; then she feels unreasonably annoyed by the polite promptness with which he falls silent, makes a U-turn, and heads toward the city. For a second she wishes intensely that something would happen to surprise her. She sees it in a complete, swift sequence, the way she dreams up those freelance scripts: Nicolò stops the car, turns to her, and bites her bare shoulder to the bone. Or an angel suddenly steps out on the road, wings and arm outstretched, and explains each of them to the other in a kindly, efficient, bilingual manner, rather like a senior UN interpreter. From the radio, which has been on since they reached the canal road, comes a fuzz of static and a few faint phrases of Sam Cooke's "Cupid." Merope looks down at her hands in her lap and when she looks up again they are passing an old farmhouse set close to the road: one of the rambling brick peasant *cascine*, big enough for half a dozen families, that dot the Bassa Padana lowlands like fortresses. Even at night it is clear that this place is half in ruins, but as they pass by she sees a figure standing in front and gives an involuntary cry.

Nicolò has good reflexes and simply slows the car without bringing it to a halt. "What is it?"

"There was someone standing in front of that *cascina*—it looked like a woman holding a child."

"That's not impossible. Some of these big abandoned houses close to the city have been taken over by squatters. Foreigners, again: Albanians, Filipinos, Moroccans, Somalians, Yugoslav gypsies. What I'm afraid we're facing is a new barbarian invasion."

She hardly notices what he says, because she is busy trying to understand what she saw back in front of the old farmhouse, whose walls, she realizes with delayed comprehension, seemed to have been festooned with spray-paint graffiti like a Bronx subway stop, like an East London squat. The figure she saw in the moonlight could have been a wild-haired woman holding a baby but could just as easily have been a man with dreadlocks cradling something else: a bundle, a small dog. The clothing of the figure was indeterminate, the skin definitely dark, the face an oval of shadow. Thinking of it and remembering her thoughts beforehand, she feels an absurd flash of terror, from which she quickly pulls back.

You aren't drunk, she tells herself in her mother's most common-sense tone, and you have taken no dicey pharmaceuticals, so stop worrying yourself at once. Just stop. When Nicolò notices that she is shaken up and asks if she is feeling all right, Merope says she is overtired and leaves it at that. She is sorry she cried out: it makes it seem that the two of them have shared some dangerous intimate experience.

Back in Milan they go speeding along the deserted tram tracks, and the moon disappears behind masses of architecture. Merope wants above all things to be back in her apartment, in her own bed, under the ikat quilt her ex-boyfriend made for her. She has to drive to Bologna for a meeting tomorrow afternoon and in the morning has a series of appointments for which, she thinks, she will be about as alert as a hibernating frog. By the time they are standing outside the thick oak carriage doors of her apartment house, in Via Francesco Sforza, her fit of nerves has passed.

Nicolò, looking a bit sheepish after the amount he has said, invites her to have dinner next week.

"I can't see how that would help either one of us," replies Merope, but she says it without the malicious energy of earlier that evening. In fact she says it as a joke, because she doesn't really mind him anymore. She doesn't give him her number, but she knows he'll get it from Clay or from someone else, and this knowledge leaves her so unmoved that for a minute she is filled with pity, for him and probably for herself as well. Without adding anything she kisses him on both cheeks and then lets the small, heavy pedestrians' door close between them.

Then she takes off her shoes and in her stocking feet runs across the cold, slippery paving stones of the courtyard into her wing of the building. She steps into the old glass-and-wooden elevator, careful not to bang the double doors and awaken Massimo the porter, who sleeps nearby. As she goes up she feels the buzzing mental clarity that comes from exhaustion. In the back of her mind have risen the words from the ghost story at the party, the baleful pronouncement engraved on a stone slab: *"Siete tutti maledetti."* And for a few seconds she finds herself laboring over that phrase, attempting with a feverish automatic kind of energy to fix it—to substitute a milder word for *cursed*—as she might correct a bad line of copy.

The phone is ringing as she lets herself into the apartment, and she grins as she picks it up: Clay is worse than a dorm mother.

"What if I decide to go to bed with somebody?" she says into the phone.

"You won't—not with him, anyway. You're not the charitable type," says Clay. She gives a loud yawn: she's probably been lying there talking to the Texan, who calls every night. "I just wanted to make sure you made curfew."

"What time is curfew at this school?"

"Oh, around noon the next day."

"Clay, shame on you. You kissed that man."

"There was no man there. It was a trick of lighting."

They start giggling, egg each other on. For the first time that night Merope is having fun; courage warms her and the dread-locked apparition by the farmhouse steps back into whatever waiting room in the imagination is reserved for catchpenny roadside omens. A few months later, she will discover that this was the night she decided to stop living in Italy; that here, in a small burst of instinct, began her transition to somewhere else. But at this moment on the bare edge of a new day in Milan, only one image comes to mind: herself and Clay in evening dresses out of a thirties film, fox-trotting together like two Ginger Rogerses around and around an empty piazza. Full of bravado, they laugh loud American bad-girl laughter as they dance; they whirl faster until they outrun gravity and start to rise over the worn gray face of the city, their satin skirts spinning out in a white disk that tosses casual light down on factories and streetcar lines, on gardens, palaces, and the bristling spires of the Duomo.

Merope sits down on the bed and wedges the phone between her shoulder and ear. "Did you see the moon?" she asks.

Brothers and Sisters Around the World

"I took them around the point toward Dzamandzar," Michel tells me. "Those two little whores. Just ten minutes. They asked me for a ride when I was down on the beach bailing out the Zodiac. It was rough and I went too fast on purpose. You should have seen their titties bounce!"

He tells me this in French, but with a carefree lewdness that could be Roman. He is, in fact, half Italian, product of the officially French no-man's-land where the Ligurian Alps touch the Massif Central. In love, like so many of his Mediterranean compatriots, with boats, with hot blue seas, with dusky women, with the steamy belt of tropics that girdles the earth. We live above Cannes, in Mougins, where it is always sunny, but on vacation we travel the world to get hotter and wilder. Islands are what Michel prefers: in Asia, Oceania, Africa, the Caribbean, it doesn't matter. Any place where the people are the color of different grades of coffee, and mangoes plop in mushy heaps on the ground, and the reef fish are brilliant as a box of new crayons. On vacation Michel sheds his manicured adman image and with innocent glee sets about turning himself into a Eurotrash version of Tarzan. Bronzed muscles well in evidence, shark's tooth on a leather thong, fishing knife stuck into the waist of a threadbare pareu, and a wispy sun-streaked ponytail that he tends painstakingly along with a chin crop of Hollywood stubble.

He loves me for a number of wrong reasons connected with his dreams of hot islands. It makes no difference to him that I grew up in Massachusetts, wearing L. L. Bean boots more often than sandals; after eight years of marriage, he doesn't seem to see that what gives strength to the spine of an American black woman, however exotic she appears, is a steely Protestant core. A core that in its absolutism is curiously cold and Nordic. The fact is that I'm not crazy about the tropics, but Michel doesn't want to acknowledge that. Mysteriously, we continue to get along. In fact, our marriage is surprisingly robust, though at the time of our wedding, my mother, my sister, and my girlfriends all gave it a year. I sometimes think the secret is that we don't know each other and never will. Both of us are lazy by nature, and that makes it convenient to hang on to the fantasies we conjured up back when we met in Milan: mine of the French gentleman-adventurer, and his of a pliant black goddess whose feelings accord with his. It's no surprise to me when Michel tries to share the ribald thoughts that run through the labyrinth of his Roman Catholic mind. He doubtless thought that I would get a kick out of hearing about his boat ride with a pair of African sluts.

Those girls have been sitting around watching us from under the mango tree since the day we rolled up from the airport to spend August in the house we borrowed from our friend Jean-Claude. Michel was driving Jean-Claude's car, a Citroën so rump-sprung from the unpaved roads that it moves like a tractor. Our four-year-old son, Lele, can drag his sneakers in red dust through the holes in the floor. The car smells of failure, like the house, which is built on an island off the northern coast of Madagascar, on a beach where a wide scalloped bay spreads like two blue wings, melting into the sky and the wild archipelago of lemur islands beyond. Behind the garden stretch fields of sugarcane and groves of silvery, arthritic-looking ylang-ylang trees, whose flowers lend a tang of Africa to French perfume.

The house is low and long around a grandiose veranda, and was once whitewashed into an emblem of colonial vainglory; now the walls are the indeterminate color of damp, and the thinning palm thatch on the roof swarms with mice and geckos. It has a queenly housekeeper named Hadijah, whose perfect *pommes frites* and plates of crudités, like the dead bidet and dried-up tubes of Bain de Soleil in the bathroom, are monuments to Jean-Claude's ex-wife, who went back to Toulon after seeing a series of projects—a frozen-fish plant, a perfume company, a small luxury hotel—swallowed up in the calm fireworks of the sunsets. Madagascar is the perfect place for a white fool to lose his money, Michel says. He and I enjoy the scent of dissolution in our borrowed house, fuck inventively in the big mildewed ironwood bed, sit in happiness in the sad, bottomed-out canvas chairs on the veranda after a day of spearfishing, watching our son race in and out of herds of humpbacked zebu cattle on the beach.

The only problem for me has been those girls. They're not really whores, just local girls who dance at Bar Kariboo on Thursday nights and hang around the few French and Italian tourists, hoping to trade sex for a T-shirt, a hair clip. They don't know to want Ray-Bans yet; this is not the Caribbean.

I'm used to the women from the Comoros Islands who crowd onto the beach near the house, dressed up in gold bangles and earrings and their best lace-trimmed blouses. They clap and sing in circles for hours, jumping up to dance in pairs, wagging their backsides in tiny precise jerks, laughing and flashing gold teeth. They wrap themselves up in their good time in a way that intimidates me. And I've come to an understanding with the older women of the village, who come by to bring us our morning ration of zebu milk (we drink it boiled in coffee) or to barter with *rideaux Richelieu*, the beautiful muslin cutwork curtains that they embroider. They are intensely curious about me, *l'Américaine*, who looks not unlike one of them, but who dresses and speaks and acts like a foreign madame, and is clearly married to the white man, not just a casual concubine. They ask me for medicine, and if I weren't careful they would clean out my supply of Advil and Bimaxin. They go crazy over Lele, whom they call *bébé métis*—the mixed baby. I want to know all about them, their still eyes, their faces of varying colors that show both African and Indonesian blood, as I want to know everything about this primeval chunk of Africa floating in the Indian Ocean, with its bottle-shaped baobabs and strange tinkling music, the *sega*, which is said to carry traces of tunes from Irish sailors.

But the girls squatting under the mango tree stare hard at me whenever I sit out on the beach or walk down to the water to swim. Then they make loud comments in Malagasy, and burst out laughing. It's juvenile behavior, and I can't help sinking right down to their level and getting provoked. They're probably about eighteen years old, both good-looking; one with a flat brown face and the long straight shining hair that makes some Madagascar women resemble Polynesians; the other darker, with the tiny features that belong to the coastal people called Merina, and a pile of kinky hair tinted reddish. Both are big-titted, as Michel pointed out, the merchandise spilling out of a pair of Nouvelles Frontières T-shirts that they must have got from a tour-group leader. Some days they have designs painted on their faces in yellow sulfur clay. They stare at me, and guffaw and stretch and give their breasts a competitive shake. Sometimes they hoot softly or whistle when I appear.

My policy has been to ignore them, but today they've taken a step ahead, got a rise, however ironic, out of my man. It's a little triumph. I didn't see the Zodiac ride, but through the bathroom window I saw them come back. I was shaving my legs—waxing never lasts long enough in the tropics. Squealing and laughing, they floundered out of the rubber dinghy, patting their hair, settling their T-shirts, retying the cloth around their waists. One of them blew her nose through her fingers into the shallow water. The other said something to Michel, and he laughed and patted her on the backside. Then, arrogantly as two Cleopatras, they strode across the hot sand and took up their crouch under the mango tree. A pair of brown *netsuke*. Waiting for my move.

So, finally, I act. Michel comes sauntering inside to tell me, and after he tells me I make a scene. He's completely taken aback; he's gotten spoiled since we've been married, used to my American cool, which can seem even cooler than French nonchalance. He thought I was going to react the way I used to when I was still modeling and he used to flirt with some of the girls I was working with, some of the bimbos who weren't serious about their careers. That is, that I was going to chuckle, display complicity, even excitement. Instead I yell, say he's damaged my prestige among the locals, say that things are different here. The words seem to be flowing up into my mouth from the ground beneath my feet. He's so surprised that he just stands there with his blue eyes round and his mouth a small *o* in the midst of that Indiana Jones stubble.

Then I hitch up my Soleiado bikini, and march outside to the mango tree. *"Va-t'en!"* I hiss to Red Hair, who seems to be top girl of the duo. "Go away! *Ne parle plus avec mon homme!"*

The two of them scramble to their feet, but they don't seem to be going anywhere, so I slap the one with the straight hair. Except for once, when I was about ten, in a fight with my cousin Brenda, I don't believe I've ever seriously slapped anyone. This, on the scale of slaps, is half-assed, not hard. In that second of contact I feel the strange smoothness of her cheek and an instantaneous awareness that my hand is just as smooth. An electric current seems to connect them. A red light flickers in the depths of the girl's dark eyes, like a computer blinking on, and then, without saying anything to me, both girls scuttle off down the beach, talking loudly to each other, and occasionally looking back at me. I make motions as if I'm shooing chickens. *"Allez-vous-en!"* I screech. Far off down the beach, they disappear into the palms.

Then I go and stretch out in the water, which is like stretching out in blue air. I take off my bikini top and let the equatorial sun print my shadow on the white sand below, where small white fish graze. I feel suddenly calm, but at the same time my mind is working very fast. "My dear, who invited you to come halfway across the world and slap somebody?" I ask myself in the ultra-reasonable tones of my mother, the school guidance counselor. Suddenly I remember another summer on yet another island. This was in Indonesia, a few years ago, when we were exploring the back roads of one of the Moluccas. The driver was a local kid who didn't speak any language we spoke, and was clearly gay. A great-looking kid with light brown skin pitted with a few acne scars, and neat dreadlocks that would have looked stylish in Manhattan. A Princess Di T-shirt, and peeling red nail polish. When we stopped at a waterfall, and Michel the Adventurer went off to climb the lava cliffs, I sat down on a flat rock with the driver, whipped out my beauty case, and painted his nails shocking pink. He jumped when I first grabbed his hand, but when he saw what I was up to he gave me a huge ecstatic grin, and then closed his eyes. And there it was: paradise. The waterfall, the jungle, and that beautiful kid with his long fingers lying in my hand. It was Michel who made a fuss that time, jealous of something he couldn't even define. But I had the same feeling I do now, of acting on instinct and on target. The right act. At the right moment.

"Mama, what did you do?" Lele comes running up to me from where he has been squatting naked on the beach, playing with two small boys from the village. His legs and backside and little penis are covered with sand. I see the boys staring after him, one holding a toy they've been squabbling over: a rough wooden model of a truck, without wheels, tied with a piece of string to a stick. "Ismail says you hit a lady."

Word has already spread along the beach, which is like a stage where a different variety show goes on every hour of the day. The set acts are the tides, which determine the movements of fishing boats, pirogues, Zodiacs, and sailboats. There is always action on the sand: women walk up and down with bundles on their heads; bands of ragged children dig clams at low tide, or launch themselves into the waves at high tide to surf with a piece of old timber; yellow dogs chase chickens and fight over shrimp shells; palm branches crash down on corrugated-iron roofs; girls with lacy dresses and bare sandy shanks parade to Mass; the little mosque opens and shuts its creaky doors; boys play soccer, kicking a plastic water bottle; babies howl; sunburnt tourist couples argue and reconcile. Gossip flashes up and down with electronic swiftness.

I sit up in the water and grab Lele, and kiss him all over while he splashes and struggles to get away. "Yes, that's right," I tell him. It's the firm, didactic voice I use when we've turned off the Teletubbies videos and I am playing the ideal parent. "I did hit a lady," I say.

"She needed hitting." I, the mother who instructs her cross-cultural child in tolerance and nonviolence. Lele has a picture book called *Brothers and Sisters Around the World*, full of illustrations of cookie-cutter figures of various colors, holding hands across continents. All people belong to one family, it teaches. All oceans are the same ocean.

Michel, who has watched the whole scene, comes and tells me that in all his past visits to the island he's never seen anything like it. He's worried. The women fight among themselves, or they fight with their men for sleeping with the tourists, he says. But no foreign woman has ever got mixed up with them. He talks like an anthropologist about loss of face and vendetta. "We might get run out of here," he says nervously.

I tell him to relax, that absolutely nothing will happen. Where do I get this knowledge? It has sifted into me from the water, the air. So, as we planned, we go off spearfishing over by Nosy Komba, where the coral grows in big pastel poufs like furniture in a Hollywood bedroom of the fifties. We find a den of rock lobster and shoot two, and take them back to Jean-Claude's house for Hadijah to cook. Waiting for the lobster, we eat about fifty small oysters the size of mussels and shine flashlights over the beach in front of the veranda, which is crawling with crabs. Inside, Lele is snoring adenoidally under a mosquito net. The black sky above is alive with falling stars. Michel keeps looking at me and shaking his head.

Hadijah comes out bearing the lobster magnificently broiled with vanilla sauce. To say she has presence is an understatement. She got married when she was thirteen, and is now, after eight children, an important personage, the matriarch of a vast and prosperous island clan. She and I have got along fine ever since she realized that I wasn't going to horn in on her despotic rule over Jean-

Claude's house, or say anything about the percentage she skims off the marketing money. She has a closely braided head and is as short and solid as a boulder—on the spectrum of Madagascar skin colors well toward the darkest. This evening she is showing off her wealth by wearing over her pareu a venerable Guns N' Roses T-shirt. She puts down the lobster, sets her hands on her hips, and looks at me, and my heart suddenly skips a beat. Hers, I realize, is the only opinion I care about. "Oh, Madame," she says, flashing me a wide smile and shaking her finger indulgently, as if I'm a child who has been up to mischief. I begin breathing again. "Oh, Madame!"

"Madame has a quick temper," Michel says in a placating voice, and Hadijah throws her head back and laughs till the Guns N' Roses logo shimmies.

"She is right!" she exclaims. *"Madame a raison!* She's a good wife!"

Next morning our neighbor PierLuigi pulls up to the house in his dust-covered Renault pickup. PierLuigi is Italian, and back in Italy has a title and a castle. Here he lives in a bamboo hut when he is not away leading a shark-hunting safari to one of the wild islands a day's sail to the north. He is the real version of what Michel pretends to be: a walking, talking character from a boys' adventure tale, with a corrugated scar low down on one side where a hammerhead once snatched a mouthful. The islanders respect him, and bring their children to him for a worm cure he's devised from crushed papaya seeds. He can bargain down the tough Indian merchants in the market, and he sleeps with pretty tourists and island girls impartially. Nobody knows how many kids he has fathered on the island.

"I hear your wife is mixing in local politics," he calls from the truck to Michel, while looking me over with those shameless eyes that have got so many women in trouble. PierLuigi is sixty years old and has streaks of white in his hair, but he is still six feet four and the best-looking man I have ever seen in my life. "Brava," he says to me. "Good for you, my dear. The local young ladies very often need things put in perspective, but very few of our lovely visitors know how to do it on their own terms."

After he drives off, Michel looks at me with new respect. "I can't say you don't have guts," he says later. Then, "You really must be in love with me."

In the afternoon after our siesta, when I emerge onto the veranda from Jean-Claude's shuttered bedroom, massaging Phyto Plage into my hair, smelling on my skin the pleasant odor of sex, I see—as I somehow expected—that the two girls are back under the mango tree. I walk out onto the burning sand, squinting against the glare that makes every distant object a flat black silhouette, and approach them for the second time. I don't think that we're in for another round, yet I feel my knees take on a wary pugilistic springiness. But as I get close, the straight-haired girl says, *"Bonjour, Madame."*

The formal greeting conveys an odd intimacy. It is clear that we are breathing the same air, now that we have taken each other's measure. Both girls look straight at me, no longer bridling. All three of us know perfectly well that the man—my European husband—was just an excuse, a playing field for our curiosity. The curiosity of sisters separated before birth and flung by the caprice of history half a world away from each other. Now in this troublesome way our connection has been established, and between my guilt and my dawning affection I suspect that I'll never get rid of these two. Already in my mind is forming an exasperating vision of the gifts I know I'll have to give them: lace underpants; Tampax; music cassettes; body lotion—all of them extracted from me with the tender ruthlessness of family members anywhere. And then what? What, after all these years, will there be to say? Well, the first thing to do is answer. *"Bonjour, Mesdemoiselles,"* I reply, in my politest voice.

And because I can't think of anything else, I smile and nod at them and walk into the water, which as always in the tropics is as warm as blood. The whole time I swim, the girls are silent, and they don't take their eyes off me.

Anthropology

(**M**y cousin says: Didn't you think about what *they* would think, that they were going to read it, too? Of course Aunt Noah and her friends would read it, if it were about them, the more so because it was in a fancy Northern magazine. They can read. You weren't dealing with a tribe of Mbuti Pygmies.)

It is bad enough and quite a novelty to be scolded by my cousin, who lives in a dusty labyrinth of books in a West Village artists' building and rarely abandons his Olympian bibliotaph's detachment to chide anyone face-to-face. But his chance remark about Pygmies also punishes me in an idiosyncratic way. It makes me remember a girl I knew at Harvard, a girl with the unlikely name of Undine Loving, whom everybody thought was my sister, the way everybody always assumes that young black women with light complexions and middle-class accents are close relations, as if there could be only one possible family of us. Anyway, this Undine—who was, I think, from Chicago and was prettier than I, with a pair of bright hazel eyes in a round, merry face that under cropped hair suggested a boy chorister, and an equally round, high-spirited backside in the tight Levi's she always wore—this Undine was a grad student, the brilliant protégé of a famous anthropologist, and she went off for a

67

year to Zaire to live among Pygmies. They'll think she's a goddess, my boyfriend at the time annoyed me by remarking. After that I was haunted by an irritating vision of Undine: tall, fair, and callipygian among reverent little brown men with peppercorn hair: an African-American Snow White. I lost sight of her after that, but I'm certain that, in the Ituri Forest, Undine was as dedicated a professional who ever took notes—abandoning toothpaste and toilet paper and subjecting herself to the menstrual hut, clear and scientific about her motives. Never even fractionally disturbing the equilibrium of the Lilliputian society she had chosen to observe. Not like me.

Well, of course, I never had a science, never had a plan. (That's obvious, says my cousin.) Two years ago, the summer before I moved to Rome, I went to spend three weeks with my great-aunt Noah, in Ball County, North Carolina. It was a freak impulse: a last-minute addressing of my attention to the country I was leaving behind. I hadn't been there since I was a child. I was prompted by a writer's vague instinct that there was a thread to be grasped, a strand, initially finer than spider silk, that might grow firmer and more solid in my hands, might lead to something that for the want of a better term I call *of interest*. I never pretended—

(You wanted to investigate your *roots*, says my cousin flatly.) He extracts a cigarette from a red pack bearing the picture of a clove and the words *Kretek Jakarta* and lights it with the kind of ironic flourish that I imagine he uses to intimidate his students at NYU. The way he says *roots*—that spurious seventies term—is so shaming. It brings back all the jokes we used to make in college about fat black American tourists in polyester dashikis trundling around Senegal in Alex Haley tour buses. Black intellectuals are notorious for their snobbish reverence toward Africa—as if crass human nature didn't exist there, too. And, from his West Village aerie, my cousin regards with the same aggressive piety the patch of coastal North Carolina that, before the diaspora north and west, was home to five generations of our family.

We are sitting at his dining table, which is about the length and width of the Gutenberg Bible, covered with clove ash and Melitta filters and the corrected proofs of his latest article. The article is about the whitewashed "magic houses" of the Niger tribe and how the dense plaster arabesques that ornament their facades, gleaming like cake icing, are echoed faintly across the ocean in the designs of glorious, raucous Bahia. He is very good at what he does, my cousin. And he is the happiest of scholars, a minor celebrity in his field, paid royally by obscure foundations to rove from hemisphere to hemisphere, chasing artistic clues that point to a primeval tropical unity. Kerala, Cameroon, Honduras, the Philippines. Ex-wife, children, a string of overeducated girlfriends left hovering wistfully in the dust behind him. He is always traveling, always alone, always vaguely belonging, always from somewhere else. Once he sent me a postcard from Cochin, signed, "Affectionately yours, The Wandering Negro."

Outside on Twelfth Street, sticky acid-green buds are bursting in a March heat wave. But no weather penetrates this studio, which is as close as a confessional and has two computer screens glowing balefully in the background. As he reprimands me I am observing with fascination that my cousin knows how to smoke like a European. I'm the one who lives in Rome, dammit, and yet it is he who smokes with one hand drifting almost incidentally up to his lips and then flowing bonelessly down to the tabletop. And the half-sweet smell of those ridiculous clove cigarettes has permeated every corner of his apartment, giving it a vague atmosphere of stale festivity as if a wassail bowl were tucked away on his overstuffed bookshelves.

I'd be more impressed by all this exotic intellectualism if I didn't remember him as a boy during the single summer we both spent with Aunt Noah down in Ball County. A sallow bookworm with a towering forehead that now in middle age has achieved a mandarin distinction but was then cartoonish. A greedy solitary boy who stole the crumbling syrupy crust off fruit cobblers and who spent the summer afternoons shut in Aunt Noah's unused living room fussily drawing ironclad ships of the Civil War. The two of us loathed each other, and all that summer we never willingly exchanged a word, except insults as I tore by him with my gang of scabby-kneed girlfriends from down the road.

The memory gives me courage to defend myself. All I did, after all, was write a magazine article.

(An article about quilts and superstitions! A fuzzy folkloristic excursion. You made Aunt Noah and the others look cute and rustic and backward like a mixture of *Amos 'n' Andy* and *The Beverly Hillbillies*. Talk about quilts—you embroidered your information. And you mortally offended them—you called them black.)

But they *are* black.

(They don't choose to define themselves that way, and if anybody knows that, you do. We're talking about a group of old people who don't look black and who have always called themselves, if anything, colored. People whose blood has been mixed for so many generations that their lives have been constructed on the idea of being a separate caste. Like in Brazil, or other sensible countries where they accept nuances. Anyway, in ten years Aunt Noah and all those people you visited will be dead. What use was it to upset them by forcing your definitions on them? It's not your place to tell them who they are.)

I nearly burst out laughing at this last phrase, which I haven't heard for a long time. It's not your place to do this, to say that. My cousin used it primly and deliberately as an allusion to the entire structure of family and tradition he thinks I flouted. The phrase is a country heirloom, passed down from women like our grandmother and her sister Eleanora and already sounding archaic on the lips of our mothers in the suburbs of the North. It evokes those towns on the North Carolina–Virginia border, where our families still own land: villages marooned in the tobacco fields, where—as in every other rural community in the world—"place," identity, whether defined by pigmentation, occupation, economic rank, or family name, forms an invisible web that lends structure to daily life. In Ball County everyone knows everyone's place. There, the white-white people, the white-black people like Aunt Noah, and the black-black people all keep to their own niches, even though they may rub shoulders every day and even though they may share the same last names and the same ancestors. Aunt Eleanora became Aunt Noah—Noah as in *know*—because she is a phenomenal chronicler of place, and can recite labyrinthine genealogies with the offhand fluency of a bard. When I was little I was convinced that she was called Noah because she had actually been aboard the Ark. And that she had stored in her head—perhaps on tiny pieces of parchment, like the papers in fortune cookies—the name of every child born since the waters receded from Ararat.

I was scared to death when I went down to Ball County after so many years. Am I thinking this or speaking aloud? Something of each. My cousin's face grows less bellicose as he listens. We actually like each other, my cousin and I. Our childhood hostility has been transmogrified into a bond that is nothing like the instinctive understanding that flows between brothers and sisters: it is more a deeply buried iron link of formal respect. When I was still living in Manhattan we rarely saw each other, but we knew we were snobs about the same occult things. That's why I allow him to scold me. That's why I have to try to explain things to him.

I was scared, I continue. The usual last-minute terrors you get when you're about to return to a place where you've been perfectly happy. I was convinced it would be awful: ruin and disillusion, not a blade of grass the way I remembered it. I was afraid above all that I wouldn't be able to sleep. That I would end up lying awake in a suffocating Southern night contemplating a wreath of moths around a lightbulb, and listening to an old woman thumping around in the next bedroom like a revenant in a coffin. I took medication with me. Strong stuff.

(Very practical, says my cousin.)

But the minute I got there I knew I wouldn't need it. You know I hate driving, so I took an overnight bus from the Port Authority. There isn't a plane or a train that goes near there. And when I got off the bus in front of Ball County Courthouse at dawn, the air was like milk. Five o'clock in the morning at the end of June and 90 percent humidity. White porches and green leaves swimming in mist. Aunt Noah picked me up and drove me down Route 14 in the Oldsmobile that Uncle Pershing left her. A car as long and slow as Cleopatra's barge. And I just lay back, waking up, and sank into the luxurious realization that you can go home again. From vertical New York, life had turned horizontal as a mattress: tobacco, corn, and soybeans spreading out on either side. And you know the first thing I remembered?

(What?)

What it was like to pee in the cornfields. You know I used to run races through the rows with those girls from down the road, and very often we used to stop and pee, not because we had to, but for the fun of it. I remembered the exact feeling of squatting down in that long corridor of leaves, our feet sinking into the sides of the furrow as we pulled down our Carter's cotton underpants, the heat from the ground blasting up onto our backsides as we pissed lakes into the black dirt.

The last time before my visit that I had seen Aunt Noah was two years earlier at my wedding in Massachusetts. There she elicited great curiosity from my husband's family, a studious clan of New England Brahmins who could not digest the fact that the interracial marriage to which they had agreed with such eager tolerance had allied them with a woman who appeared to be an elderly white Southern housewife. She looked the same as she had at the wedding and very much as she had when we were kids. Eighty-three years old, with smooth graying hair colored intermittently with Loving Care and styled in a precise nineteen fifties helmet that suited her crisp pastel shirtwaist dresses and flat shoes. The same crumpled pale-skinned face of an aged belle, round and girlish from the front but the profile displaying a blunt leonine nose and calm predator's folds around the mouth—she was born, after all, in the magisterial solar month of July. The same blue-gray eyes, shrewd and humorous, sometimes alight with the intense love of a childless woman for her nieces and nephews but never sentimental, never suffering a fool. And, at odd moments, curiously remote.

Well, you look beautiful, she said, when she saw me get off the bus.

And the whole focus of my life seemed to shift around. At the close of my twenties, as I was beginning to feel unbearably adult, crushed by the responsibilities of a recently acquired husband, apartment, and job, here I was offered the brief chance to become a young girl again. Better than being a pampered visiting daughter in my mother's house: a pampered visiting niece.

Driving to her house through the sunrise, she said: I hear you made peace with those in-laws of yours.

Things are okay now, I said, feeling my face get hot. She was referring to a newlywed spat that had overflowed into the two families and brought out all the animosity that had been so dutifully concealed at the wedding.

They used excuses to make trouble between you and your husband. He's a nice boy, so I don't lay blame on your marrying white. But you have to watch out for white folks. No matter how friendly they act at first, you can't trust them.

As always it seemed funny to hear this from the lips of someone who looked like Aunt Noah. Who got teased up North by kids on the street when she walked through black neighborhoods. Until she stopped, as she always did, and told them what was what.

The sky was paling into tropical heat, the mist chased away by the brazen song of a million cicadas. The smell of fertilizer and drying earth flowed through the car windows, and I could feel my pores starting to pump out sweat, as if I'd parachuted into equatorial Africa.

Aunt Noah, I said, just to tweak her, you wouldn't have liked it if I'd married a black-black man.

Oh Lord, honey, no, she said. She put on the blinker and turned off the highway into the gravel driveway. We passed beneath the fringes of the giant willow that shaded the brick ranch house Uncle Pershing built fifty years ago as a palace for his beautiful childless wife. The house designed to rival the houses of rich white people in Ball County. Built and air-conditioned with the rent of dark-skinned tenants who cultivated the acres of tobacco that have belonged to Noah and Pershing's families for two hundred years. They were cousins, Noah and Pershing, and they had married both for love and because marrying cousins was what one did among their people at that time. A nigger is just as bad as white trash, she said, turning off the engine. But, honey, there were still plenty of boys you could have chosen from our own kind.

(You stayed two weeks, my cousin says, jealously.)

I was researching folkways, I tell him, keeping a straight face. I was hoping to find a mother lode of West African animism, pithy backwoods expressions, seventeenth-century English thieves' cant, poetic upwellings from the cyclic drama of agriculture, as played out on the Southeastern tidal plain. I wanted to be ravished by the dying tradition of the peasant South, like Jean Toomer.

(My cousin can't resist the reference. *Fecund Southern night, a pregnant Negress,* he declaims, in the orotund voice of a Baptist preacher.)

What I really did during my visit was laze around and let Aunt Noah spoil me. Every morning scrambled eggs, grits, country ham, and hot biscuits with homemade peach preserves. She was up for hours before me, working in her garden. A fructiferous Eden of giant pea vines, prodigious tomato plants, squash blossoms like Victrola horns. She wore a green sun hat that made her look like an elderly infant, blissfully happy. Breakfast over and the house tidy, we would set out on visits where she displayed me in the only way she knew how, as an ornamental young sprig on the family tree. I fell into the gratifying role of the cherished newly-wed niece, passed around admiringly like a mail-order collectible doll. Dressing in her frilly pink guest room, I put on charming outfits: long skirts, flowery blouses. I looked like a poster girl for *Southern*

Living. Everyone we visited was enchanted. My husband, who telephoned me every night, began to seem very far away: a small white boy's voice sounding forlornly out of Manhattan.

The people we called on all seemed to be distant relatives of Aunt Noah's and mine, and more than once I nearly fell asleep in a stuffy front room listening to two old voices tracing the spiderweb of connections. I'd decided to write about quilts, and that gave us an excuse to go chasing around Ball County peering at old masterpieces dragged out of mothballs, and new ones stitched out of lurid polyester. Everybody had quilts, and everybody had some variation of the same four family names. Hopper, Osborne, Amiel, Mills. There was Gertie Osborne, a little freckled woman with the diction of a Victorian schoolmistress, who contributed the "Rambling Reader" column to the *Ball County Chronicle*. The tobacco magnate and head deacon P. H. Mills, tall and rich and silent in his white linen suits. Mary Amiel, who lived up the road from Aunt Noah and wrote poetry privately printed in a volume entitled *The Flaming Depths*. Aunt Noah's brother-in-law Hopper Mills, who rode a decrepit motorbike over to check up on her every day at dawn.

I practiced pistol-shooting in the woods and went to the tobacco auction and rode the rope-drawn ferry down at Crenshaw Crossing. And I attended the Mount Moriah Baptist church, where years before I had passed Sunday mornings in starched dresses and cotton gloves. The big church stood unchanged under the pines: an air-conditioned Williamsburg copy in brick as vauntingly prosperous as Aunt Noah's ranch house.

After the service, they were all together outside the church, chatting in the pine shade: the fabled White Negroes of Ball County. An enterprising *Ebony* magazine journalist had described them that way once, back in 1955. They were a group who defied conventional logic: Southern landowners of African descent who had pale skins and generations of free ancestors. Republicans to a man. People who'd fought to desegregate Greensboro and had marched on Washington yet still expected their poorer, blacker tenants to address them as Miss Nora or Mr. Fred. Most of them were over seventy: their sons and daughters had escaped years ago to Washington or Atlanta or Los Angeles or New York. To them I was the symbol of all those runaway children, and they loved me to pieces.

(But then you went and called them black. In print, which to people raised on the Bible and the McGuffey Readers is as definitive as a set of stone tablets. And you did it not in some academic journal but in a magazine that people buy on newsstands all over the country. To them it was the worst thing they could have read about themselves—)

I didn't—

(Except perhaps being called white.)

I didn't mean—

(It was the most presumptuous thing you could have done. They're old. They've survived, defining themselves in a certain way. We children and grandchildren can call ourselves Afro-American or African-American or black or whatever the week's fashion happens to be.)

You—

(And of course you knew this. We all grew up knowing it. You're a very smart woman, and the question is why you allowed yourself to be so careless. So breezy and destructive. Maybe to make sure you couldn't go back there.)

I say: That's enough. Stop it.

And my cousin, for a minute, does stop. I never noticed before how much he looks like Uncle Pershing. The same mountainous brow and reprobative eyes of a biblical patriarch that look out of framed photographs in Aunt Noah's living room. A memory reawakens of being similarly thundered at, in the course of that childhood summer, when I lied about borrowing Uncle Pershing's pocketknife.

We sit staring at each other across this little cluttered table in Greenwich Village. I am letting him tell me off as I would never allow my brother or my husband—especially my husband. But the buried link between my cousin and me makes the fact that I actually sit and take it inevitable. As I do, it occurs to me that fifty years ago, in the moribund world we are arguing about, it would have been an obvious choice for the two of us to get married. As Ball County cousins always did. And how far we have flown from it all, as if we were genuine emigrants, energetically forgetful of some small, dire old-world country plagued by dictators, drought, locusts, and pogroms. Years ago yet another of our cousins, a dentist in Atlanta, was approached by Aunt Noah about moving his family back to Ball County and taking over her house and land. I remember him grimacing with incredulity about it as we sat over drinks once in an airport bar. Why did the family select him for this honor? he asked, with a strained laugh. The last place anyone would ever want to be, he said.

I don't know what else to do but stumble on with my story.

Aunt Noah was having a good time showing me off. On one of the last days of my visit, she drove me clear across the county to the house where she grew up. I'd never been there, though I knew that was where it had all begun. It was on this land, in the seventeen forties, before North Carolina statutes about slavery and mixing of races had grown hard and fast, that a Scotch-Irish settler—a debtor or petty thief deported to the pitch-pine wilderness of the penal colony—allowed his handsome half-African, half-Indian bond servant to marry his only daughter. The handsomeness of the bond servant is part of the tradition, as is the pregnancy of the daughter. Their descendants took the land and joined the group of farmers and artisans who managed to carve out an independent station between the white planters and the black slaves until after the Civil War. Dissertations and books have been written about them. The name some scholars chose for them has a certain lyricism: Tidewater Free Negroes.

My daddy grew tobacco and was the best blacksmith in the county, Aunt Noah told me. There wasn't a man, black or white, who didn't respect him.

We had turned onto a dirt road that led through fields of tobacco and corn farmed by the two tenant families who divided the old house. It was a nineteenth-century farmhouse, white and green with a rambling porch and fretwork around the eaves. I saw with a pang that the paint was peeling and that the whole structure had achieved the undulating organic shape that signals imminent collapse.

I can't keep it up, and, honey, the tenants just do enough to keep the roof from falling in, she said. Good morning, Hattie, she called out, stopping the car and waving to a woman with corn-rowed hair and skin the color of dark plums, who came out of the front door.

Good morning, Miss Nora, said Hattie.

Mama's flower garden was over there, Aunt Noah told me. You never saw such peonies. We had a fishpond and a greenhouse and an icehouse. Didn't have to buy anything except sugar and coffee and flour. And over there was a paddock for trotting horses. You know there was a fair every year where Papa and other of our kind of folks used to race their sulkies. Our own county fair.

She collected the rent, and we drove away. On the road, she stopped and showed me her mother's family graveyard, a mound covered with Amiel and Hopper tombstones rising in the middle of a tobacco field. She told me she paid a boy to clean off the brush.

You know it's hard to see the old place like that, she said. But I don't see any use in holding on to things just for the sake of holding on. You children are all off in the North, marrying your niggers or your white trash—honey, I'm just fooling, you know how I talk— and pretty soon we ugly old folks are going to go. Then there will just be some bones out in the fields and some money in the bank.

That was the night that my husband called from New York with the news we had hoped for: his assignment in Europe was for Rome.

(You really pissed them off, you know, says my cousin, continuing where he left off. You were already in Italy when the article was published, and your mother never told you, but it was quite an item for the rest of the family. There was that neighbor of Aunt Noah's, Dan Mills, who was threatening to sue. They said he was ranting: *I'm not African-American like they printed there! I'm not black!*)

Well, God knows I'm sorry about it now. But really—what could I have called them? The quaint colored folk of the Carolina lowlands? Mulattos and octoroons, like something out of *Mandingo?*

(You could have thought more about it, he says, his voice softening. You could have considered things before plunging into the quilts and the superstitions.)

You know, I tell him, I did talk to Aunt Noah just after the article came out. She said: Oh, honey, some of the folks around here got worked up about what you wrote, but they calmed right down when the TV truck came around and put them on the evening news.

My cousin drums his fingers thoughtfully on the table as I look on with a certain muted glee. I can tell that he isn't familiar with this twist in the story.

(Well—he says.) Rising to brew us another pot of coffee. Public scourging finished; case closed. By degrees he changes the subject to a much-discussed new book on W. E. B. Du Bois in Germany. Have I read about that sojourn in the early nineteen thirties? Du Bois's weirdly prescient musings on American segregation and the National Socialist racial laws?

We talk about this and about his ex-wife and his upcoming trip to Celebes and the recent flood of Nigerian Kok statues on the London art market. Then, irresistibly, we turn again to Ball County. I surprise my cousin by telling him that if I can get back to the States this fall, I may go down there for Thanksgiving. With my husband. Aunt Noah invited us. That's when they kill the pigs, and I want to taste some of that fall barbecue. Why don't you come too? I say.

(Me? I'm not a barbecue fan, he says. Having the grace to flush slightly on the ears. Aren't you afraid that they're going to burn a cross in front of your window? he adds with a smile.)

I'll never write about that place again, I say. Just one thing, though—

(What?)

What would you have called them?

He takes his time lighting up another Kretek Jakarta. His eyes, through the foreign smoke, grow as remote as Aunt Noah's, receding in the distance like a highway in a rearview mirror. And I have a moment of false nostalgia. A quick glimpse of an image that never was: a boy racing me down a long corridor of July corn, his big flat feet churning up the dirt where we'd peed to mark our territory like two young dogs, his skinny figure tearing along ahead of me, both of us breaking our necks to get to the vanishing point where the green rows come together and geometry begins. Gone.

His cigarette lit, my cousin shakes his head and gives a short exasperated laugh. (In the end, it doesn't make a damn bit of difference, does it? he says.)

Un Petit d'un Petit

I 'm swatting fallen leaves with a hockey stick in front of the Victorian castle where I dream through school hours with other captive heroines, when a car pulls up. The car is a station wagon, green as the Philadelphia suburbs around us. And the girl behind the wheel is wearing green as well, a pleated tunic that means she goes to Chew Academy, our rival down the road. She rolls down the window and leans out with the air of a baroness addressing a roadside peasant. "Have you seen Dogface?" she asks.

I don't know her, but from the car and the nickname—an elegant sibling appellation for my best friend, Edie—I know she has to be Edie's older sister Gus, whose beauty is a tribulation to the rest of the family. "Big eyes and big tits" is the capsule description I've heard of Gus, but what strikes me is the phenomenal whiteness of her skin as she sits there in all that green, a pallor like candle wax that culminates in an incandescent burst of red-blond hair. She has bound up this hair with a silk scarf in a topknot that makes her look like a fifties movie star, and the impatient majesty with which she sits behind the wheel discounts any idea I might have that she is just a schoolgirl like me. All in all, an unsettling apparition to face beside a hockey field on a bleak fall afternoon. As I stand transfixed in my sweaty gym clothes and graceless fourteen years, she looks

me over with amused contempt. I direct her to Edie down at the
Old Gym and continue on my way, only now with the feeling of
stepping along on invisible stilts, my head high above the thinning
treetops. It's the same feeling I get every September when I fall in
love with that year's English teacher.

For some time after that, worshiping Gus is a private luxury like
a certain kind of candy I hoard in my locker: a shell-shaped bitter
chocolate with an Italian name. It goes on outside of my friendship
with Edie, which is another story altogether: a normal adolescent
catalog of lachrymose confessions, gut-wrenching fits of mirth,
and shared musing on future lives of art and turpitude. And it has
nothing to do with the broth of intimacy and rivalry that simmers
around Edie and Gus. It's an undemanding crush in which I simply
allow myself to relax into bedazzlement whenever she flashes by. My
encounters with her at Edie's house and in other places take on an
intensity that encloses the details in a magnified wall of sensation so
that in my memory they line up gleaming like a row of crystal balls.

At a New Year's Eve party, I watch her clowning with her guitar,
surrounded by clusters of infatuated boys. In a wailing, cornball
voice, she sings "Dona Dona":

> On a wagon bound for market
> There's a calf with a mournful eye . . .

It is Gus's party, which Edie and I have been allowed to attend
on sufferance because a freak blizzard has thinned the ranks of her

friends, students from prep schools and colleges up and down the
East Coast. Snow dervishes spin against the windows and make the
fire sputter in the sitting room of the bland suburban house filled with
Boston and Philadelphia antiques. The prettiest girls wear jewel-
colored Indian dresses, and the most desirable boys are dressed
like ranch hands or factory workers. It's not a costume party, just
the seventies. They all keep moseying out into the storm to ingest
various chemicals, though at the time I'm aware only that some
Olympian mischief is going on. Mousy and prim in a wool A-line
skirt and matching sweater, I sit sipping a digestive liqueur made by
monks, a drink I chose because it was in the least intimidating bottle.
No one talks to me, and I have spent most of the evening feigning
absorption in a coffee-table book of nursery rhymes rendered wit-
tily in nonsensical French. *Un petit d'un petit s'étonne aux Halles*—
Humpty-Dumpty sat on a wall. Edie, prettier and bolder, has just
abandoned me to chat up a Haverford sophomore when Gus crosses
the room and stops in front of me.

"You! What have you got on your legs?" she asks, in the loud,
flippant tones of a social triumphator, who knows that whatever she
says or does will add hugely to the general jollification. A numbness
comes over me, as I observe the firelight gleaming on her bright
hair and slightly prominent white teeth: it is the swift anesthesia that
is nature's gift to bird or beast in the talons of the raptor. Dreamily,
I am aware that her friends have paused in their talk to observe us.
She is peering at my tights, a glistening silver pair on which I have
spent my allowance in hope that, as I read in a teen glamour magazine, they will add the all-important touch of holiday sophistication.

"It's sort of a style called the wet look," I say, trying to fold up
my poor silly legs and stick them out of sight.

Gus laughs with dreadful clarity, flashing her carnivore's overbite, setting off ripples of laughter around us. "Wet!" she exclaims to her audience. "Looks more like slime!" It is a moment of debacle that strikes my idolatrous heart with a complicated mixture of pleasure and pain. And it leaves me strangely without bitterness—in memory merely becoming a static, faintly allegorical scene, like an engraving in an old pornographic book.

A few months afterward, I watch Gus in a movie that must still exist in some school archive. Shot by Edie for an art project, it's a five-minute eight millimeter that shows Gus with a boyfriend, a cousin. There is a beach of egg-sized granite pebbles; the Maine sea crumpling like gray taffeta beyond; two improbably beautiful teenagers (who seem mature and sophisticated to me) in foul-weather jackets, mugging for the camera with the energy of a pair of healthy young setters. The whites of their eyes are as clear as skim milk. He feeds her a stone, she dumps seaweed on his head; even through the amateurish focus comes a sense of the aimless reciprocity of perfect happiness. Like any spectator I anticipate with relish the doom of that happiness, doom Edie tells me has existed from the start in the big shingled summer houses barely visible in the background of the film, houses full of aunts and uncles who play New England Montagues and Capulets. Edie's film doesn't show, but somehow implies, the endless family councils on inbreeding and the real-life medieval finish, in which Gus is packed off to college in France. The film earns Edie an A in art. I make her show it to me three times.

At about the same time I wear one of Gus's old dresses to the May dance at school. As if by chance, not even admitting anything to myself, I've chosen it over an array of my own dresses, out of a mass of things from a closet at Edie's house. The dress is apple green satin with silver buttons, too large for me in the bust and in every way so extremely unbecoming that it seems like a statement of some kind. There is a snapshot of me wearing it, standing in my garden before the dance, and my expression is both dreamy and stubborn.

Four years pass, and I attend a wedding in Rhode Island, in a small brown Episcopalian church with a view of Narragansett Bay. A cool clear July day, sunlight on the pearls of the Philadelphia and Providence aunts crowding the church, Gus in old lace and wildflowers in front of the altar. She has cropped her hair to an inch long and looks disturbingly fey, like a garlanded Peter Pan. The mascara on her lashes stands out against blanched cheeks. She wears a slightly demented look of joy. Beside her is a Frenchman, who exactly fits the image I carry in my brain under the heading "Frenchman": dark, brachycephalic, handsome; with a short man's swagger and a brilliant smile that makes a sudden white rift in a face tanned the color of walnuts. The intelligence circulating like a breeze through the groves of the aunts is that this is a choice far more imprudent than marrying a cousin. This ravishing niece from the poor end of the family might have recouped many things with a judicious marriage. But instead of being the kind of Frenchman she could well aspire to—a baron with rolling vineyards, a vulgar but fetchingly solvent property developer with half of the Côte d'Azur in his pocket—the man is a travel agent and tour leader, who first wooed Gus over the Atlantic, with champagne swiped from First Class. An accomplished charmer trailing an untidy string of ex-wives and girlfriends, he knows enough to disarm the aunts with boasts of his peasant roots. He is from the Vercors, the high plateau where the French resistance fighters hid in limestone caves.

Edie and I are photographing the wedding, and we have dressed like men, in white linen trousers and jackets and bow ties. We want to look original and decadent and hope to upstage the bride. I am in college now, my virginity long gone, sure of my looks and puffed up with the importance of my own romantic dramas. My schoolgirl crush seems as distant as chicken pox. This is confirmed after the cake and the toasts, when people are getting seriously drunk on a lawn that runs down to a private dock, and the bridegroom comes up to me. "That outfit doesn't work," he says in French. "You should show off your body."

He looks me over with the matter-of-fact brazenness of a man who feels entitled to any woman at any time. And suddenly—the novelty of this feeling is breathtaking—I am afraid for Gus. The newlyweds sail off in a Herreshoff sloop that, like the sweeping lawns and the long gabled house sprawled above, seems to be part of Gus's dowry but in reality belongs to yet another distant relative. Before leaving they stand on the dock, the groom's arm tightly around her, swapping jokes in French with the crowd. Tipsy uncles are hollering colloquialisms. "He never calls me darling," Gus complains gigglingly to her audience. "*Il m'appelle sa boudin:* he calls me his blood sausage."

Now this tale skips years and continents and alights in the middle of a wet autumn in a working-class suburb of Paris near Orly Airport. Jets take off overhead, so close that you can see the wheels retracting into their bellies, drowning out sounds of life in the narrow streets where sycamore trees are cropped into knobs like arthritic hands, and small houses with pointed tile roofs stand behind meager fences in gardens the width of hallway carpets. Gus's wrought-iron gate is enameled a flaking tan, and has an annoying long French key that must turn four times before the gate opens with a metallic groan. She has given me the key because I am staying with her since I walked out on my Parisian boyfriend after a summer of love and literature at the Sorbonne.

We stand in the kitchen, where Gus is fixing lunch. She mixes hunks of day-old bread with grated Gruyère and slices of a cabbage we bought at the outdoor market this morning. Before putting it in the oven, she sluices it with homemade onion soup. Her hands have a deftness that seems a bit show-off. This is a peasant dish, she tells me. Her husband ate it when he was a boy in a hilltop village half destroyed by German bombs. She has spent two scorching summers there, mainly in a kitchen plucking fowl and pickling cucumbers among female in-laws dressed like lay sisters in black.

Her kitchen is small and dark like all the other rooms in the house. In the living room hang a few watercolors of Maine islands. The kitchen looks out on rain and a wall covered with a vine whose leaves are turning the shiny yellow of children's slickers. In a tiny driveway sits a battered but jaunty red MG. This car belongs to Gus's husband, and she is not allowed to drive it when he is off leading tours. He is often away on long trips to Brazil, Yemen, Australia. Sometimes he flies with his mistress, who is a flight attendant he knew before he met Gus. Sometimes this woman, who has black hair and an ungenerous nature, parks outside their house in the middle of the night and screams insults.

There is a hard jauntiness in Gus's voice as she speaks of her troubles that makes me feel almost as young and insignificant as I did when she was a debutante. We're not exactly friends, not like

Edie and me; yet a nameless bond has grown between us. She is six months pregnant and, except for her swollen belly, impossibly thin. Her skin and hair look almost phosphorescent in the Parisian autumn gloom. One afternoon when we go mushroom hunting in a nearby wood, I look at her sharp profile and pipestem wrists and for some reason remember the French trick rhyme I was reading at the party when she laughed at my tights: *Un petit d'un petit s'étonne aux Halles.* On a hillside dotted with cowpats, she holds up the basket of mushrooms—cèpes and pieds de moutons—and we bend over to smell them. There is no real fragrance, just a breath of moisture and decay.

Three years later when I'm living in Rome, she comes to visit me for a weekend. By then I have a cushy job at the United States Information Service. I live on Via Giulia and have a terrace in crumbling buff-colored stone and am quite the girl about town, with an Italian boyfriend and a Siamese cat. I've learned how to dress, where chic Roman women buy their underwear and shoes. Gus arrives with her second daughter on her back. The first little girl is rusticating with her grandparents in the Vercors. This baby is a round-headed blond cherub of eleven months who sucks with Rabelaisian vigor at her mother's huge pearly breast. Gus has pink cheeks now, and talks about nettle teas and herbal ointments for eczemas, and mothers in Africa who nurse children until they are five or six. She has let her hair grow out into limp fair wisps that cling to her head in an unbecoming way that makes me think of feathers on ducklings, and she wears an embroidered Afghan shirt, out of style in Rome right now. My boyfriend teases me about "the hippie mamma," and I feel vaguely insulted that he is not falling in love with her.

But that evening when we drive down Via Veneto in my little

convertible, I see that Italians in nearby cars are turning to stare at us. Why is it that they are looking, that some wave, and somebody even honks? I turn around and see that Gus, like a woman casually shrugging on a wrap, has reassumed her old glamour. She and the gorgeous baby, both sitting tall and wearing big broad grins, are parading through the Roman night like a Hollywood Madonna and child.

We meet in Maine, after a space of several years. We are on an island in the Penobscot, a place ringed with granite boulders, where the locals speak in accents out of Sarah Orne Jewett, and the smell of woodsmoke carries for miles through the pines. There is a cove with three farmhouses that belong to Edie and Gus's family, the same ancestral cove where in the long-ago film Gus and her cousin fed each other stones in perfect bliss. I am staying in the oldest farmhouse with my husband of one year. Speaking of bliss, we are at the accomplished stage in love when the sense of miracles has become triumphantly quotidian. There are the usual sea urchins and blueberries and gray mornings that become incandescent noons and hordes of freckled children in dinghies; and across the way is Edie with a dull husband, and somewhere around the edges is Gus, alone, in a cloud of rumor about the Frenchman. My husband wins a Fourth of July swimming race across the cove, and in the midst of the cheers and my own delirious pride, as he emerges from the icy water like a blue-lipped god, I glimpse Gus and note with surprise that she like everyone else is a small unimportant figure in the foreground of my idyll. A month later she surprises me again, with a letter that plunges in medias res. "Watching the two of you has shaken me, put a mark on me, knocked me out of my niche of cowardice. I know now what is possible, if I find the courage to go after it."

The letter is written in the exquisite spidery handwriting of all the women in their family, and a pine tree is sketched rather brilliantly at the top. But I forget to respond, busy as I am with marriage, with inhabiting another person.

Life intervenes. The death of Edie and Gus's mother, the remarriage of their father, Edie's tumultuous divorce. The births of my children, my own divorce, my work, my life in Europe. All stories worth recounting. But on this peculiar path I am tracing, the next milestone comes in the form of a letter that contains an article clipped from the *Times* of a coastal town in Massachusetts. The article describes the opening of a French restaurant called Le Maquisard in a white elephant of a frame house in the town, and has a photograph of the proprietors: Gus and the Frenchman. The letter, from Edie, tells me that Gus grabbed her daughters and left France one morning, and that the Frenchman disappointed a number of women by following his wife. At present they are reconciled among the beurre noir and dried cèpes of this new mad venture, which is going great guns, at least with the summer people. I look at Gus's face in the photograph: an oval of tiny gray dots that tells me nothing except that she is still beautiful. Her position at the side of the Frenchman has, to my mind, a provisional look. I reread the letter and ponder the wonderful seductiveness of action, of clean, defiant acts; and the tedium of consequences.

A number of years scurry past with the undignified haste of startled geese. Suddenly I hear gravel crackle under tires, and Gus pulls up the driveway in a tall blue Jeep and peers out at me with a quizzical tilt of the head that reminds me of our first meeting near the hockey field. This happens in Newport, where I've rented a house and am soaking up the American summer with an expatriate's melancholy gusto. She looks the same—just sharper around the edges, the way we all do. And something completely unexpected has come out of hiding: a rueful good humor that signifies a talent for living. She's not a glamour girl or a martyr anymore, and she has left behind the garlicky romantic dramas of the restaurant business. Of all the roles I never envisioned for her, she is a teacher, filling the occasionally receptive minds of high school students in her coastal town with irregular French verbs and tidbits of Pascal. Her eyes, under the unchanged long lashes, hold a proper pedagogical irony. She slams the car door and walks over to plant a kiss on the foot of my six-month-old son, who is propped on my shoulder. "We're going to talk for twelve hours!" she announces.

The forerunner of this visit was a wedding announcement that arrived months ago at my house in Northern Italy. A snapshot showed Gus in bone-colored satin beside a man whose expression of uncomplicated devotion was as American as the name engraved on the announcement. A fellow teacher, who courted her over a long bitter New England winter. Now, sitting in a wicker chair on my rented porch, she talks on about him, blushing and excited as she never was as a teenager. It's love, of course, straightforward and divine, arrived at last according to its own mysterious timetable. She holds my son and tells me she longs to have a child with her new husband, but wonders if she's too old, that they were so crazy about each other when they first met that her breasts filled with milk. We eat corn on the cob and blueberry pie and gradually drift into that helium sphere of giggling late-night confidence where straight news takes on phantasmagoric color and exaggeration. Is it

really possible that the Frenchman has been reborn in the Church of
Christ and settled down contentedly beside a Vermont lake? Until
past midnight we discuss our men. Mine is Italian, and faintly like
the Frenchman, as hers is faintly like my American ex-husband. We
exchange queasy smiles over this.

Noontime next day finds us at Gooseberry Beach, surrounded
by rich people in sensible bathing suits and canvas hats. In the cold
Atlantic we jump and splash with exaggerated girlish gestures. Gus
is wearing a black suit as shiny as a mussel shell, and we are engaged
in the sly game of women over forty, covertly scanning each other's
bodies for signs of wear. She has the same startling white skin as
ever, only twining over her chest and collarbone is a large vein I
don't remember, sinuous as a vine.

She is telling me about her teenage daughters, beautiful bilingual
girls who divide their year between New England and France. How
creative they are, and how patient with the quirks of father and
stepfather; how one is learning to fly, and another will study soil
conservation in Madagascar. She shows a picture of a small Cape
Cod house on a pastoral road. With vegetables and chickens in the
back, and a tent permanently pitched for visitors from Boston and
France. We scoop holes in the sand and our talk assumes a desperate
velocity as the hour draws near for Gus to drive back to Massachusetts. As if finishing up a complicated board game, we attempt to
comment on every single person we both know. Mercurial Edie;
friends from Paris; my brothers; her raft of handsome tragic cousins; the boy who owned the guitar Gus played at that New Year's
party. And me, of course. "I always thought you were incredibly
interesting," she says, sifting a fistful of sand.

This is untrue, but she seems to believe it. And for a minute the array of past scenes we share undergoes a drastic shift in perspective. As if the effulgent young goddess who sat wreathed with admirers, playing the guitar badly in a New Year's blizzard, had actually been trying to impress me with her clowning. The funny thing is how little the truth matters now, just as it doesn't matter whether we are really friends. Now we are simply a pair of women, not yet old, each trying in vain to create something useful out of her memories: something protective, perhaps, like foul-weather gear.

With clothes in mind, I tell her about wearing her green dress to the dance. "You're kidding," she says. "That Jackie Kennedy thing? That was one of the ugliest dresses I ever had."

"I know," I say. "It looked terrible on me."

At four o'clock Gus climbs into her Jeep and backs up, swearing softly in French as she struggles with the clutch. She calls out to me to keep my pecker up, and I shout something bawdy in return. Then, through the windshield, I watch her bright head catch the afternoon sunlight, flare up and fade as she disappears down the street, past lofty elms and Victorian houses. I pause for a minute in the driveway, wondering where and when we'll see each other next, and as I do it occurs to me for absolutely the first time to wonder whether there is a hidden logic to this sparse set of encounters across oceans and years. Like a science fiction story, where isolated flashes from space turn out to be parts of a coded dispatch. And even if there is no interstellar communiqué, I think, there certainly exists some dull celestial chamber of protocol where the number of my meetings with Gus has already been fixed. Standing in the deep summer shade, I try, for a few heartbeats, to guess how many we have left.

Dancing with Josefina

"Thanks, I'd love to." So, if I recall correctly, begins a Dorothy Parker monologue, set in similar circumstances. But what I actually say is *"Sí, gracias."* Adding a coy dip of the eyelashes that any film director would nix as being over the top, but which to my mind gives me the authentic air of belonging to the local population of nubile señoritas. There is no need to move to the center of the dance floor, since we are already there, already molten with the heat, crushed in the pullulating Friday night crowd at Bobby's, a harbor club where the jump-ups get so packed and wild that the pilings shudder like an earthquake, and eels and remoras swarm to devour the beer vomit in the spotlit sea below. We're in the Bay Islands of Honduras, which are the usual Caribbean crucible of races. The mob of dancers swirls with teak- and amber-colored faces, legacy of Hispanic sailors, English pirates, Maroon slaves, Mosquito Indians. Over the alternating beats of salsa and reggae rises the buzz of Spanish and the lilt of island English. Adrift in the whole mad brew are a few Americans. Me, for example, an unabashed tourist. And my husband, Rory, and our expatriate friend Mitch, who are presently hailing me with Dos Equis bottles out of the sweltering press at the bar. And also this gentleman, quite a senior gentleman,

97

who left his little cluster of friends—gray-haired fellows with a lot of rum under their belts, yachtsmen's brick complexions, and the look of timid but relentless hunger that marks the sex tourist—to squeeze up next to me. He put a large pinkish paw on my elbow—respectfully, it must be said—and, in halting phrasebook Spanish, asked me to dance.

It's rare to have the opportunity to make mischief with such ease. So simple to break off eye contact with husband and friend across the room. To give that little falsely modest flicker of the lashes and make a simpering reply in the few words of Spanish I know, and begin moving thorax and pelvis in a way that suggests that I pulled on my scanty cotton dress in one of the shacks that stand on stilts out in the water, in the town named after a buccaneer who holed up there to feast and fornicate. Easy to pretend that I am not a coddled North American black woman, aged thirty-one, the kind of young woman this man might encounter in an investment bank, or see on the podium at an academic conference. That I am much younger and poorer, that the genes for my dark skin arrived from Africa along the thoroughfares opened by the conquistadors, rather than the more northerly Protestant channels of the Georgian slavers. That the boundaries of my education were marked not by a graduate degree but by the dusty walls of the island elementary school, where geckos scuttle and boards hide the windows the hurricane shattered. That I'm not married to Rory, a white lawyer from Delaware, who might be this man's nephew, or son. And that perhaps I'd be just desperate enough to trade a few blow jobs for a charm bracelet, or a pair of running shoes, or even the fata morgana of a U.S. passport.

"*Sí, gracias. Bailamos.*"

It would be too easy to detest him immediately, so I'll take my time. Dispassionately I observe how he starts to wag his buttocks, in innocent khaki shorts, to the truly wonderful music, which the deejay has magicked into a weird dub fusion: a Caribbean male voice intoning salacious directives over a Latin beat. It's hot muscular sound that you have to obey, and, packed around us, gorgeous Honduran kids, their faces incandescent with sweat, are humping away as if their lives depended on it. My partner makes it clear that he would like to hump me too—his friends, after all, are watching. They loosed a faint cheer and raised their glasses when we started dancing. But I keep myself a hygienic inch from his soaked polo shirt and make it look like seductive teasing. I improvise an undulating mishmash of bumps and grinds with a sort of samba-limbo-macarena flavor. I've never been a good dancer, but I once had a Puerto Rican boyfriend who made me appear to have rhythm. The guy in front of me, of course, belongs to a whole different category of bad dancing: the juggernaut school. I haven't looked at him closely yet. Except to note that he's large and red and old.

"Cómo te llamas?" Shouted over the music.

What's that? Oh, a name, a name. Maria would be too absurd, and for some reason, all the other names that spring to mind are unequivocally Nordic. Helga—no. Although Frieda brings to mind magnificent Kahlo, Mexican icon with her baroque costumes and Byzantine monobrow. Gabriela—no. Erendira? Let's stay away from magic realism.

"Josefina," I reply. Congratulating myself on a good serviceable choice, with an imperial resonance to it—Napoleon's consort was, after all, a Caribbean girl. And as I announce my alias, I begin— with my lashes still modestly lowered—my inventory. Age: mid-sixties. Genre: American Anglo-Saxon or Celt. Accent: from what I can gather, mid-Atlantic. Feet: large, size twelve at least, in battered blue-and-white Top-Siders—an upper-middle-class indicator, like the khakis and the shirt with the midget alligator and the diver's watch. Sunburnt freckled arms and legs with the muscle mass of a former team player: football or hockey. And a belly that on a woman would mean pregnancy of about seven months.

I get irritated as I observe this belly jiggling insouciantly to the beat. What whacking arrogance it takes for the possessor of a Brobdingnagian gut like this even to dream of aspiring to dancing with a pretty girl thirty years younger. Yet wherever I've traveled in Africa, Asia, and Latin America, I've seen similar woeful sights. Dropsical bellies, spindling shanks, speckled pates, wistful salt-and-pepper attempts at Hemingway beards, Frank Zappa ponytails made up of a few white hairs. All displayed by visiting men— tourists not interested in antiquities, because they're in ruins them-selves. These cruel signs of sovereign time would be touching if they weren't always exhibited at the sides of dewy local beauties— young goddesses, in fact, whose skin is black or brown or yellow. My honeymoon flight from Frankfurt to Bangkok was packed with Frenchmen, Americans, Germans, Italians. All of them well over fifty. All of them with the same expression of complacent anticipa-tion—consumer anticipation, like housewives headed for a reliable supermarket. I was tempted to get up and make a speech. What a sight that would have been: Susanna lecturing the elders. But what would one say but "Shame"? And shame, it is well known, is in the eye of the beholder.

Some oaf just stomped on my foot and nearly blew my cover. Not the guy I'm dancing with, who is surprisingly nimble, a bit like a boogying Santa. No, it was a local kid crushed up next to us— actually not an oaf but a teenager with a shaved head, a child's face, and steel muscles under a sweaty Ziggy Marley T-shirt. The kind of partner I should be dancing with—would love to be in bed with, in all honesty, though out of respect for my dear husband, Rory, standing five yards across the crowd, I'll suppress the thought. Rory will howl when he hears the tale of Josefina and the American. And at the same time—how well I know the covert twists of his white-boy preppy mind—he'll find it exciting, a confirmation of his fantasies about the brown girl he married. But that's another story. Another dance.

The thing is, what happens to Josefina if she stays away from tourist men? I've seen a wedding here on the island: a cascade of nylon lace framing the scared face of a fifteen-year-old bride seated with her boy-husband on a pair of straight chairs in the shade of a thatched house on stilts. The fundamentalist preacher thundering about obedience for wives and hellfire for adulterers, while in the background, the wise women of the village flick flies off the macaroni and the iguana stew. After the ceremony come the babies and the work, and the swift shriveling of youth and beauty like sea grapes in the sun.

"*Y abajo . . . Y abajo . . .*"

This song is endless. My partner looks as if he's about to have a coronary. Certainly it must take special skills to deal with a guy like this—nursing skills, perhaps. I've never had an old one, though I've been hit on by plenty. "*Ils sont tellement gentils,*" said the Senegalese massage girl at the hotel in Dakar, telling me about her sixty-year-old French lover, and the other elderly tourists who helped her buy a moped and a condominium. "*Quand ils font l'amour, il n y'a pas de problème. C'est vite, vite! Et après il y'a toujours le cadeau.*" Practical words from an eminently pragmatic mademoiselle. Mitch, our friend who left the States to become a vacation realtor and beach bum, says that a few girls have escaped from the island to become hostesses in a high-end nightclub and brothel in Antigua. Where they earn a fortune. And when they come home to visit, he reports in an aggrieved tone, they go out dancing dressed up like princesses. And if the wrong man tries to cozy up to them, they look him in the eye and say: I choose my partners.

The music is winding down now, and so is this pointless joke. I'm sweatier than ever and feel not mischievous but strangely melancholy. Weighted, as if I'd swallowed a piece of pig iron. Any minute now, my partner will ask Josefina if she wants a Coke or a beer. And I need to get away, to remember that I'm on vacation. To go drink rum with Rory, to make him jealous by dancing outrageously with some beautiful island boy. Or better yet, to steal off by myself. I'll shove through the roistering throng on the stairs to reach the upper deck, where stars and planets look down blandly through the tropical night.

"Quieres una Coca-Cola? Una Cerveza?"

Valiant Josefina. Before answering she lifts her eyes—eyes with all the subtle fascination of jungle and reef and incorrigible poverty—and for the first time looks directly at her partner. And— most amazing of all—the face of this American is quite ordinary. The face of a professor, an accountant—or a father-in-law like mine. Someone who pays his taxes and worries about dry rot. A little drunk, a little stupid, a little horny and confused, like all the rest of us. Gray hair, a sunburnt nose with a few broken veins, and a blue gaze as limpid as a child's. Impossible to hate.

"No, gracias." Said gently. For a fraction of a second, as the next song begins, I link eyes with him. You know me, I say silently. I'm not an exotic dream, not a victim; and with me you can't hide behind a foreign mask. My name isn't Josefina, it's Rachel Moore, and I may have gone to school with your daughter. I married someone

who could be your son. I know who you are. Recognize me: it's the only hope you have.

"No, thank you," I repeat in calm, clearly enunciated English, as the music gets louder. "It was fun, but I have to go now."

And since I'm suddenly not interested in observing his confusion, I turn and push my way deep into the surging crowd. There, in the press of overheated bodies, my feet at last grab the rhythm, and for a few delirious minutes Josefina and I dance all on our own.

The Golden Chariot

A musical comedy, or traveling minstrel show, starring a middle-class American Negro family and their brand-new 1962 metallicized Rambler Classic. All of them headed on an epic summer vacation trip across America, from Philadelphia to the Seattle World's Fair.

Time: August 3–24, 1962

Cast:
EARL B. HARMON, Ed.D., a high school principal
GRACE HARMON, his wife, elementary school teacher
WALKER HARMON, their son, a college freshman
RICHARD HARMON, their second son, age fourteen
MAUD HARMON, their daughter, age ten
The gold Rambler Classic

Music:
No gospel, Dixieland, bebop, doo-wop, ragtime, Delta blues, rhythm and blues, Memphis sound, Philly Soul, or Motown. Just 1962 summer AM middle-of-the-dial radio. Especially three songs: "Portrait of My Love," by Steve Lawrence; "Things (We Used to Do)," by Bobby Darin;

and "Sealed with a Kiss," by Brian Hyland. These songs
play over and over again, fading in and out of the pebbly
roar of static that joins cities and towns, ranchland and
mountains. The static is the real music.

SCENE I

*(Sunrise. Somewhere heading away from Philadelphia on the Pennsyl-
vania Turnpike. DR. EARL HARMON is driving the Rambler while the rest
of the family sleeps around him. The roadsides in the burgeoning light are
dense with Virginia creeper, and the speeding car shines like molten gold.
The peaceful hills are dotted with black-and-white Mennonite cows.)*

DR. HARMON: Oh, it's the AAA that gives us the bedrock of secu-
rity, the courage to take this leap. American Automobile Asso-
ciation. The name inspires confidence. All those A's, like the
NAACP. The opposite of the KKK. The AAA guidebook tells
us that it includes only hotels, motels, inns, TraveLodges, camp-
sites, and guesthouses where, and I quote, no discrimination
is made according to race, color, or creed. And there you are,
there's the whole country open to us, like one big guesthouse.
They can't slam the door in your face if they're in the guide.

Avoiding humiliation, that's been the thing. I'm roughly the
color of Gandhi, but I would never go around in sandals and
a diaper or flop down and let some Mississippi cracker spit on
me. Oh, I went down to Birmingham because it was the right
thing to do, but I kept well in the middle of the ranks as we
marched along down streets lined with what looked like zoo
animals to me. It was really just Southern white folks, offering
their famous hospitality. They were howling for nigger blood,

but it wasn't going to be mine. I made sure I was protected by a solid wall of sharecroppers, and then later I headed up a first aid station where we treated the minor wounds of confrontation, my smooth brown hands on my simpler brothers' work-roughened skin. *Ebony* published a photo of me wearing a Red Cross armband, my brilliantined hair rippling back like Desi Arnaz's, an old black Alabama church deacon staring at me like I was the savior of the world.

Not everyone has to confront. I swallowed enough humiliation for a lifetime in Philadelphia when Mordecai Jackson and I were the first colored students at Central High, and they used to take fresh shit, I suppose it was their own, and put it in our lockers, in our desks, in our lunch bags, in our gym suits. Months of shit. There were some white boys with prolific intestines in that school, or maybe they bought it by the pound.

Now I live in a suburb where I don't have to smell shit unless they're spreading it on a lawn, in a five-bedroom fieldstone Colonial that the slick Irish realtor who was busy changing the neighborhood gave away to me for eighteen thousand the way he gave houses away to Hobell Butler and Melvin Durant and all the other Negro dentists and judges and preachers and doctors who left the old Philadelphia row-house neighborhoods to the poor niggers from the South. We're in a greener ghetto, and we like the walls. My oldest boy is in a good Quaker college, and the other two are on scholarship in private school, and my wife doesn't have to work if she doesn't want to. Education and integration are the keys to the future, as I tell the seniors at my school; and my kids have the future unlocked, with ushers handing them in.

It's time to give them the biggest present: the country. Not the South, where the air stinks of barbecued black flesh, but the West, the direction the covered wagons rolled. And in a gold car that's not one of those niggerish Cadillacs or Lincolns, but a Rambler, begotten by American Motors. Discreet luxury, one of the new metallic paint jobs, and a padded dash. Praise the Lord, as my mother would say, we are rolling towards the Pacific in a sort of temple, elect, protected under the signs of American Motors and AAA. Safe, as usual. Safe.

SCENE II

(Along the southern edge of Lake Superior, between Sault Sainte Marie and Ironwood, Michigan. About three in the afternoon of the third day. Beyond fields and woods come occasional glimpses of the lake in dry brilliant sunshine. MAUD HARMON *in the backseat opens her mouth into the air rushing in from the front, and lets the wind dry her tongue.)*

MAUD: A good thing about this trip is the bottle caps. Coca-Cola is having a contest in honor of the World's Fair and what they do is print a picture of a different city of the world in each bottle cap, you just peel up the cork, and there it is: Bangkok, Paris, Amsterdam. Whenever we stop at a gas station, I dash over to the Coke machine and worm my hand into the hole where the caps drop down after people open their Cokes. I'm lucky I have skinny hands. I have dozens of bottle caps now, my pockets rattle. I have all the countries now except Brazil and Denmark; they didn't print any of Russia because they're Communists. It's for a contest, but I don't think about that, I just like having all those cities. I like things that make you think about anything far away, whether it's other countries or millions of years ago.

Among the books I brought with me is one about Marco Polo and another about digging up fossil men in Africa. Another is *Ivanhoe*. Sometimes I dream that I'm flying over the heads of my mother and father and brothers, gone somewhere else. They're sad but I'm not.

There was a big storm last night, which was our second night away from home. We were in a town called Mackinaw, which is a name that reminds me of old fish and worn-out raincoats, in a white little house that was part of a sort of motel near Lake Huron where the floor, if the three of us kids stood in one place, caved in about five inches, and where we had to wash the plates in the kitchen part *before* we ate dinner. Mom fixed minute steaks and corn on the cob and sliced tomatoes and the wind howled like a ghost story and the house shook like a giant was slapping it back and forth and I was disappointed that the roof didn't blow off.

In the morning I went outside before anybody else and met a white boy on the shore of the lake, where the waves were slamming down like ocean waves. This boy came out of the bushes and he had a long green man's jacket that came down over his spindly legs like toothpicks, and hair cut so short it looked like a smudge on his head. He said his name was Spencer and that his dad owned land beside the lake and then asked like a retard was I a Negro. I said no I was a Polish Chink from Bessarabia, which was a joke I got from my oldest brother, Michael, and then I told him we were going to the World's Fair, and that's our car I said, that new gold one. It was funny to be talking to a white boy in the summer, I'm used to them at school, but we don't see each other after school or in vacations. This Spencer was quiet for a minute and said he'd show me something, and then he showed me that almost all the rocks on the shore had fossils in them, shells and sponges and trilobites. I picked up about fifteen fossils until my mother called me to come in and get my hair braided, and then it was time to eat breakfast and drive off in our golden chariot and leave old Spencer there waving like a little white doll in the middle of all of his million-year-old shells. See you later, alligator, I said. I felt sorry for him, stuck there while we set off to see the world.

SCENE III

(Bemidji, Minnesota. RICHARD HARMON stands at the foot of the giant statue of Paul Bunyan and his blue ox, Babe. Sixth day, about eleven in the morning. In the distance, paddleboats on Lake Bemidji.)

RICHIE: Well, eighth-grade history was good for something. The Mississippi starts here. At least I think it does. This would be a great home movie, but this cheap family doesn't even own a movie camera. Our friends do, but not us. Our mother says it's more educational to look than to take pictures, so we're traveling with the oldest Kodak in the USA, and we get to take a few crummy slides. On the *Wonderful World of Color*, people in the commercials are always filming each other in front of Pikes Peak or the Golden Gate Bridge. And what are we doing? We're not even modern. In exactly eight years, when I'm finished with high school and college, I'm going to be a famous photographer and I'll have the best equipment there is.

I buy photo magazines to check up on the new cameras, and because they're good for nudes. Every issue you get has two or three good ones. All the girls in the photo pix are white, the way all the girls in *Playboy* are, the way everybody is, everywhere in the movies, on TV, in everything we watch or read. I know five or six really cute Negro girls from school or those pathetic Jack and Jill parties, girls so fine I'm half scared to ask them to dance or to say anything to them, but somehow they don't seem as real as the white girls in the pictures that make you touch yourself. It's like they exist less. It's like our family exists less than *Father Knows Best* or *Leave It to Beaver*. We're going across the continental United States of America in this fabulous car, but it's like no one can see us. It's too bad that we didn't bring a movie camera. We could make a television show of ourselves.

SCENE IV

(Eighth day. Devils Lake, North Dakota. Sunset in a motel parking lot with arid hills beyond. GRACE HARMON *stands in front of stacked wooden boxes of empty soda bottles.)*

GRACE: These wide spaces scare me. The light is too strong. I don't know what to do with it. I feel unwelcome, caught like a cockroach out in the open. I like small places inside, places like my shiny kitchen when I have pots on all the burners and everything under control, the smell of greens cooking with ham bones, of chicken roasting, of yeast rolls and tapioca pudding. Or church, when the service has just finished, and we ladies are all standing in our gloves and hats à la Jackie Kennedy, and greeting each other and chatting so close that you can smell everyone's Arpège perfume and Alberto VO5 hair cream. There is a sense of salvation, and relief, because the Holy Word is still floating around us in the air, and yet we're all going home to eat soon.

Once when I was still a student at Philadelphia Normal

School, I sat next to Eleanor Roosevelt at a tea to benefit the work camps, and she said to me that I must try to see as much as I could of this great country of ours. She was kind, but like an elephant in pearls, and it made me angry that she didn't stop to think that most of our great country didn't want to see me.

And I had traveled. The year before that I went with my cousin Minerva down to Palm Beach to work the winter season as a butter-water girl at the Fontainebleau Hotel. That was an experience: the dining room long as a football field, with all those dried-out white faces bent over their food, with Minerva and I and all the other pretty colored girls in our ruffled caps, skimming round tables where never in our lives could we have sat down. The manager's son, who was our age, used to walk around in jodhpurs and riding boots, not saying anything, just looking us over with hard blue eyes. We felt naked. That's the way I feel now, standing here under this big sky.

SCENE V

(Glacier National Park, looking over the Canadian border toward Waterton Lakes National Park and Calgary. A curving highway through a swarm of snowcapped peaks, resonance of early afternoon light over heights and distant forests. WALKER HARMON is behind the wheel, smoking a cigarette.)

WALKER: One Winston and they're on my ass. They haven't been uncool enough to say anything yet, but Mom is muttering to herself and staring out at the Rockies as if she'd like to bite them off, and Pop looks like I just punched him in the stomach. Well, it had to be done, it's ridiculous that I'm eighteen and in college and doing half the driving and can't act like the hell I want. This trip is a mistake. It shows up what's wrong with this pitiful family. The fight for civil rights is in the South, so we go west on a sightseeing expedition. My roommates at Oberlin, Joel Kagan and Marty Hubbard, are both down in Greenville, Mississippi, registering voters. Joel's sister from Bryn Mawr is with them; she wears dancers' leotards and skirts from Mexico, and twists her hair up in a style called the Marienbad. White students are lining up to risk their lives, and what did I do? I came home from college in June like a good son, worked a summer job in the mail room at the Philadelphia *Bulletin*, and dated my high school flame, Ramona Jenkins, who has tits like dirigibles and allows a lot of heavy action with bra and panties firmly in place and is already talking about how she wants to marry a doctor. Instead of acting like a man and volunteering for SNCC, I came on this trip, with Pop sweating over his AAA guide, and practically shitting in his pants every night when he has to go to ask for a room in one of these little cow-town motels. Terrified that he's going to hear that word—*nigger*—that would sweep us right off the map of the USA. Sweep his precious family right off to Oz, like a black tornado.

SCENE VI

(Seattle World's Fair. High noon. The whole HARMON FAMILY stands together in the crowd.)

THE FAMILY: We are standing at the foot of the Space Needle, which was our goal. It's as tall as the Eiffel Tower, and there's a rotating restaurant up at the top. We won't go up because there's a long line, and it costs four dollars a person, and because we're not the kind of family that does things all the way to the end. This is enough for us. The Space Needle points to the Sputniks, to the stars. It's like part of a cartoon about the future, something we think we must have wanted for a long time. A prize the president might have promised us as an inalienable right. A giant ultra-modern suburban kitchen appliance out of a dream.

SCENE VII

(Heading back home. The FAMILY MEMBERS speak in turns.)

MAUD: In Oregon the Pacific was tall gray waves that turned my feet numb when I waded. There were dead trees like goblin trees scattered on sand that came from volcanoes. My father and brothers peed against one of the trees, and my mother said: "Don't look." It was the end of the country, and I wanted to stay there forever. I kept some sand in a bottle. I'd never seen black sand before.

DR. HARMON: White fellow who ran the lodge where we stayed in the Bighorn Mountains, a Pacific Theater vet, kept going on and on about the Indians when I went to pay the bill, about how they were shiftless and drank and so on. I think the son of a bitch thought I was going to laugh and chime in. Out here, Indians are niggers. Once my brother Ray, the minister who's the straightest-haired one in the family, was traveling across Oklahoma with some kind of fool Baptist tour group, and in a little two-bit café, they refused to serve him. But then the owner kind of slid up to him and asked if it was true that he was an American Indian. "No," says Ray, figuring he's not going to eat anyway. "I'm an American Negro." Damn if the cracker didn't shut up, smile, and bring him his apple pie.

RICHIE: At Yellowstone, the best thing wasn't Old Faithful, which you could hardly see because there were so many people around, or the bubbling pink sulfur mud that would probably parboil your foot if you wanted to make the experiment, it was two girls that Walker and I met at the campground canteen. They were a pair of not very pretty white girls with hair the color of grass when the green is burnt out of it at the end of the summer, one of them with pimples and one with a bow clipped on over her bangs. They started talking to Walker, who was very cool and said he was in college and that impressed them into wild giggles and "Oh," they said to me, "you look older than fourteen, you look at least twenty." They went crazy over the Golden Chariot, and I showed them how the front seats flipped all the way back. We would have taken them for a ride except Mom was waiting for the hot dogs. "They were ready, little brother," said Walker, who the whole time had had this sort of constipated look on his face, that he gets when he tries to act suave. "It's a new age, the great and glorious West, gateway to the future. Be cool and the white chicks will flock like pigeons, they think we've got the Space Needle between our legs."

GRACE: When we got to Cody, Wyoming, we stopped in a big general store that had traps and skins hanging from the ceiling and dusty old pickup trucks in the parking lot and we went in and all three of the kids bought blue jeans. No one we know wears blue jeans, except for white teenagers on television. The kids walk differently now: they amble like cowboys; they look, even little Maud, as if they all of a sudden know about distances, as if they're about to gallop away from me into a Technicolor sunset.

THE FAMILY: In the Black Hills of South Dakota, we, the Harmon family and our new car, were present at an historic event: the first intercontinental television broadcast using the Telstar satellite. At the base of Mount Rushmore we stood in a crowd looking on as the huge indifferent sand-colored faces of the Founding Fathers traveled magically across outer space to Paris. The Harmons, latest issue of the combination of a few Mid-Atlantic coastal Indians with certain unwilling West Africans shipped abroad for profit by their own warlords, which combination lightly mixed with the largely undistinguished blood of English debtors and Irish bond servants, stood and cheered with the rest of the crowd watching itself on an outdoor screen. Though we still can't vote or eat or pee with white men in many states, we love our country. Didn't we learn patriotism at school? We feel enlarged by a sense of history and destiny, even though inside each of us, in the dark space at the very center, is a secret question mark.

MAUD: The USA is like a big board game, Monopoly or Clue. We've been following signs for days along the highway: Burma-Shave; Little Stinker; and ads for the Corn Palace, in Mitchell, South Dakota. There it is, smack in the middle of the country, a royal palace really built out of corn. Cars all around it from every state. And if you look up in the sky, clouds of crows just gobbling it up.

RICHIE: I've grown three inches since I turned fourteen, and I have the biggest appetite in the family. I've been eating my way across America, and I say that the best root beer floats on the road are at A & W and the best barbecue is the Piggly Wiggly chain. I won a bet with my sister by drinking four bottles of Coke in less than five minutes in the backseat, when we were driving through the Badlands. And, out of intellectual curiosity, I ordered shrimp in Iowa, a thousand miles from either ocean. In Chicago, we went out to a restaurant run by Jewish people, and it was the best place I ever ate in my life. Papa Stein's. When they brought the meat, it looked like a rib out of an elephant, and they even served pickles that were made from whole tomatoes. The real Papa Stein himself, a cool old white-haired guy with a Mad Professor accent, came over to our table to say hello. Like we were celebrities or something.

WALKER: In Chicago, I didn't go out to dinner with everybody else. I stayed in the hotel, which for once was a deluxe one, a Holiday Inn—AAA of course. I had to get away from them all, to breathe. I wanted to think about how I could start living my own life. After a while I opened the curtains, and you could see the big city just lighting up in purple dusk, and I turned on the radio, and a wild tune stole out of that radio that was like the breath of the city. Jazz like I've never heard before. Spilling out of some big mysterious black heart hidden out there under the lights. I sat and smoked a Winston, and for a few minutes, everything fell into place. The family trip doesn't bother me anymore: I knew it was the last time for me. And that I was where I needed to be.

THE FAMILY: So we returned, dashing across the last few states to Philadelphia, overcome by a sudden desperate urge to sleep in our own beds. Back East, nothing much was changed. It was still August 1962, the cicadas still at their summer wars in the treetops. Our new car, unmarred by the dust of prairies and alkali flats, was still a sumptuous gold. Were we the same? That was a question not one of us, for a long time, would think to ask. Not until years had passed, and other, far more sophisticated vacations had been taken—jaunts to Europe and Africa and Asia, paid for by credit cards and boosting us to a palmy level of worldliness we'd never dreamed of. Not until we Harmon children had gone our separate ways, and looked back suddenly to realize that this was the trip by which we would judge all others. A journey that defined the ambiguous shape of our citizenship, when we moved across our country feeling as apprehensive as foreigners and at the same time knowing that every grain of dust was ours. And a private moment of glory, the kind every family has just once. When the highway belonged to us, and our car was the best on the road. "Swing low, sweet chariot," sang Dr. Harmon for a joke, as we turned the corner of our suburban street. And the Rambler Classic carried us home.

MUSIC. CURTAIN.

Interesting Women

Interesting women—are we ever going to be free of them? I meet them everywhere these days, now that there is no longer such a thing as an interesting man. It's the same for all my girlfriends, whether they're in the States or in Hong Kong, where I'm now living. They come back from vacations or parties and announce proudly—with an air of defiance—that they met the most fascinating woman. What a refreshing change it would be if the new acquaintances were gorgeous lesbians or bisexuals whose intoxicating charm fed straight into hot, wet tumbles between rented sheets! Instead, these encounters are always drearily platonic. More than anything—and I speak from experience—they turn out to be schoolgirl crushes in disguise, instant friendships that last as long as it takes to swap tales of love and desperation. In short, an ephemeral traffic of souls that is about as revolutionary as flowers pressed in rice paper.

My hotel in Thailand is swarming with interesting women. I am probably one of them, though I try not to be. My husband, Simon, metallurgist and tireless *père de famille*, is presently looking over strip mines in Hunan Province, so I'm free to reinvent myself. I plan to occupy six days of Easter vacation with conspicuous idleness—no sightseeing, eating and drinking without compunction, binges of in-room movies with our twelve-year-old daughter, Basia. And, when I sit by the pool, I even bend back the cover of the book I'm reading, so no one can see that it's literature.

This hotel is the kind of place where guests read worthy books: it has, of all things, a library on the beach, where one can come in covered with sand and, under lazily revolving ceiling fans, open a glass case and consult *The Oxford English Dictionary*. It also has a meditation pavilion, and a high-tech gym, and bougainvillea garlands placed on the beds in the bungalows every morning; it has a view of an opalescent bay strewn with distant islands of surpassing beauty, and a chef with California leanings, plus a mad French owner who bestows on each guest a handwritten guide that mingles facts about the medieval kingdoms of Ayutthaya and Sukhothai with information like "The hotel grounds are kept secure at night by dogs trained to bark only at Thai faces."

On my third afternoon here, in a lazy moment, I fall into a conversation from which I sense that I will not be able to extricate myself without relating the usual set pieces of emotional history. I am pulling a kayak up over the sand, after a jaunt on the lagoon with Basia. She is still in her kayak, skimming around the shallow waters inside the reef, and I am huffing and puffing, scratching my feet on broken coral, and exchanging cheerful insults with her. "You're a wuss," she calls. "Go ahead, desert your only daughter!"

A slim shape emerges from the palms behind me, and I see that it belongs to a woman I have been observing idly since I arrived. I've seen her by the pool, drinking gin-and-tonics with a pair of Swiss anthropologists, husband and wife, who live in Bangladesh and are here with their adopted baby son. I eavesdropped on an emotional discussion they had about child prostitution and AIDS in Bangkok, and noted that this woman was demanding some kind of attention, not sexual, from her new acquaintances, which the couple, focused on their gorgeous, dark-skinned baby, couldn't give. And at odd moments of the day, I have been aware of the woman sitting, not reading, in a deck chair pulled into one of the furthest clefts of the elephant-colored rocks that loom over the water. I judge her to be in her early fifties, about ten years older than I am. Looking good without pushing it, still in the game. No matronly straw hats or designer sunglasses. Over various stylish bathing suits she wears a white pareu, expertly tied, and she walks barefoot with the lounging gait that in the Far East often marks members of the great diaspora of Westerners who imagine that they are not tourists.

"Is it hard?" she asks, coming up beside me and indicating the kayak.

"It's easy, as long as you don't go outside the reef."

"I'll do it tomorrow. It's on my list of things that scare me." She looks at me knowingly. "I was very good at canoeing at camp," she goes on, with a sibylline smile.

An American East Coast accent. Upper-class. The old traveler's game of placing a compatriot arranges itself in my thoughts like a fragment of Anglo-Saxon verse: clearly Caucasian, so Jewish or Gentile? A wandering WASP wastrel, or Irish, Italian? Camp? I imagine her at some posh backwoods establishment with secret midnight hazings and awards inscribed on birch bark. But Maine or Blue Ridge? Up close, she's a funny mix of elegance and uncouthness. Her body has a thoroughbred length of bone, but her limbs look slightly wasted—a tropical bug, perhaps, or simply borderline anorexia. Her armpits and legs are unshaven but her toenails are meticulously manicured, painted a glossy orange-red. She is wearing an Indian nose ring, and bangles around her ankles. Her hair, short and raked back from her face, is orange-red as well, the cheap, untempered henna color one sees in fakirs' beards; and her sun-weathered face with its short, arrogant nose and hooded gray eyes—no surgical work that I can discern—displays a peculiar expression of rueful good humor that reminds me of a street urchin in a thirties movie. It is amusing to see her studying me at the same time.

"Taos," she says. And everything is clear. Of course she wasn't born there, because no one like her is ever born in Taos; people like her are reborn there. A horsey childhood in northern New Jersey and Madrid, where her father owned chewing-gum factories, she tells me. Then twenty years as a banker's wife in London, where she ran a shop that imported South American textiles. Then the divorce and the move to New Mexico, which she initially discovered when she was "doing a Thelma and Louise" with a friend. "After all those years in England, I realized that I didn't want to be buried among the Brits. I got to Taos, and knew I could die there." Now that the kids are grown, she is traveling through the East by herself. Roughing it, mostly—she's at this pricey hotel, which fits her style but not her present budget, for a few days of R and R. She has just finished moving from ashram to ashram in India, and was at Poona, where the faithful live on in the waning rays of the glory of the Maharishi.

We are sitting on the powdery sand, our legs stretched out into transparent water the temperature of amniotic fluid. There is too much information, I worry, moving between us too fast. But I'm on vacation, and after a while, I let myself go. Sitting there in my black bikini, the water from my hair dripping down my shoulders, I describe the fancy Santa Fe wedding I once attended, where aristocratic Florentines and Milanese, wearing spanking-new cowboy boots, boogied with Texas millionaires. I complain about the rootlessness of my life as an expatriate wife blown by multinational winds from Massachusetts to Birmingham, Warsaw, and now Hong Kong. Shamelessly, I lament the superficiality of the travel articles I write for two quite reputable magazines back in the States. Then I get to the hard stuff. Showing off to this adventurous new acquaintance with chitchat about cities and jungles we both know, I touch scornfully on the inability of men to appreciate canopic jars and shaft tombs, to deal with knavish cabdrivers, to tolerate bedbugs. I observe that women are better travelers than men, and superior beings altogether. And then I drop the word *ex-husband*—that password that functions as a secret handshake in the freemasonry of interesting women.

It is five in the afternoon, the time when it rains for ten minutes every day at this season. Steel gray thunderheads loom over the bay and, as a long-prowed fishing boat motors hastily by, there is a distant flare of lightning under an arcade of black cloud. Basia has beached her kayak and is chasing crabs on the rocks, circling closer and closer as she eavesdrops on us. By now, we're engaged in an orgy of divorce talk, slapping away at the mosquitoes that began attacking us once the shore breeze died down. My new friend is telling me in detail exactly how the Filipina maid was bribed to testify against her. And I respond with the well-worn saga of my perfidious lawyer, a woman who, after helping arrange the official dissolution of my brief first marriage, moved in with my ex-husband. Perched above us on the rocks, Basia gives up any pretense of not listening. "You can come and sit beside us, you beautiful girl," says the woman, whose name I still don't know. She speaks to my daughter with a tender familiarity that sends a wary prickle down my spine.

I have to be careful what I say, I think, as Basia climbs down and settles near me. But it's hard. Impromptu confession can be as irresistible as sex. At least I keep my revelations rigorously in the past, and avoid the slightest spilling of guts about my second husband, Basia's father, Simon. Although at other times I can go on for hours about him and his controlling love, his occasional stupid infidelities, and his still more annoying blind devotion—revealing itself more and more over the years—to a fantasy ideal of a family. Or about my two miscarriages after Basia, and how Simon's prolonged and noisy grief left nearly no room for mine. Of none of this do I speak as I watch Basia sitting in the warm sea, her arms crossed to protect her twelve-year-old breasts, those impertinent brand-new breasts that already, I note, attract attention from old and not-so-old lechers around the hotel pool.

Basia is as tall as I am, and wears a larger shoe; she is one of the new, giant breed of American children created by overnurturing parents, and she has the precocious social aplomb of most expat kids. She goes to an international school where kids have tongue studs and Prada running shoes and get alternating lectures on the importance of getting into the right college and of avoiding STDs. However, when it comes to matters other than sex, ambition, and controlled substances—small matters like distinguishing honest people from charlatans—Basia is still as innocent as custard pie. Now she is openly hoarding the specious information we are exchanging. And I feel a flash of alarm that changes to annoyance at her presence. Later, back at our bungalow, I will scold her unfairly, poor baby, for butting into adult conversations.

The rain comes on, cooler than the water where we are sitting. The three of us raise our arms and turn up our faces to the hard drops that rattle down as if someone were tossing handfuls of coins. Up from the lagoon, as if in response, leap entire schools of tiny silver fish. In a minute, the sun pokes through; the daily rainbow bridges two dark banks of clouds, and, on cue, a fashion shoot appears on the beach in the distance, as it does every morning and evening: photographer, dressers, models, minions, trunks and tripods and diffusers. Tonight it's the two male models in long bathing trunks: a sculptural blond with a strange, chopped haircut, and a black guy with a shaved head and a body that makes one realize that sometimes just a body is enough. "Look at that," I say.

"Don't stare at him, Mom!" begs Basia.

"Oh, he doesn't mind being stared at," says our new friend. "He's used to it. It's an element. You learn to breathe in it, and then, if you're not careful, you have to have it. It used to be part of my life," she goes on after a pause. "People turning around to look. Now that phase is over. It's not important anymore."

Basia looks so inclined to take this statement as a pearl of wisdom that I rise abruptly from the water and say that I'm chilled to the bone. I grab my reluctant daughter, and we head off to shower, leaving our new acquaintance reclining in the sea. Before departing, I introduce myself and ask her name. "Silver," she says.

"Is that your real name?" I blurt rudely.

"One of my real names." The voice drifts out of the darkness, which in tropical style has fallen like a sudden curtain.

At dinner, predictably enough, it is Basia who defends Silver while I roll my eyes over that ridiculous New Age alias. "I think she's cool," says Basia, taking a tiny spray of green peppers out of her milky soup. "She's really, really mysterious." At the tables around us, people with careful, moderate tans are wearing pale clothes and sitting over hurricane lamps whose amber glow makes the dining terrace look vaguely like a shrine. A real shrine sits nearby, under the mango tree, a tiny spirit house that is a replica of the hotel, with candles, fruit, and flowers around it. The hotel, recommended by my editor, has been a disappointment, I think: pretentious; arrogantly overpriced; hardly any kids, and none Basia's age. Instead, it's a perfect hideaway for upscale lovers: without turning around, I can count two honeymoon couples, an enamored pair of Englishmen, and a German businessman with his young mistress.

"Mysterious? Oh, please, sweetheart," I say. "She's the classic kind of woman who is very beautiful and lives for that, and then the beauty fades, and she goes and gets spiritual. Like Bianca Jagger."

"Who?"

"Bianca Jagger was one of the most beautiful women back in the seventies. Way back before you were born. Now she's not so beautiful, so she's involved in saving humanity."

"Silver doesn't want to save humanity."

"She wants to save her soul. Same difference."

Basia giggles and crunches the ice from her Diet Coke. "But I thought you liked her. Why are you trashing her?"

"I am not trashing her," I say untruthfully, and I wonder why I am bothering to be malicious about a woman I've just met, who seems more like than unlike me. That's it, of course. That and the fact that I revealed a great many intimate facts of my past to a complete stranger down on the beach. Why, I wonder? Am I becoming an embittered woman of a certain age, maddened at the sight of romantic couples, and driven into serial episodes of pathetic self-revelation as my daughter flowers into maidenhood? For a second, I wallow in gloomy speculation.

Basia stares across the candlelight at me. She is wearing a green tie-dyed dress and her round, seraphic face is deeply tanned, an irritating fact that reminds me of our daily battles over sunscreen and hats. It is Simon's face, but my eyes look out of it, and whenever she turns those eyes directly on me I experience an eerie jolt of total recognition. "Mom? Are you missing Daddy?" she asks.

"Not right this second," I reply, with bravado. But suddenly I do miss Simon. He would have added a bit of male ballast to the unbearable lightness of this female vacation. He would have fussed about the price of drinks and worried about hepatitis and bilharzia and insisted on renting mopeds for horrible family excursions. He'd have insisted on daily screwing at siesta time—not such a bad idea, that—and at least once he would have attempted to amuse both of his girls by turning on MTV and dancing around in a pareu, imitating Cher. He would have laughed at Silver. I take a forkful of rice and try to think of something wise and maternal to say, but Basia has stolen most of my lines. "We'll call him tonight," I mutter.

One of my weak points, as Simon continually tells me, is my untrammeled curiosity. The next morning, when I should be horizontal under a palm tree, reading disguised literature, I agree, in a moment of wild perversity, to share a taxi into town for a morning's shopping with Silver. At breakfast, with Basia out having a half-day diving lesson, my new acquaintance looked interesting to me again.

I have misgivings already, when I have to wait in the taxi for fifteen minutes, as Silver, at the front desk, calls the States to shout endearments to her boyfriend, who, it seems, is a retired oil-field engineer. Flies swarm sociably into the rear end of the taxi, which is a rump-sprung *tuk-tuk* with aluminum seats. The driver, one of the few fat Thai men I've ever seen, occasionally turns to regard me with lazy amusement. Finally Silver appears, with a crisp white Indian *kurta* pulled over her pareu, and asks me whether I mind making an extra excursion. Before she moves on to the other islands she wants to visit—Bali, Lombok, the Moluccas—there is something she wants to do here. A program of meditation and yoga coupled with high-colonic irrigation.

"Enemas! You're crazy!" I say. I say it in the downright tone of an old Methodist churchwoman.

Silver looks thoughtful. "One thing I really got to understand in India is that the body can't be separated from the spirit," she says. "You can't make any real progress toward enlightenment unless your body is clean. You don't know how much toxic stuff you've been carrying around with you for years."

And then, as the driver heads toward town, she tells me about a man she knows who did colonic irrigation and found that the encrustations in his guts had included a dozen little round pellets of metal, slightly bigger than buckshot. It turned out that when he was six he used to bite the heads off his toy soldiers, and they'd stayed with him.

"Excuse me if I'm too blunt, but the whole thing has always sounded to me like getting buggered for your health," I say. "People talk about the benefits, but why doesn't anybody talk about the erotic part of it?"

It's impossible to offend Silver. She simply smiles, rakes back her hennaed hair, revealing a narrow band of white at the roots, and shakes her head at me with a tinge of pity. Then she tells me that in Goa she heard of two places on this island, health centers where one can go on retreats for meditation and purification of both ends of the body. She wants to find them—and this, I discover, is the main purpose of our shared outing. "Come on," she says. "We can get our shopping done, and then set off and look. One of the places is over by the caves. I heard it used to be good, but the owner, a German guy, has turned into an alcoholic, and it may have gone downhill. If it doesn't look promising, we can always go find Cornelia, the American woman who runs a retreat in the bush. They say she's the best, if you can find her."

She looks at me with her urchin's smile, and I recall wondering earlier how this frail-seeming woman had managed to travel alone but unscathed through the backwaters of half of Asia. Now I see how: an exuberant opportunism protects her as absolutely as angels guard saints and children. Already I know that I'm going with her and that I'll probably get stuck with the taxi fare, too.

Silver pats my shoulder as we rattle along. "Come on. It'll be an adventure." She's astute enough not to press any spiritual points. "Cornelia went to Wellesley," she adds brightly.

In the port town, a fat, naked baby with brass anklets crawls around, laughing, on the floor of a shop that sells cheap viscose pants, sundresses, and cotton bathing suits from Bali. The baby's parents are eating noodles in the back of the shop, and keeping a weather eye on Silver, who is going through the racks of clothes and pulling out things with magisterial gestures as if she were shopping at Saks. I catch sight of a black-and-white pair of pants which I immediately know will look good, and buy them. "You move fast," Silver observes.

A pronouncement on my entire uncontemplative life. But part of my haste is due to a suspicion that I might end up paying for her purchases as well. "Yes," I say, and move on to the next shop, arranging to meet her afterward at a café on the waterfront. Wandering through a market past heaps of coriander, lichees, and jackfruit, I ponder whether I should simply escape back to the hotel in one of the many bush taxis that pass me, crammed with country people. But I'm held there by my curiosity, which seems to grow stronger in the heat, like a kind of jungle itch. I wait for Silver in the café, which looks out on two long, decayed jetties that stretch into the flat dazzle of the straits. Around me, waiting for ferries, killing time, sit golden Australian boys with dive gear and many large, ugly foreign men looking like assorted Calibans beside tiny, beautiful Thai prostitutes. A jeep pulls up and a tattooed American girl jumps out and hands around invitations to a full-moon beach party on a far island: live music, magic mushrooms. I stare out over the blazing sea that is as motionless as gelatin, and punish myself by rereading a Chinese poem I found in a book borrowed from the hotel library:

> How sad it is to be a woman!
> Nothing on earth is held so cheap.
> Boys stand leaning at the door
> Like gods fallen out of heaven.
> No one is glad when a girl is born.

Silver appears, and we get back in the taxi and race toward the first of our anal destinations. We drive along the bay, away from the stylish south of the island, where the good beaches and fancy hotels are. Soon our taxi stops in a palm grove gray with fallen, withered fronds. A large, faded signboard reads EMERALD CAVE HEALTH SPA. Below is a list: "Thai Massage; Yoga Classes; Vegetarian Cuisine; Detoxification Cures; Pranotherapy; Gymnastics." Nine or ten thatched bungalows form a semicircle around a larger bungalow, and beyond gleams the incorruptible sea. After the green-velvet lawns and manicured hibiscus of the hotel where we are staying, the place looks ominously neglected.

Silver disappears into the office, and I walk down a path toward the beach. A small outdoor restaurant with white-plastic tables and chairs is deserted. A Thai woman with square-cut hair and a scowl uncharacteristic of the friendly islanders peers out at me from behind the bamboo bar, and then vanishes. Nearby, three cats are sleeping under a Ping-Pong table with a broken net, and on a deck chair outside an open-air cubicle containing a treadmill and a few barbells sits an enameled tin bowl that once held someone's lunch and is now black with flies.

Music fills the air—a Chopin nocturne. For a minute, I think it is live, produced by the German gone to seed. But then the music shifts to Peruvian flutes, and I realize that it's a cassette, broadcast through speakers wired to the palms. A man, a Westerner, brown-haired and pasty-skinned, is snoring in a hammock at the edge of the beach. I turn and walk quietly back to the car.

Silver comes back with her hands full of papers describing what Emerald Cave can offer. On one is a list of health products with names like Hatha Purge, on another a Xeroxed diagram showing rolls of tubing and a kind of plastic-and-metal table for attaching over a toilet.

I look at it all. "Don't do this," I say to her, overturning my vow not to get involved. "At least, don't do it here."

"It's very cheap," she says stoutly. "My funds aren't what they were."

"Don't."

She looks at me as Basia does when I get tough. "Well, then, we'll go find Cornelia," she says.

Locating Cornelia involves a return to town and a stop at a bakery popular with trekkers, where we look for a notice posted on a bulletin board, and a dive with the taxi down a path into the bush past a huge, unpacific-looking water buffalo. Hours pass, as we jolt over red mud roads. All spirit of independence withers within me. Desperately thirsty, flapping my hands feebly at the mosquitoes that billow into the back of the truck at every stop, I realize that

I've undergone a minor conversion to a vaguely Eastern worldview: sweat and fatalism. At one point, the taxi bounces over a bridge across a vine-filled gorge where water is falling among clouds of orchids, a paradise I know I visited in dreams all through my childhood. "Please stop for a minute," I say in a faint voice, but the place is past, never to be found again in this incarnation. And we head onward toward Cornelia.

It is late afternoon, and the taxi driver has begun to give us ominous glances over his shoulder, when we pull into a clearing in the middle of a huge palm grove. Before us is a modest concrete house with a heap of coconuts against one wall. ISLAND WELLNESS CENTER is written on a small sign posted on a tree trunk. A thin, deeply tanned woman in a plum-colored leotard and a pair of loose batik pants comes out on the veranda and looks at us.

"Are you Cornelia?" calls Silver, clambering nimbly out of the truck and advancing with the triumphant air of Stanley sighting Livingstone.

The woman acknowledges her with a spare, formal nod. I instantly dislike her.

In a matter of minutes, Silver and Cornelia have clasped hands like long-lost friends, gazed into each other's eyes, and vanished into an office with screened windows, leaving me on the veranda with a portly, yellow dog, who studies me tranquilly. The reddening sun is level with the tops of the acres of palms surrounding us, and I think with a pang of Basia, who must be fretting because I've run off and left her. Beside the heap of coconuts, our driver, who has plainly given up hope of an early dinner, squats companionably to smoke with a couple of young men who drove up behind us in a truck full of gas canisters. From inside, where the two women are sitting, comes a murmur of excited voices. The door opens and Cornelia beckons to me. "You can come in," she says, as if she were speaking to a small child.

I tiptoe inside and settle on a low rattan stool in a corner of the room beside an overflowing bookcase, where I see Castaneda's *Journey to Ixtlan*, and *Back to Eden* by Jethro Kloss. More books crowd the desk where Cornelia sits, and on the wall behind her hangs a Thai anatomy chart, dense with notations in green ink.

"We do a lot of work in the sea," Cornelia is telling Silver. "Breathing and movement. You live in one of our huts down by the beach. They are very basic, of course. No hot water. You'll be fasting and doing the high colonics every morning and evening, before meditation. The results of the colonics can be amazing. People reexperience fragments of past lives."

Cornelia has a phenomenally narrow torso, and breasts with sharp nipples that show clearly through her leotard. Her frizzy, sandy hair is dusted with gray. She has a penetrating voice, and a look in her pale eyes which I recognize as subtle orneriness. She, I see immediately, is another interesting woman. She has already made it clear that she speaks fluent Thai, and has given a quick, disdainful sketch of her rejected past life, not omitting Wellesley.

Silver is staring at her, bedazzled. I feel a pang of the kind of jealousy I haven't felt since Girl Scouts, when my troop leader—one of those dear, old-fashioned closet lesbians—liked my best friend better than me. Just yesterday Silver was staring at me like that as I rattled on about my ex-husband's shenanigans and the rigors of a writer's life. Evidently I wasn't ethereal enough for her. And besides, getting a taste for these chaste female encounters can lead to incredible promiscuity. Another day, another soul laid bare.

I clear my throat and announce—philistine that I am—that I have to get back to the hotel, and Silver and Cornelia wince with annoyance. They agree that Silver will begin her cure in a day's time, and then they embrace.

"I think you are absolutely beautiful," says Cornelia to Silver.

"You are exactly what I have been looking for," says Silver to Cornelia.

Silver and I ride back to our hotel in silence and arrive there at dusk, just in time to view the underlings of the fashion shoot trudging up from the beach lugging equipment and screens with the weary air of peons returning from the fields. I pay the entire taxi fare without a murmur and run to find Basia. She is lolling under the mosquito net in our bungalow, watching MTV broadcast from Kuala Lumpur and finishing the last of the forbidden M&Ms from the minibar. She is so happy to see me that she forgets her twelve-year-old's dignity and jumps up and hugs me like a much younger child. "I thought you'd never come back!" she tells me. "I thought I was going to be stuck watching 'An Evening with Aerosmith'!"

Her mouth drops open when I describe Silver's quest. "Oh God, Mom—you mean she's going around looking for places to get her ass washed out?"

"Don't use crude words to show off," I say coldly. "And it's her colon, really."

"It's still her butt. Remember that joke: Are there rings around Uranus? Is there intelligent life on Uranus?"

We look at each other and snicker. Then I tell her about the man who swallowed the heads of toy soldiers and we collapse on the bed and sob with laughter. We're still laughing on our way to dinner. Outside the dining room, Basia stops to inspect the spirit house as she always does, touching with the tip of one finger the minute plastic figures set inside it and the fresh offerings of fruit and flowers around them. On our first night at the hotel she read aloud to me from the guidebook a passage explaining that these tiny houses are set up for wandering guardian spirits. In the light of the candles set on the miniature carved veranda, Basia half resembles a little girl looking over her dolls, and half—with her flimsy dress, tumbled hair, and glowing sunburn—a nymphet in a romantic soft-porn photo. A familiar wave of emotion sweeps over me, an even mixture of tenderness, envy, and general terror of the future. At the same time, I wonder how I could have left this angel even for an hour for such a poor substitute as Silver. It occurs to me, as it often does, that I am supposed to be setting an example for Basia. And what a cock-up I make of it, sometimes.

Basia turns away from the little house and looks over at the lamp-lit diners at the restaurant tables. "I'm still thinking about those toy soldiers," she says in a dreamy voice. "I wonder what Silver will find." A pause and a giggle. "I wonder what *you* would find."

Next day, I keep to myself, as one is entitled to do in a hotel that has a library. When Simon calls from Hunan, before breakfast, I don't say a word about my daylong excursion but instead wax lyrical on the joys of solitude until, through the crackling Chinese static, he asks me suspiciously what I've been up to. "Just the usual sex with hotel waiters," I tell him.

From my lounge chair in the shade beside the pool, I observe Silver's movements on the last day before her retreat. After bidding me a cheerful good morning, she breakfasts garrulously with the assistant manager, who dreams of opening a luxury hotel in Rangoon; she meditates on the rocks by the bay; and by late afternoon she is one of three torsos emerging from the water at the far end of the pool, drinking cocktails with the black male model and one of the stylists from the shoot. When she sees me watching, she holds up her glass. "The last gin-and-tonic!" she calls. *"Vive la folie!"*

I don't see Silver again. She goes off to Cornelia and a cleaner life without saying good-bye. Once or twice, she drifts through my thoughts in her white sarong with her cocky grin. But almost immediately I banish her, and for the last part of my vacation I set about being indolent and uninteresting.

Still, it happens that on the day before I leave I find myself in the library, deep in conversation with a woman I have just met. She is younger than I am, twenty-eight or twenty-nine, and English: blond, with a pudgy, tanned body packed into a girlish bikini; entertainingly foulmouthed, with a Geordie accent. She came to the hotel a couple of days ago, with a tall Jordanian husband covered in gold chains; two blond, black-eyed toddlers; and a pair of male attendants in white robes and Arab headdresses, who carried suitcases and looked after the children, even changing diapers. Leaning on a table covered with weeks-old foreign papers in the dim, low-ceilinged library, she looks at me and says, "I envy you, being practically alone on holiday. Sometimes I get so fucking sick of the lot of them—"

Mice scurry in the palm thatch on the roof. *The Oxford English Dictionary* looms behind us, in its glass case, locked away against the ravages of suntan oil and salt air. Across the room, Basia, reading *MAD* magazine in a varnished planter's chair, has stopped turning the pages. In the woman's surly blue eyes I can see skeins of experience poised to unwind, and the password trembles on my lips.

The Visit

As we agreed, you are waiting for me in Piazza Crimea on the corner between the taxi stand and the bus stop, at the hour of the afternoon that always scares me to death. Two-thirty, the time when the butcher's shop and the pharmacy in the piazza are shuttered in steel, and the good burghers of Turin are digesting their *agnellotti in brodo*, and a paralyzed stillness hangs over the whole peninsula of Italy. It's a dangerous hour of daylight ghosts, an hour when I can't write or sleep. Instead I try always to be doing something definite, like making love or drinking strong coffee, nursing the baby, having my hair washed, or reading a scandal magazine. Otherwise, if the sun is shining, one could be vaporized in that deadly silent brightness, or if it is overcast or foggy, one might feel one's soul leached away, particle by particle, into damp gray nothing. You could have taken the train from Milan at any time, but it was I who suggested this hateful time of day.

There you are under the sycamores, a slender woman of my own height and weight, looking dismayingly elegant in a black ski jacket and narrow black pants. Oddly flattened, a theatrical silhouette. A female stage Mephistopheles, or a sexy transvestite Hamlet. And your entourage of sycamores—a mottled platoon of them leading up to the Crimean war memorial—makes me think of college writ-

137

ing seminars, when I stuck lyrical sycamores into all of my prose. "Parti-colored branches searching the heavens . . ." One of my best stories from those days describes a professor whose trousers fall down as he strolls beneath the sycamores of the Cambridge Common. It dates from the time when I was about to marry R, the young man who years later would marry you. R is no longer husband to either of us, but his quondam presence in our lives has formed the frail bond that connects us. Not sisters or lovers or yet friends, we are certainly not strangers.

I stop the car and get out and kiss you on both cheeks. We are used to the greeting; we both know Italy well enough to have picked up the customs of the country. But already I feel my disadvantage planted and growing, established in the exaggerated strength with which I grabbed your shoulders and pressed my lips against your face. I wanted to show you that I was relaxed enough to be very happy to see you. All I did, however, was leave myself open to one of those ironical glances of yours, the mute comment of a West Coast earth child, disdainful of all pretentiousness. In the shadow play that lies behind all of our encounters, I am the false, frothy artist type; you, somehow, the genuine human article.

I grab your bag, which is slightly larger than an overnight bag, and wonder how long you are going to stay. On the phone, I urged, no, insisted, in my frivolous way, that you stay for two nights, but we both know that that's probably too much. You have the excuse, anyway, that you have little time. You don't live in Italy anymore; you're on vacation here from the Oregon town where you moved after you divorced R. Where you are a consultant to fiber optics companies run by callow billionaires. Where you live with a dog that used to be my daughter's puppy. Why do I feel secretly possessive about your life?

What are you writing nowadays, you ask me as you get into the car. I've been following the magazine and wondering . . .

It occurs to me that you might feel possessive about my life.

We drive away from the city center up into the hills, or the Hill, as they call it, winding past walled villas, green stretches of park with rust-colored beeches, the turn-of-the-century Ospedale San Vito, with its peeling stucco towers streaked with water stains. As we go higher, we drive through patches of November fog. Your presence is making me rattle along like a tour guide about the history of this area where I've come to live with my second husband, who's an Italian businessman. About the court of the Savoy kings, and the Juvarran villas the courtiers built for summer rustication, out of the heat and malaria of the Po Valley. About Fiat, and the postwar invasion of automobile workers who constructed their socialist dream in the smoggy industrial flatlands below.

And every so often, you'll prick the bubble of my rhetoric by saying something droll. Yes, you're droll. You have a sexy, slightly adenoidal voice. So, you say, do you hang out with Gianni Agnelli? What's the Italian word for Motown—*Mottocittà?*

From the corner of my eye, I see you sitting as always like a wary child, with your cropped head thrust forward and your hands in your lap. You are wearing the most beautiful scarf I ever saw, black with a design of peacock blue. Its changing colors and heavy fringe match your eyes. When I compliment you on it, you say that it's from a movie wardrobe, that a well-known actress wore it in a recent role. Someone in your family, I recall, is in the film business. Once, when R was still married to you, he stopped by my house on a casual errand, wearing a pair of oversized jeans that he told me proudly had been worn by Gérard Depardieu. They hung alarmingly low on him, like a rapper's jeans, and caused me to muse for a second on exactly why it was that a wife—a recently married second wife— would present her husband with Depardieu's trousers. Why he wore them to visit his first wife was, I thought, fairly obvious.

We get to my house at three-thirty, a few minutes before my daughter gets off the bus from the American School. Piles of raked leaves dot the garden, and someone as usual has left the side door wide open.

It's very big, I say of the house, in my tour guide's voice. But we don't have the time or money to keep it as it ought to be kept up. It's old, over six hundred years, and there used to be a pair of round towers, though it was never a real castle, just a fortified farmhouse. You are silent, so I babble on. Down the hill are the outbuildings, but they belong to our neighbor, a lawyer with a shady side business of selling used luxury cars. That bulldozer is him trying to dig out the old fishpond, which there is officially some city ordinance against doing. Imagine, all the land that we can see, with those modern suburban houses, used to be vineyards that were attached to this place. You are still silent, walking beside me as I carry your bag, your profile inexpressive as a face on a cameo; and I am running out of things to say. I tell you that there are supposed to be secret tunnels joining the cellars of our house with all the other old villas on the hill, that this hill is a warren of underground passages.

We pause alongside the back garden wall, where the stone urns are full of yellowing geraniums. From here, on those rare clear blue days that sometimes descend on Turin without warning, one can see green slopes sweeping down to the city; streets and buildings and factories as if in a diorama; and beyond the Po, rising into the sunlight, the snowcapped wall of the Alps. The mountains are extraordinary presences, angelic witnesses to our lives. But today they are hidden, and the line of the hillside fades off into the usual smoggy haze.

Even so, you look out over the wall and say: I think it's beautiful. And you have such a winning way of saying it, as I have heard you say other things in the past: an earnest tone with a curious submissiveness to it, that gives one the feeling of having won a small but valuable prize. Suddenly I love you. I invite you into my house.

Your bag is full of presents for my daughter, formerly your stepdaughter, presents of a perfection that I am not sure I would ever be able to manage. We are upstairs in the attic playroom having a gift opening, one of those tiny misplaced Christmases that expatriates, always celebrating things minimally or out of season, get used to. You've brought a CD of UK garage music that the twelve-to-fifteen-year-old crowd desires ardently this year; another CD of Christmas carols miaowed by a computerized chorus of felines; a floppy stuffed cat and dog; a T-shirt from your local microbrewery; and, most marvelous of all, a fantastic array of kids' magazines, the kind that Theodora can never find on the international newsstands here, with subjects ranging from Internet pet exchanges to feminist water polo.

Theodora sits with her long legs crossed Indian-style, so we can see the mud caking the soles of her size nine Doc Martens, bending her flat-chested eleven-year-old body over the gifts, pushing back a single skinny braid she has made at the front of her hair, a braid tipped with an orange bead and a tiny piece of tinfoil. She knew you were coming, and was excited about it, but when she gallumphed in from school, ready for her snack, and saw you and me together, she turned mute. I was embarrassed, but you wisely sat still and waited, and now she is giggling and chattering as she tears wrapping paper. She is the nominal reason for this visit, after all. I have a snapshot from six years ago, of Theo sitting on your lap, her head lolling back in an abandoned attitude of perfect confidence. It scared me at the time: I thought you might steal her. Some years later, I was scared at the idea that you might vanish forever from her life: that, instead of the stepmother she learned to love, you might become a woman who left her father's house one spring night, and stepped into nonbeing. Theo already has too many memories that hover on the verge of being apocrypha.

The baby is awake from his nap, and crawling around shredding wrapping paper and making noises like an engine that needs a muffler. As usual, his fat toothless face wears an expression of expectant hilarity, as if he were awaiting the punch line to the joke of the century. His Sri Lankan nanny is crawling after him. We've put on the British CD, and the clamor of young black female voices makes it seem that there are a lot more of us in this attic with its posters and toys and cushions, that we've been transported to an intimate noisy paradise of women and children. I leaf through *National Geographic World* and find an article on the Hubble telescope. New galaxies, it appears, have been discovered, not just a few dozen, but billions, and those billions crammed into a visual space the size of my fingernail, like angels on the head of a pin. Theo is looking at some snapshots you brought of the Fourth of July celebrations in your hometown. Shaggy-haired, Gore-Tex-clad Oregonians are reveling in patriotic weirdness.

Mom, look at these two guys, says Theo. They're dueling with foam swords on this board over a mud pit.

Just wanted to give you a little taste of home, you say, with a half smile.

Strangely enough, these pictures fill me with real contentment, as though I'd been missing something without knowing it.

The phone starts ringing, and it's my editor from New York. I have to correct last-minute details of an article on Fellini that is closing the next day. Specifically, we're thrashing out whether Fellini for decades nourished an illicit passion for a woman the Italian scandal sheets call Fatty. And whether in his famous sketches he drew "thousands of penises" (my words) or "hundreds of penises" (fact checker's specification). I have to keep jumping up from dinner to discuss these matters, and I fear I'm neglecting you. Theodora devoured a plate of tortellini and dashed upstairs to do her homework. My husband, home from the office at eight-thirty and, knackered as usual, is eager to stretch out in front of the television and watch one of those big Italian variety shows in which platoons of scantily clad girls wag their butts and lip-synch Spice Girls tunes. My husband knows and likes you, the more since he enjoys acting grandiose and liberal about our mutual ex-husband. But it is clear that in the labyrinth of his Mediterranean male brain, this visit is a foreign female caprice. It's woman's work, *my* work, and aside from opening a wonderful 1982 Barolo, and making a few obligatory flirtatious comments on your unchanged beauty, he's leaving me to it.

I'm sorry I have to bore you like this, I say, as the phone rings for the fifth time. I didn't expect it. I promise that if you stay tomorrow night, we'll go out, we'll take you to one of the grand old Piedmontese restaurants, with their magnificent heavy pastas and polenta and boiled and fried meats. It's white truffle season, I add, almost pleadingly.

You're sitting with a full glass of wine that looks like a globe of ruby. I don't mind, you say, I've never seen a writer at work before.

I have to turn around and get a look at you. Droll again?

Much later, I finish, and go upstairs to find you in Theo's room, sitting in the dark beside her bed. I kiss Theo, and she grins at me blankly from the borderland between sleep and waking, and tells me that you checked her Latin for her. I feel a pang of jealousy, and a sudden illumination—it occurs to me for the first time that the two of you, a few years ago, did indeed have a real life together, of homework and bedtimes. I used to feel that my daughter melted into mist when she left for her father's house. Now, for a second, I feel strange, insubstantial, standing at my daughter's bedside with you, as if we are twin fairy godmothers. And suddenly I wonder what it is, apart from the bare physical fact, that makes a mother. What it is, for that matter, that makes a wife.

The baby gets me up twice during the night, but I'm awake anyway, thinking of you up in the guest room under the eaves, with British *Vogue* on the night table, and an anemic ivy plant snaking down the wall. Are you awake too? My husband huddles at the other side of the bed, as if he knows that I'm not present for him.

I'm thinking of the many times you have passed through my life. First in anecdote, as R, courting me, naïvely—how men live to regret this—confided far too many details of his earlier loves. And you were the earliest of all. An image: a small California town, citrus groves on the edge of the desert, and you and R at fifteen, eerily similar in unisex bell-bottomed jeans and Pre-Raphaelite hair, feeding the ducks under monumental palms in the park. Hand in hand, venturing inside the gigantic troubling maze of romance that we all enter so lightheartedly and find so hard to leave. A snapshot from that time used to prick my heart cruelly. I'd sneak it out of the box where R kept old pictures, and study your face, as you sat in Polaroid murk, cross-legged, arms clutched in the wary position you've never lost, gazing apprehensively at somebody out of the picture.

I knew about your childhood troubles, your fragmented family, and envied you even that. I could not summon up an aura of melancholy even faintly equal to that which you wore so seductively, like one of those girls who looks well in vintage clothes. You were the kind of girl Smokey Robinson and Linda Ronstadt had in mind as they sobbed out their lyrics. And then there was the fact that the adolescent romance between you and R had foundered in college, giving you the consummately enchanting quality of absence, the perfume of the vanished woman.

So many things I knew about you, as if we were best girlfriends. The fights, the reconciliations, the devastating letters, the elegiac lovemaking in a hayfield in France.

When I finally met you, at a beery Oakland reunion of college friends, I was happily married. You, the ex-girlfriend, were annoyingly beautiful, but you wore a pair of designer high heels that dispelled any uneasiness on my part. A romantic legend, I thought, would not need a pair of flashy shoes. I felt your power was neutralized. And I liked the way you kept dipping your head, checking me out through your thick Welsh eyelashes.

Years later, when R and I had moved to Rome and I, in a mo-

ment of epic distraction, left R, I wasn't entirely surprised to find
you suddenly, mysteriously, back in his life. You came to Europe on
a visit, and decided to stay on; but this, and that swift, subsequent
marriage are merely the facts. You had perpetually been present, as
a kind of mist that coalesced into a presence after I departed. Theodora, who was five, came back from her father's house one day,
speaking in a portentous voice of "the other," and that was you. You
had always been the other.

We all socialized nobly for a time in Rome, in our cramped expatriate circle: I'm thinking particularly of a time when the three of
us shocked a Pakistani friend by sitting in a giggling row at Theodora's school Christmas concert. And of a rather elegant Thanksgiving dinner I gave where you came in a loose Jean Muir dress, and
my friends came sidling up to me and hissed delighted speculations
as to whether you were pregnant.

You knew so much about me—as much as I knew about you.
I could see the knowledge flickering uneasily in your eyes. You
couldn't quite dislike me.

Then one afternoon I came to pick up Theodora, and realized
that for you things in your new Italian life, in that brief marriage,
had reached one of those obscure points of no return we all have
experienced. Your face was a study in controlled desperation.
Caught in my own role, I could say nothing. But I wasn't surprised
when the phone call came that told of shock, a sudden wild flight
to America. You were almost instantly back on your feet, but then
came the usual stunningly sordid debris of wrecked vows. Bits of
them floated downstream through my life.

Hurt and furious, R wanted to cancel you from the record. You
weren't supposed to exist anymore. But Theodora missed you and,
to my surprise, at the outset of a new marriage, I missed you, too.

So with Theo as an excuse, the first feelers went out, the telephone calls, the letters. Little nearly imperceptible stirrings, the movements of a breaking cocoon. This visit is the outcome, the emergence of a new form of life. And I haven't got a clue as to what kind of animal it will turn out to be.

Over on the far edge of the bed, my sleeping husband mumbles gibberish that sounds like tag ends of Latin. *Veni, vidi, vici.* He, too, has indissoluble links with extinct partnerships. I picture an endless mazurka of former wives, husbands, lovers, children, and assorted hangers-on, not excepting au pairs, cleaning women, and pets, and suddenly the whole thing makes me sick. I lie awake another half hour, furious at myself for inviting you, and at you for using up the air in my guest room.

You said you wanted to go along when I drive Theo to school in the morning, and when I knock on your door at seven, you emerge dressed, with the groomed, cold-shower flush that professional people have in the early morning. And you are carrying your black overnight bag.

I just remembered that I promised to have drinks with friends at the Principe di Savoia tonight, you say, as you and I and Theo clump down the freezing cold stone steps to the kitchen. It's all done correctly, discreetly, with impeccable regard for dignity, yours and mine. And with a slight implied rebuke for something overbearing and yet insincere in my insistence on your staying a second night. I am put in my place, and though it irks me I have to admire you for it. You don't take even the subtlest shit from anybody.

———

The American School is ten minutes away in a nearby suburb, a beautiful medieval town with a sixteenth-century Savoy castle looming over it. I had hoped for clear weather, but the November fog is so thick this morning that we can see only the silhouette of a tower and a soaring brick parapet. The car winds slowly through the labyrinth of slick cobblestone streets, as trees and pedestrians loom and vanish, and the fog lights of other cars shine in cone-shaped beams around us. Signs of provincial commerce—frutteria, trattoria, bar, supermercato—slide in and out of sight. We drop Theo off at the school gate, and you get out and hug her and tell her you'll write to her. I know you will, says Theo, in a serene voice that makes me want to cover her with kisses. She stands clutching her book bag, smiling and waving sleepily at us through the fog.

And at last we are on our own. We drive into the center of Turin, and I take you first for breakfast to one of my favorite bars, an Art Nouveau place frequented by opera fans, set under the arcades near the Teatro Regio. Then we cross the bridge over the Po on foot, and poke around the fashionable shops near the Gran Madre church; and end up lunching on roast kid and potatoes at a hole-in-the-wall restaurant in Via Mazzini. The whole time, in fits and starts, we have the conversation that is the occult reason this whole visit occurred.

It is not nearly as much fun as similar conversations have been in the past. Once at college, when I had been battling a roommate of mine for the affections of a scoundrelly med student, we both came to our senses over a bottle of tequila and in one epic night probably talked the wretch into a premature grave. Ah, those are the ribald confidences between unbuttoned ex-consorts that rightfully strike terror into the heart of every male. Incantatory insults to every gasp of his sexual performance, shrieks of witchy laughter over each stitch of his wardrobe and every pimple on his poor vulnerable ass.

But what you and I have to say about the man in the matter has a surprisingly wan quality. There is no blood, no tears, no sweat, no sperm in any of it. With a great many words, we compare a few notes, settle a few minor questions, chuckle with a curious sound of mortification. Out of some bizarre sense of etiquette, that has to do with your being the guest, we talk more about you than about me. We keep coming close then veering away from a central mystery that seems in my imagination to shine like a big incandescent globe between us. The question in its bare simplicity is whether or not we were really married to the same man.

Not whether or not we fucked him, because that, as we have seen, creates a farcical camaraderie between two women. Not whether we were both in love with him, because that shifts things into the banal rose-colored light of the eternal triangle. Not even whether we both lived with him, since that is simply within the classic tradition of ex-girlfriends swapping complaints about his farts, his blissful indifference both to laundry and to the historical grief and pain of female existence, his annoying party trick of dancing the boogaloo with a bottle of Dos Equis balanced on his head.

No; whether or not we were both married to him, feeling the weight that is marriage. The extra dimension, whatever it is, that gives simple lovemaking an affiliation with eternity; that makes one able to view a mole on the back of a strong young male neck—a reddish mole we both are familiar with—with a feeling of investment, an instinct that a great deal of knowledge still waits to be accumulated about this and other details. The sense, in a word, of possession, the mysterious ingredient in marriage that nobody at all understands.

Is it possible that we were both involved in this way with the same man? As I listen to the pathetic little confessions we are making, creating two portraits of astonishing dissimilarity, my good sense tells me that the answer is no. Your R was not my R. What the hell, then, is the connection between us?

I watch you drinking a *latte macchiato* in the bar, surrounded by dark curving wood and stained-glass nymphs. We have paused in our reminiscences, and you are telling me about the house you bought on the Skagit River, how you drive to work each day through the fern-covered trees down one of the most beautiful stretches of highway in the state. I can tell by the calm, downbeat way you talk about this that you are happy nowadays, perhaps happier than you have ever been. Though you don't brag, it is clear that, as usual, men are courting you. One suitor is a Chinese stockbroker from Vancouver, and another swain is the local vet, a guy who saves racing greyhounds. You don't want to live with anyone at present. Your dream is to buy a ranch with your brother.

Through the windows of the bar, we can see the cavernous seventeenth-century stone arcade where African street vendors have spread out their wares on blankets. No other foreigners in Italy look quite as misplaced as these blue-black Senegalese, wrapped up like Siberian grandmothers against the freezing fog. Cross-legged on the pavement, they sit as motionless as the cheap wooden statues they are selling, along with counterfeit Vuitton luggage. And I wonder what remarkable antipodean memories of love and devastation are unrolling behind their still eyes, while the two of us review what is, after all, only a minor domestic drama. A common one, at that. Near the vendors, a newsstand displays a headline: SCANDAL IN PARIS: DEAD MITTERRAND HAD TWO WOMEN.

At lunch I ask you: Why did you run away like that? The question just pops out, and it's the only spontaneous one I've asked you all day. Over the dish of roast meat and rosemary potatoes, in the middle of the chattering lunchtime crowd with two old waitresses rushing to and fro.

Your blue-green eyes, suddenly glacial, hook into mine and hold them. Didn't you run away too? you ask, in a voice that chills presumption, and silences me. You pick up your empty water glass and drink an imaginary drop.

Yet in the wake of this rebuke, I experience a sensation of perfect happiness. A sensation so brief and slight that if it were pain it would be called a twinge. And it's not even really happiness: it's a kind of satisfaction, as if together we have solved a complicated problem. There is no reason for this, and no way to explain it, so I say nothing. But I take a minute to admire you as you sit across the table from me—to gloat over the shape of your face and lips and hands, almost as if I were a susceptible man. As if I were our ex-husband, R, falling in love with you all over again.

The inauspicious hour of the afternoon has rolled around again, and it is time to get you to your train. As we walk across the river, the sun is burning off the fog, but for some reason the temperature has dropped. I am wearing a down vest, and I'm freezing; my impulse is to take your arm, the way Italian women do when they walk together on the street, but I don't. Below the bridge, the Po is mud-colored and swollen from the November rains. On the other side of the river we pass a travel agency outside of which, to promote tourism in China, someone has set up a peculiar pagoda-shaped booth in garish red, with gold dragons at the corners and lanterns hanging from the eaves. It looks so sinister that we have to giggle.

I wouldn't go near there, you say. It's either an opium den or one of those UFOs where they snatch humans for research.

Maybe it's just a Chinese time machine, I say. You and I could end up rival concubines in the Forbidden City.

More laughter. We walk on toward the car, close together but not touching.

As we drive to the station, I feel a growing relief that this visit has gone off so well. Twenty-four hours. We got along marvelously, and it was so good for Theodora, I can imagine myself saying to my friends. She's a lovely person, a strong, wonderful woman. I'll inflate my own image with every admiring adjective I apply to you. At the same time, I can hardly wait for you to get out of the car. And I know from the winged restlessness of your glance that you are impatient as well.

And now the kiss, once more a shade too forceful; and then you walk swiftly into the station entrance between the taxicabs, and the sleepy porters leaning on their metal carts. You seem to dart, a slender black figure with a black bag, the peacock scarf fluttering airily behind you, and as you go you remind me of a figure from a children's book. Peter Pan, maybe; or that capricious and slightly sinister little shadow of the Robert Louis Stevenson poem. A bit of past magic flickering out of sight.

Driving home up the hill, I turn on the radio, and tumble into the voluptuous sense of solitude one has after any guest leaves. Rounding a curve, I see in the distance that, as the mist thins, a phantom outline of the Alps has begun to sketch itself on the sky beyond the city. I think of you, probably already leaning your cheek in relief against the upholstery of a first-class compartment, pounding through the rice paddies and cornfields toward Milan, and eventually America. And I feel sorry that I wasn't able to show you the mountains from my house.

I drive on, still glad to be alone but feeling strangely diminished now that you are not beside me anymore. All the rest of the afternoon I go around feeling that I've lost something. Something as essential and indefinable as a shadow. I wonder if you feel the same way. Maybe you'll tell me, when I visit you.

About Fog and Cappuccino

During my second autumn in Milan, I would always stop in at the Delinquents' Bar on my way back from dropping my daughter off for school. The bus from the American School stopped in front of the Hotel Milan, and so from our apartment in Via Monte di Pieta we had a long walk through the fog. At that opaque morning hour the streetlights still made big blurred cat's-eyes in the muffling gray; the legendary shops of Via Montenapoleone and Via della Spiga, which just a few hours later would be filled with hordes of reckless women battling for luxuries, were shuttered. The antique palaces that had been turned into banks and boardrooms for the making and reshuffling of new money and new ideas were still unlit, revealing themselves through the thick numbing atmosphere in Piranesian glimpses of barrel vaults and muscular caryatids. It was a purgatorial landscape through which to guide a six-year-old girl every morning, a landscape that illustrated my dreary bemusement at finding myself, at my own initiative, suddenly unmarried and making a new home in a foreign city.

My daughter, the subject of much guilty pondering, was, in fact, obstinately cheerful in the midst of the fog. Full of oatmeal and orange juice, she skipped along in her dark blue jacket and mittens, chattering and laughing at the top of her lungs. While walking she

155

liked to play a game called Torture and Forgive, in which she would
pretend to crush my fingers, squeezing them as tight as she could
in her own small, fierce grasp, and then raising my hand to her lips,
where she would undo the damage with kisses. On our route, there
were certain things we couldn't look at because they brought bad
luck: a monstrous rubber plant in the window of a pharmacy; the
flyblown diamond earrings in the grimy showcase windows of the
Hotel Milan, which apparently had not been refurbished since Verdi
died there, and was famous for its cockroaches. We stood with our
backs to the diamonds until the school bus came. When my daughter stood on the steps of the bus and I kissed her cold red cheeks,
her face would blaze out at me from her dark hood like a fiery rose.

Then I was alone and it was time for my cappuccino. In Italy
cappuccino has not taken on the overblown dimensions it has acquired in America, and remains a spare and seemly breakfast drink.
Whether it is good, really good, depends not just on the lightness
of its foam, the perfection of its mixture of strong coffee and bland
milk, the correctness of its temperature. To my mind, it has to
incorporate a slight taste of misery as well, a tinge of bitterness or
sadness that has nothing to do with the provenance of the beans
but is drawn from the surroundings in which it is drunk. From this
point of view, the cappuccino served in the Delinquents' Bar was
nearly perfect.

The D.B. was a neighborhood bar of mine—in fact, it was on
the ground floor of my apartment house—and was really called
Bar Opera, in honor of the fact that La Scala was a block away. I'd
renamed it because it was a gathering place for a peculiar subspecies
of the generally fashionable denizens of central Milan: ten or fifteen
sidewalk loan sharks and ruffianly small-time dealers in gold and
jewelry. These men spent their mornings hanging about the side-

walk in front of the great stone facade of the Monte di Pieta Bank, which was a few doors up the street and had since the Middle Ages been the public pawnshop of Milan. There they lay in wait for the desperate souls whose offerings were too scanty for the official exchange. Often the carabinieri would pull up, and they would scatter like a flock of vultures, to regroup a few minutes later around an old man brandishing a pair of silver forks, or a woman in a worn fur coat who furtively displayed a set of cameos. It was an odd sight in a neighborhood where the normal uniform for men and women was English sports clothes, or suits by Armani, Valentino, and Versace; where chauffeurs and bodyguards hung about idly outside gateways through which manicured gardens could be seen like glimpses of Arcadia. Yet the Milanese are pragmatic enough to comprehend the sudden ascents and collapses of fortune—to see that the easy wealth they seek and enjoy must have its spectral reverse side in the gray mornings at the Monte di Pieta.

So one by one the delinquents used to materialize out of the fog as I sat on a high slippery stool, sipping my cappuccino and glancing through *La Repubblica*. They would order coffee and grappa, greeting each other with a weary matutinal precision, like employees checking in at an office. In looks they were a brilliant cast. Their leader was a short muscular fellow, wide as a refrigerator, with a fixed carnivorous grin and glistening gelled hair that seemed to begin at his eyebrows and swept back all the way to the base of his fat neck, where it turned up in a dandified flip. His principal colleague was a tall pimply blank-eyed lad with a straw-colored pompadour and an anarchic snaggle to his teeth; he dressed in striped suits, and never have stripes looked sadder or scarier.

Giovanni and Giacomo, the father and son who owned and ran Bar Opera, detested their clientele. They once confided to me

that they had removed most of the tables inside to discourage the
delinquenti from sitting down and doing business there, but they
dared not do more. There was some low-level odor of Mafia there
that I never felt like investigating. They had reason to feel annoyed,
because just a hundred yards away other bars were packed with
well-heeled businessmen, fashion models, elegant housewives and
their little yapping dogs; while the Bar Opera attracted only this
louche company that seemed to be an interior manifestation of the
fog in the streets. It was partly the proprietors' own fault, since they
hadn't bothered to gentrify the place with smoked glass mirrors and
little islands of green plants; and because they served horrible stony
pastries, too obviously bought day-old on the cheap. Father and son
floated wanly behind a dented aluminum counter in a brown cavern
of nineteen-fifties paneling lit by a grimy chandelier that seemed to
have been looted from a provincial dance hall. Giovanni, who came
from a mountain village near Bolzano, still retained a hearty phys-
iognomy that went with his crisp Austrian accent, but Giacomo,
who had clearly grown up on an urban caffeine diet, was a forty-
year-old with the face of a schoolboy preserved in formaldehyde.
And there was an heir, a pale sprout of a ten-year-old who appeared
after school and pumped coffee with the deadpan ease of a pro.

The two of them treated me well, probably because they felt I
gave a minimal touch of class to the place. Each morning, they paid
me respectful compliments on my attire, and adorned my cappuccino with the stylized flower in chocolate powder that is the mark
of a skilled barista. With the delinquents themselves I established
one of those relationships between cordiality and aloofness that a
solitary lady in Italy must set up with the shopkeepers in her area if
she is to be considered a lady. I said good morning and nodded with
a certain formality, and they did the same. If the truth be told, I was

happy to see them, had begun to consider them a sort of family, and would have loved to know more about who they were and what they did. This, however, was impossible, for my own good, and for their clear view of the world. In a certain sense, I measured my dignity by not having recourse to their company and services, but the possibility, I told myself, was not so far removed that I could afford to be casual. Only once did it happen, one morning when I burst into the bar wearing blue jeans and a conversable American grin, that the great stout slick-haired leader stole up to me on light feet like Count Fosco and inquired whether he could buy me a grappa. I declined lightly and civilly, but that day, staring into the dregs of my coffee and milk, I saw an abyss.

Cappuccino is a morning drink, but in those days I drank it all day with my friend Nelda. She'd appear at my door after lunch, when I'd finished writing and she was on a break from her job of showing apartments to rich foreigners. She carried an umbrella against the eternal drizzle and wore a hooded mushroom-colored raincoat that like the rest of her clothes was slightly too large for her, and that made me think of the poem "An Old Woman of the Roads."

"Oh, to own a little house . . ."

Nelda was no old woman, but she was Irish, and in spite of being one of the most beautiful girls I have ever known, had about her a faint raggle-taggle air that inspired visions of a weary rainswept vagrant life. The hems of the long peasant skirts she favored were sometimes trampled and wet. She had once been the pampered young wife of a doting Milanese banker and had her nightgowns handmade out of plum-colored silk satin. Now she lived in a studio apartment with a decor that seemed to require underwear dripping in the bathroom. She had some Georgian silver teapots from her mother, and a NordicTrack squeezed alongside the sofa. She was always on the phone to the Philosopher, the man for whom she'd left husband, children, and fortune, a fifty-year-old anarchist from Bologna who spent most of his days getting stoned on a futon, like some wonderful period piece from the seventies. Nelda would call him up and ask what he was doing, and he would reply, shamelessly: "Thinking." I could imagine him with his neat D. H. Lawrence beard, reclining on a bare futon decorated with graceful brownish blossoms of ancient sperm stains. Nelda worshiped the Philosopher. She told me that, unlike overstressed businessmen his age, who couldn't get it up, he could make love three times a day.

"Oh," she would sigh. "If only I didn't have to be unfaithful to him." For she saw him only on weekends, and in the splendor of her loneliness was generous with her spare evenings. The only men she disdained were Irishmen, "because I don't like pink penises." She liked all other colors. She told me about a young prince from Ghana, a shy polite boy of twenty who had the biggest one she'd ever seen. "It looked like a weapon. I said: 'That thing is not coming anywhere near me,' and he said: 'Look, Nelda. You've had babies. If *they* could get out, *this* can get in.' "

Nelda's eyes, as she told me these things over cappuccino, had the unnerving clarity of a kitten's. She seemed born without the capacity to regret anything, and she gave me courage. I felt that if one day I informed her that I'd gone to the zoo, jumped into a cage, and made love to a chimpanzee, she would have found not just an excuse for me but a way of explaining that it had been urgently necessary for my mental health that day to have sex with another species of primate. At the same time, she had a curious loopy sense of practicality that appealed to me in that disordered stage of my existence, and with it she spent a surprising amount of energy trying to redirect my life. For someone who lived in a way I associated with cheese rinds and the ends of candles, she thought in the economic terms of a great demimondaine. An industrialist was courting me, and she told me that I should simply ask him to buy me a big expensive apartment in the best part of Milan.

Though I had no intention of following her advice, I amused myself by letting her show me an array of apartments whose prices were redolent of abused expense accounts: ten-room penthouses in the Montenapoleone or Magenta district, full of dirty wall-to-wall carpet. These places all had vast wet terraces covered with tubs of moribund oleanders, terraces from which you could sometimes view the prickly spires of the Duomo, and the wasteland of fog pierced by the sparks of the streetcars far below.

One November afternoon after we'd looked over a particularly dismal apartment in Via Visconti di Modrone, Nelda continued her rehabilitation campaign by convincing me that I had to track down a man I'd known briefly that summer in Sardinia. This was a lawyer from Varese who wore white patent-leather loafers, and who had astonished our little seaside colony of mothers and children by manifesting a sudden devotion to me as apparently respectable as it was intense. He would arrive at my door with flowers in the early evening when all the ladies, babysitters, and children were assembled on their condominium terraces, and take me out to one of the cheaper restaurants on the Costa Smeralda. He made the sign of the cross before he ate. On our third date, he asked me to marry him, and bear many children in an ancient brick farmhouse in the swampy midst of the Varese rice paddies, where frogs are so common they are included in risotto. He vanished quickly when I showed little enthusiasm for the project, and I had forgotten his last name. However Nelda seized on the idea that he was the man for me.

"He may have seemed dull, but dull men can be the best husbands. There's no disappointment, because you know what you have."

She said we should get a detective and find him. I didn't want the man, but the idea of sleuthing in the Northern Italian provinces had a dark frivolity that appealed intensely to me. So we made an appointment—telephoning, of course, from a bar—with a detective whose face had the benign look of a father confessor as he stared out of a half-page ad in the Milan yellow pages. His offices, on a fashionable street near Piazza San Babila, were big enough for a whole law firm and lined with dark green leather, and his beautiful receptionist had a brisk air of high-class tartiness. Seated at a mahogany desk littered with telephones, the famous investigator was small and bald, and wore the bland sacerdotal smile of his advertisement; he spoke, however, in a fast rough voice with a trace of a Calabrian accent. At once he began to ask me questions in a way that was so vulgar that it gave me a thrill. Instinctively, I prepared my body and mind to follow unexpected mysterious orders, as if I were visiting a medical specialist.

"Did you—" He made a back and forth motion with his fist.

"I don't understand," I said.

Nelda poked me. "Don't act like a fool," she whispered.

"Excuse me, Signorina, but I have to be blunt. If I am to help you, it's important that I know everything. Did you have relations with this man?"

"Yes—well, no, not in the sex way that you mean. Well, not in any way, really."

"How often did you see him?"

"We met on the beach, and then we went out for dinner four times."

"What did he talk about when you were together?"

"About the fact that I was, well, a goddess—"

"A what?"

"A goddess." I said the Italian word clearly, and the investigator wrote something down on a small pad of paper. "And he wanted me to come and live with him in an old farmhouse in the rice fields—"

"He asked her to marry him!" broke in Nelda. The investigator smiled fatuously at her, as men always smiled at Nelda. After a few minutes, he telephoned a minion and demanded information on restaurants on the Costa Smeralda. Then he put down the phone and said: "Signorina, it's a clear case of breach of promise. I'll find the individual in question for you, but it won't necessarily be an easy path. For expenses I'll need immediately from you a check for three million lire."

Something I was never afterward able to reconcile with any idea of sanity was the unmistakable pleasure with which I drew out my checkbook and wrote a check for the outrageous amount of money—twice what an office worker would earn in a month, and money that I could not easily spare. I did it with a promptness that clearly surprised even the investigator. It was obvious that the desperate women he preyed on usually required at least a minimum of convincing. He had his mouth open, showing an unharmonious array of dental work, when I tore off the check and handed it to him with a flourish. "Signorina," he stammered, "I want to explain—"

But I waved him aside with a gesture I didn't know I possessed, the gesture of a grand duchess. *"Trovalo a tutti costi,"* I said. "Find him at all costs, my dear Mr. X."

As we left—as in some psychiatrists' offices, the exit was different from the entrance—Nelda squeezed my arm affectionately, like a mother proud of a clever child. I felt weak with relief. It seemed that there was a climactic folly in what I had just done that laid to rest whatever shades had been haunting me. I had paid a tithe to hell, and it could now absent itself from my mornings and afternoons. We went out onto Corso Monforte, where at three in the afternoon the streetlights were already lit, and the umbrellas of the crowds of shoppers sliced through the drizzle. The expensive shops shone through the fog like caves of warmth, full of treasures that could nourish and heal, and the women lingering in front of the bright windows all looked like children on Christmas morning. Soon I would be picking up my daughter from the school bus and could forget the perverse adventures of my afternoon in the clasp of that small exacting hand. "Let's stop somewhere," said Nelda, in a happy voice. "And have a coffee."

Needless to say, the detective never found anyone, though the two times I called him, he said: "I have a very promising lead, Signorina. It is a matter of days."

I lost my money as I had known I would. Shortly thereafter, Nelda borrowed my black leather Azzedine Alaïa jacket and set off for a long visit to the Philosopher. And what did I do? In the weeks that followed, I abandoned the Delinquents' Bar and began to wander the streets of the city among the coffee-break crowds, searching for the perfect cappuccino and the perfect bar to drink it in. Each bar I entered was for a few minutes a small shelter that I considered for myself. I was convinced that imbibing caffeine in some places brought you luck, and in others brought you failure and general woe. The beauty of the bar had nothing to do with it, nor did seediness guarantee good fortune. The glossy tearoom on Via Montenapoleone would have seemed to have been an obvious cliché, to be avoided, but in fact those mirrored rooms stuffed with marrons glacés and people whose faces, above their furs, had the same gleam of expensive candied fruits, felt lucky; just as the sinister artists' hangout down on Via Brera had something indefinably wrong about its atmosphere and its cappuccino.

The barmen in some places were skilled at producing a crisp, dry halo of milk foam, and in others produced a creamier nimbus. Some could draw flowers with the powdered chocolate sprinkled on top; and one lost master, hidden from the world in a tiny establishment on the glum middle-class shopping street Viale Piave, presented his cups sketched with a tiny, ephemeral chocolate face that regarded one pensively as one pensively drank.

I drank many nondescript cups of milk and coffee, and a few great ones, but a poker-faced film-noir angel never did spring up beside me and tap me on the shoulder. At the same time I received an assignment from a magazine to write about Milan high life; and one evening, fastened into a black velvet dress and lined up on a white couch in a row of other women, like a line of drinks on a counter, I met the man who was to become my second husband. And then there was love, the indescribable, and my mornings in bars became something much more ordinary: the concluding acts of trysts. My lover, a small, elegant, good-hearted man, whose mixed aristocratic Venetian and Sicilian blood gave him ancestral depths of worldliness and cunning that I could only guess at, quickly put the delinquents at the Bar Opera in their place, shouldering up to the counter and ordering for me with a rich man's impregnable self-confidence. I could see the delinquents were impressed; they were, after all, consummate material men, and he exuded success on their terms. There was fatherly approval in their eyes as they regarded us together. I was no longer that disquieting figure: a female stray, a waif who had to pay for her own coffee.

A year later, when my daughter and I left Milan, and went to start a new life with my husband in Torino, one of the first things I did in that city, out of a sort of reflex, was to start looking for a place to have my daily cappuccino. I visited the extravagant Art Nouveau bars along Via Po and Corso Vittorio, where the courtiers of the Kingdom of Italy had languished in the mid-nineteenth century, nibbling lobster sandwiches among the brass and stained glass and polished wood, and chatting in their French-accented Italian of the latest vicissitudes of the House of Savoy. For a few weeks I went to a small pizzeria and bar in a rustic village center not far from my house in the hills overlooking the city, a bar frequented by a sort of village idiot called Il Matto, who went around in a triangular sheep-skin cap, sometimes clutching a piece of raw meat. Il Matto was considered picturesque, and I tried to feel privileged as I clutched my cup and listened to his high-pitched chatter, but the cappuccino was watery, so I abandoned the village square for an establishment I had discovered down by the river Po. This tiny place, called Il Bar del Buon Caffe—the Bar of Good Coffee—had an unrecon-structed postwar interior of apple green linoleum and aluminum tubular trim that suggested an American diner.

Inside, a strange tight-lipped Piedmontese family with the verti-cal faces of Visigoths served small floral cups of the best cappuccino I had ever had in my life. A wall plaque in folkloric Piedmontese dialect informed customers that the proprietors had indeed won some kind of regional coffee-making contest. There were only two small tables, squeezed against the windows, and at ten-thirty in the morning a crowd of well-heeled Torinese housewives, in their uniform of streaked blond hair, earth-colored tweed and cashmere, and handmade sport shoes, would press in with their umbrellas and bags of shopping. I liked sitting there with my wonderful drink—

the powdered cocoa on top was mixed with raw sugar—breathing in the expensive perfume of these women, and listening to their breathtakingly pedestrian talk about golf and suntans and servants. Torino had weather as bad as that of Milan, but in that atmosphere I felt that I had banished uncertainty and melancholy from my days, that perhaps I had actually found my bar. It was agreeable to belong somewhere, to a region, to a family, to a man.

I said as much to a new acquaintance at a party, a tall skeptical-looking surgeon who had the nondescript features of the Torino upper classes, prematurely wrinkled from a lifetime of winters spent skiing in the Alpine snowfields. He laughed when I told him about the bar. "I'm sorry to disillusion you," he said. "But that is a rather naughty little place. It's notorious for being the starting point for *Belle du Jour* adventures. A lot of those bored wives are waiting for telephone calls about personal ads, or to meet strange men as previously arranged. People say that some of them get paid for it."

He laughed again as he saw my expression. "Strange, I didn't think you were a prude."

I wasn't shocked at the goings-on in the Bar del Buon Caffe, but rather at the stupid ease of my own self-deception. I should have realized, I told myself, that no matter how solidly planted one feels, the daylight hours are always times of random searches, of changing shapes in the traffic and in the fog along the street. It occurred to me then that for the rest of my life the delinquents, in one form or another, would be peering over my shoulder. I ended up deriving a curious comfort from the idea. It was a thought that went well with the taste of strong coffee and milk.

The Pulpit

Once upon a time, O Best Beloved, some years before your quick feet and lucent curls were seen upon the earth, your father was a student courting me. Through a long Boston winter he escorted me, in the time-honored mode of the university suitor, to the symphony, to small, dank ethnic restaurants, to ocher-colored foreign films at the Brattle, and on glacial strolls beneath the elms of Harvard Yard. And I have to confess that on many of these occasions I behaved in a capricious and bad-mannered fashion, yawning openly and pleading exhaustion at 10:00 P.M. My private name for him was the White Boy, though he was certainly not the only white boy in my life, confined as I had always been by the aspirations of a middle-class black family to the narrow channels of East Coast private education. But there was something about him that seemed whiter than the others: white in the sense of inexperience and blandness, a sort of hapless innocence that to a romantic girl of any color seems worse than all the seven deadly sins. This irritating naïveté was joined to another quality that I couldn't define, but that seemed equally intolerable, and all in all I had decided to be busy for his future invitations. I'd just come to this decision when I found myself drinking Guinness with him—for the last time, I vowed—in one of those historic college bars where every wooden booth is a palimpsest of carved letters recording extinct love affairs and dead politicians, and whose cracked leatherette cushions bear the buttock prints of jocks long gone to seed. And, as if my soon-to-be-rejected companion had read my thoughts, he looked at me with a pair of ingenuous blue eyes that were part of the problem and began to tell a story.

He described a summer seven years earlier, in the late nineteen sixties, when he was working for a civil rights group in western Alabama. The place, which I'll call Tenlow County, was a vast chunk of cotton country adrift in rusticity. So much so that the seismic upheaval in Southern life that had begun in the same state almost a decade and a half before with an intrepid laundress on a Montgomery bus had scarcely rippled the old feudal reign of injustice over local plantations and towns. Things were about to change, however. In Tenlow County that summer an election was approaching that promised to be one of the great theaters of confrontation of that peculiarly confrontational year, when all of America was as candidly divided—between old and young, long hair and short, stoned and straight, hawk and dove—as the squares on a chessboard. The facts were simple: several thousand black men and women, most of them sharecroppers, were for the first time in their lives intending to vote. And a smaller group of whites, the people who ran things in the county, didn't want that to happen. A constellation of civil rights organizations had moved onto the scene, and young volunteers had come from all over the United States to help with the voter registration drive. Your father—whom from now on I'll call Y.F.—and his best friend McGinty drove two thousand miles from their town in Southern California. They were both seventeen.

Now at first, as I sat in the bar watching the foam evaporate on my Guinness and trying to shut my ears to the yammering of some Winthrop House oarsmen in the next booth, I felt annoyed by this story. How unsubtle, I thought, to try to seduce a black girl with tales of your youthful prowess in the civil rights movement. I myself, with a battling Baptist minister for a father, and siblings who always seemed to be integrating some school or other, had been weaned on civil rights legends. So I wasn't the slightest bit charmed, and was tempted to invent a morning conference with my adviser that would allow me to end the evening even earlier than usual. But for some reason I kept listening.

What intrigued me at first, I think, was just how ordinary a story it seemed. Ordinary like a fable or a page from a reading primer, something I seemed to have heard many times before. And how the voice in which he told it, with its flat California vowels and suburban syntax, suited the words as an instrument suits a particular melody. It began in fact as a fabulously commonplace story and a proper way to approach the sixties, a period about which it is almost impossible to reminisce without entering the realm of myth or parody. Y.F. made no attempt to paint pictures with language, yet whatever he said spurred me to fill in the spaces with my own visions.

He said: *We drove,* and I saw a stretch of desert highway and a battered Volkswagen carrying a pair of teenagers with faces out of the great Anglo-Saxon diaspora. Beautiful boys, almost twins, with long hair the color of the bleached flatlands around them, and straight teeth, and bodies whose rude health had just previously been the province of conscientious mothers and pediatricians. And carefully tattered jeans patched like Appalachian quilts. Boys who listened to the car radio as if their lives depended on it; which in a sense was true, since the radio poured out the statistics of the faraway yet curiously intimate war that in a few years might devour those healthy bodies. From the radio, too, came some of the best music of all time, rock, country, and soul masterpieces, which they accepted casually as the soundtrack to their own inimitable adventure. Of course they felt themselves to be on a mission, burning with a pure revolutionary flame, yet on the road they acted like fraternity brothers, stealing dips in motel pools, lifting cheeseburgers from indignant carhops, hanging moons at girls in passing cars. They'd been friends since childhood, but their friendship was not important to the story.

Their conversation I imagined as a torrent of leftist politics that was neither as superficial or as muddled as both of them were later to pretend, in times when it became fashionable to jeer at oneself in the sixties. Something else easily mocked in later days was the uncomplicated belief both of them had that the bad old world could be hammered to pieces and then put to rights. Already at the beginning of their trip this belief had been severely tested in a Tucson park, where they tried to engage in a bit of comradely dialogue with a group of Mexican kids. When their new acquaintances—in an efficient but not acrimonious fashion—knocked them down and relieved them of their watches, Y.F. and McGinty had the good sense not to discuss the matter. They put their reflections on hold and drove on to Alabama.

They'd expected to be foreigners in Tenlow County, but what actually happened was that, for the first time in their lives, they became minorities. The powers-that-were in Montgomery and Washington had bowed to the pressure for separatism that was already fragmenting the civil rights movement, and had channeled most other young white volunteers out of the field. At the first meeting of the voter registration volunteers, held in the county seat of Barreville in the Tinley Temple African Methodist Episcopal church, the two arrivals from California were the only Caucasian faces in the crowded pews. And those faces turned red as Chinese flags when the Reverend Emmanuel Basnight, pastor of Tinley Temple and local head of the voting drive, suddenly paused in the midst of an emotional invocation of justice to point his finger at the two of them. "The world is watching Tenlow County," he thundered. "And the proof is that these two white boys have come all the way from California to help us win the vote! Stand up, boys!" They tottered to their feet, grinning feebly as the congregation burst into hallelujahs. And for the rest of the summer, as if they had been formally christened, Y.F. and McGinty were known, to their concealed irritation, as the White Boys.

When I heard that, I sent an innocent smile down into my mug of Guinness.

As the story went on, it was easy to picture Tenlow County. Just the deep South, a part of the world as contaminated by myth as the late sixties period itself. A region I'd never visited, but which was familiar to me from books and newspapers and my parents' dramatic reminiscences. Familiar as the dark woods in every fairy tale. A sea of cotton in the boll, strewn at intervals with plantation houses, moribund Greek Revival towns, shacks clustered in the unchanged patterns of slavery. Crushing heat that felt more like doom than weather, and a halo of buzzards over every tree. Dirt roads, kudzu, juke joints, and the lingering perfume of original sin. Black earth and—everywhere, everywhere—black people. Neither Y.F. or McGinty had ever before sat at a table or in a classroom with a black person, but that summer there were days when the White Boys felt a shock of surprise at the sight of each other, and at glimpses of their own wan faces in mirrors.

They lived for two months in a shotgun house on the outskirts of Barreville, guests of a widow who was half blind with diabetes.

There they learned to appreciate pigs' ears and collard greens, and helped out their elderly hostess with an officious gallantry that would have amazed and enchanted their mothers back in California. Each morning they shoveled down a plate of grits and raced over to the storefront headquarters of the voter registration project, where they received marching orders from Reverend Basnight. This gentleman, since baptizing them with their nickname, had remained a remote, awe-inspiring figure who made it clear that his public enthusiasm had nothing to do with his private feelings. It was clear, in fact, that he was disposed to like or trust the White Boys about as much as he did the white men who spat tobacco in unison outside the town hall. Tall and thin, with skin the color of an old penny and a face as angular and humorless as that of a Byzantine saint, he would hand out the day's assignment while regarding them with a cold skeptical eye that left them shuffling and itching to be off. Then they'd take the battered dusty Volkswagen bumping down back roads and pull up in front of a cluster of shacks. "Good morning to you," one of them would call out. This was usually the glib outgoing McGinty, who had mastered a theatrical Southern accent. Old people, children, and anyone else who wasn't working in the fields came out to stand in the dust and stare at the long-haired white visitors and their outlandish little car. "How do, we're working for Reverend Basnight over at Tinley Temple, and for the election. We want to make sure that every grown man and woman in Tenlow County gets to vote. We're going to have a revolution here! Going to put you in power."

Old and young, their audience stood with wary faces while the visitors spoke of education and jobs and black people in charge, and handed out leaflets that displayed the proper ballot symbol, a red rooster. The blinding sunlight and those shuttered faces gave Y.F. a feeling of vertigo. At times, though he never told his friend, he was overcome by the impression that a fundamental mistake had been made: that it was really he and McGinty who needed information and hortatory phrases. That the black strangers standing barefoot in front of him had a secret hoarded strength that made talk of power and revolution simply presumptuous. And that no election would ever bring to an end the old sad story that lay like a dark river between them. These gloomy thoughts sometimes became so pressing that he had to go back to the car and pound his head to dislodge them.

At the ends of the long exhausting days, the White Boys hung out with the other young volunteers at backwoods roadhouses that throbbed like funky hearts in the night. There they could buy beer without showing ID, and argue about Fanon and Marcuse with black college students who, in their Afro hairstyles and city clothes, drew as many stares from the locals as the White Boys themselves. Though many of the black volunteers did not approve of their presence, or even of their existence, the boys had such a winning eagerness to heap ashes on their own heads for the sins of their race that a grudging camaraderie sprang up. Even romance made an appearance. McGinty flirted with the belle of the summer, a doe-eyed Spelman sophomore, who galvanized the male population of Tenlow County with tight leotards and armloads of silver bracelets. And Y.F. yearned after Reverend Basnight's daughter Nicolette, whom he did not describe to me, but whom it is easy to imagine as one of those wayside flowers one finds in rural ministers' households. Nicolette almost certainly had a pretty, virginal face the color of rosewood and a genteel straightened coiffure held back by a stretch hair band. She didn't frequent the juke joints, of course, but chattered with prim vivacity to Y.F. as she worked the mimeograph machine in the office. Mostly she expatiated on her love for the novels of Pearl Buck and her dream of studying medicine at Howard University; and she never let Y.F. so much as touch her hand.

In its last two weeks, the campaign went into overdrive. A New York, Washington, and Atlanta delegation swept into town, and suddenly Tenlow County was indeed watched by the rest of the country. Y.F. and McGinty were no longer the only white faces in the campaign, which the national press was describing as one of the test cases of the decade. Famous journalists and political luminaries arrived at rallies or sauntered into Reverend Basnight's Sunday services, appearing and disappearing as casually as the restless Olympians in the *Iliad*. An atmosphere of marvels hung in the thundery August air. Rumors about the opposition grew daily more sensational: it was whispered that Governor Wallace had issued a secret order for the bombing of black schools and churches, that the Klan was preparing a preelection night of terror. In reality, their opponents put up little resistance. Perhaps the powers of Tenlow County were simply confident that white rule was part of the climate on their ancestral soil. But most likely the lack of opposition sprang from dawning pragmatism, for after nearly two decades of bitter struggle the most obdurate segregationists had begun to recognize through the smoke the lineaments of the second great lost Southern cause.

In any case, the campaign had from the start the feeling of being directed by a conscientious Providence. On election day the biggest problem was not harassment but a fearful inertia on the part of the new voters. Y.F., McGinty, and the other volunteers had instructions not to let anyone stay home and spent hours cajoling people out of their houses and ferrying them to polling stations. In the early evening, when Y.F. was on his own in a hamlet in the eastern corner of the county, trying to talk a particularly reluctant old man off his front porch, he saw a van pull up and two men get out. One of them was a photographer, and the other he was stunned to recognize as a great civil rights leader, a legendary figure who was the right hand of Martin Luther King, and whom he had seen in newscasts parting ravening mobs like Moses dividing the Red Sea. And, because it was a day of wonders, this hero clapped Y.F. on the back and boomed—in a mighty voice, like a bell cast in a supernatural foundry: "Good job, son. We'll take it from here." And in a grand popping of flashbulbs he escorted the old man into his van.

Of course they won. Everything happened the way it is supposed to happen in a saga of the good fight and *summum jus*. The poor, the downtrodden, the orphans of history triumphed, as two thousand new voters swept into power the first black officials since Reconstruction. The next day hundreds of sharecroppers, dressed in their Sunday clothes, poured into Barreville for the victory celebration, held in the newly integrated high school. In the front of the auditorium, the great civil rights leader stood at a pulpit lectern transported from Tinley Temple AME. Beside him stood a white senator from New England. They took turns telling the ecstatic crowd that the world was going to change, that with prayer and hard work you could wipe out injustice the way you could erase an error in arithmetic. Then they embraced, black and white, as the delirious spectators roared *amen*. Choirs from five black churches sang thunderously. Reverend Basnight, his lean face radiant and softened, raised his arms to heaven and thanked the Lord in strenuous panegyric. Then came an epic fried chicken banquet, and then a famous deejay arrived from Montgomery and the party started. It was a love feast. Dissolved in the sweltering mass of celebrants, the White Boys boogied, for the first time that summer feeling invisible. Y.F. found the prim Nicolette and managed a heated slow dance and a kiss: another victory on this night when no star was unreachable.

The next day was the last in Alabama for Y.F. and McGinty, and it was then that occurred the small mishap upon which hinges this entire story. A minuscule tragedy, especially in light of the magnitude of joy still hanging in the air, but a tragedy nonetheless in that it pointed out a mysterious flaw in the scheme of—what? Of everything. But I am getting ahead of myself, as my suitor in the college bar did not do. In a few words he sketched for me a picture of that last morning after the party, when the volunteers, bleary-eyed and hungover but still euphoric, were set to cleaning up. When the school had been swabbed down and every empty bottle collected, the White Boys had one more task: to transport the pulpit lectern from the school auditorium back to Tinley Temple AME. They set out driving an ancient flatbed truck, and a few minutes outside town met with a slight mishap.

It is easy to imagine the two in the cab of a dinosaur of a truck out of a Walker Evans photograph. Behind them on the flatbed, lashed with a clothesline in McGinty's special bowline hitch, lay the tall lectern. Y.F. drove, McGinty propped his feet up in the passenger seat, both talking eagerly about the election and the party. Then a lurch, Y.F. struggling with the archaic clutch, as the old truck gave a fierce jerk to the right and took a lumbering bound into the drainage ditch. The boys catapulted onto the dashboard, realizing simultane-ously that they were unhurt; the engine gave a series of elephantine shudders and stalled; and at the same time there was a rumble and a splintery crash as the pulpit lectern, bursting free from its clothesline bonds, tumbled off the flatbed and onto the blacktop. There fol-lowed, one imagines, an almost reverent moment of silence.

When they'd said *fuck!* about a hundred times and scrambled out of the cab, Y.F. and McGinty found the lectern lying in the road. It was hard to believe that so short a fall could have caused so much damage. The impact somehow had been perfectly angled to split the varnished pine boards that made up the sides, and the whole thing, still attached by nails, but with strips of raw wood showing, lay collapsed as if flattened by a giant thumb. The White Boys stood there for a second, digesting the fact that they'd smashed up part of Reverend Basnight's church, a central part, one that famous men had been clutching and making speeches over just the day before. And because five minutes earlier they'd been adrift in pure exaltation, the wreck took on an apocalyptic significance. It seemed to Y.F. that the lectern was the pulpit itself, the heart of the church and of the people who had sheltered him for two months. And the accident had resulted from a kind of violence he'd had inside of him without even knowing, like some dupe tricked into carrying a briefcase that held a bomb. The thought of telling the news to Reverend Basnight, and watching that angular brown face lose its glow of triumph and harden into grim exasperation, was unbearable. As was the thought of the others, of Nicolette. Y.F. didn't say, but I am sure the two boys had tears in their eyes. They were not many years out of childhood, after all.

Anyway, that was the moment when I fell in love with your father. As he sat in a bar in Cambridge, Massachusetts, telling me the story, and also seven years earlier, when he stood on a road in Alabama beside a broken pulpit from an African Methodist Episcopal church. Don't ask me why, but it's a fact. There was something that caught my heart—abruptly, the way catastrophes and miracles occur—in the picture of the two White Boys standing and staring at what looked exactly like the ruin of all good intentions. And in the image of how they must have picked up the pieces, tried to start the truck, kicked at weeds, and then begun jogging miserably back to town.

Of course the story doesn't end there. That same afternoon they got the truck out of the ditch, and the pulpit to a carpenter in Barreville. The carpenter was a Tinley Temple member who promised to rebuild it free of charge. To their amazement no one was angry with them—not even Reverend Basnight, who actually stretched his Byzantine mouth in a dry smile and joked that even the Liberty Bell was cracked. And Nicolette said nothing but slipped Y.F. a piece of pink stationery inscribed with her address. It was only Y.F. and McGinty who were crushed: all their gorgeous sense of accomplishment had collapsed like a card castle, and suddenly they couldn't wait to get home to California. Late that night, without saying good-bye to anyone, they took off out of Tenlow County, racing as if the Klan were after them. It was strange how it turned out, that the only white men who scared them in Alabama turned out to be themselves.

The rest, as they say, is history: your history, darling. After all, without that splintery crash on the blacktop, the tale would not have existed and you might never have been born. Now that you have reached the age of the White Boys, I am passing the story on to you as a kind of heirloom, unencumbering, but also undefined. There are so many questions that come with it. Why, for example, does it *stick*? Why, though your father and I are now long divorced, and divided by a carefully groomed terrain of indifference, do I still feel that it is important? And what is the actual story—just the tale of the pulpit, or my listening to the tale of the pulpit? Is it a story about black people and white people, or men and women? And, behind all these words, what is the flickering presence I keep glimpsing, insubstantial as the shadow of a fly? Is it something funny, or something sad, or something completely different?

Your father remembered the misery he felt on the country road outside Barreville when he had almost forgotten what the election meant for Tenlow County. The accident became the definition of that Alabama summer, and the image stayed sharp and clear through his senior year in high school, through the waning of the sixties, and the perfectly natural death of his friendship with McGinty. It stayed with him as he set aside his raw idealism, and grew slowly into tolerating the knowledge that the world, the real world, wanted nothing more than to put White Boys like him into power. It remained vivid until one evening when he was in law school he found himself telling the tale to another black girl he had a crush on. A minister's daughter like Nicolette Basnight. A girl who, as the story progressed, laid aside her rudeness and indifference; and at the end suddenly laughed and raised her eyes to meet his across the table.

What's that? Did he ever write to Nicolette? You know, that's something that in all these years I never found out. My dear, that's one more question you'll have to ask your father.

Sicily

The first thing I knew about Sicily was marzipan. It's a specialty there, and whenever my stepfather goes down to visit his Palermo relatives he brings it back to us in Rome. Marzipan is candy made from almonds and is so sweet that as you eat it you feel slightly nauseous. Federico, my stepfather, says that Arabs brought it to Sicily a thousand years ago. The reason I love it is that they make it in every shape and color; they even copy things like asparagus or salami. It's a weird feeling, biting into a marzipan pork chop, because even if your brain knows that it's candy, your tongue still expects something else. When we went off to spend four days in Sicily over the May twenty-fifth school holiday, Federico bought me a little basket of marzipan clams and mussels at the Palermo airport. Mom was annoyed, as she always is when Fede buys me candy, which is often, because he has a sweet tooth himself. But I was happy, because the streaky brown-and-black shells looked completely real. Later, on the beach, I even fooled my stepcousin Ginevra by pretending to dig up a marzipan clam and then taking a big bite out of it. She screamed. It was all jealousy: she can't stand anyone showing off any more than she does.

Ginevra was part of the group of Federico's friends and family who had come from all over Italy to meet up with us for the holiday in a very tiny hotel on an island called Favignana. It takes a long ferry ride to get to Favignana, which is far out in the sea between Sicily and Tunisia. It's an island covered with the kind of white pumice stone you use in the bath, and also with prickly pear cactus. It gets unbelievably hot, so you can't stay out on the beach in the middle of the day or else you end up fried. Luckily Ginevra and I had brought our Game Boys, and Saturday after lunch we perched on the steps of the hotel terrace and played Tetris, Frogger, and Super Mario. Meanwhile Federico and the rest of the men sat at a big table and smoked and laughed and occasionally shouted over a card game called *scopone*. The women were all in their rooms taking siestas, except for my mother, who was reading in a hammock, with a sulky look on her face. Mom was sulking a lot on this trip, because she doesn't like to do anything in big groups, which she always says is the worst of many obnoxious Italian habits. But I knew she was peeved most of all because Fede was spending time with his brothers and his cousins: playing cards, drinking wine, strolling to the store to buy cigarettes, and not paying much attention to her at all. Mom is great, but one of the first things anybody notices about her is that she likes a lot of attention. She kept yanking me aside and hissing complaints in my ear: "He's reverted. It's a tribal gathering. I knew we shouldn't have come."

We were there on Favignana to watch them kill tuna. This is a Sicilian custom called *la Mattanza* that happens every year in May, when the tuna migrate. *Mattanza* means "slaughter," Federico told us, and what happens is that the fishermen from the islands guide schools of tuna into a special trap and then spear them, and there is a whole ceremony they perform as they do this, with prayers and songs. Fede said that it is a way of fishing that was already ancient when the Normans ruled Sicily in the Middle Ages, that probably it dates back to the Stone Age. Once it was a sort of festival, but nowadays hardly anyone is allowed to go out with the fishermen in the boats. But Federico's cousin knows someone in charge, so we all had permission. Mom and I love animals—in Rome we have three guinea pigs, two Maine Coon cats, a Jack Russell terrier, and five goldfish—and so at first both of us just flat-out refused to go. We'd been to Sicily before, for beach holidays, but this was completely different. But Federico laughed and said he'd be lost without the two of us, and that it was a once-in-a-lifetime experience. It would be an introduction to the sanguinary depths of the Sicilian character. "My character," he said. "You foreign girls only know the civilized side of me."

"Ignorance is bliss," said Mom. But she had the absentminded look she gets when something intrigues her.

We're American, my mother and I, though I was born in Rome and get teased because I speak Italian with a Roman accent. Mom is from Kenwood, California, which is where I spend summer vacations with my grandparents. She's tall, with long hair the color of brown leaves, and every Italian who sees her says the same thing: *"la classica Americana."* She says that means being beautiful and not very bright. When she was in college she did some modeling, and I have a scrapbook of yellowing magazine pictures showing her in plaid skirts and woolly sweaters, peering out of covered bridges or pretending to chat with bearded old lobstermen. Now she and her friend Elsa run an English-language bookshop in Trastevere, where I work sometimes on Saturdays. My dad is American too: he's with Reuters. When I was a baby, before my parents got divorced, they lived together in Rome; now Dad's in Manila, and I only see him a couple times a year. I've lived with my mom and with Federico for five years, since I was six. Fede is a law professor at the University of Rome, and was born in Palermo, and is a lot older than Mom. He's short, with a funny rubbery face, and he can speak perfect American English, and if I beg him, he'll do a hilarious Mafioso imitation in Sicilian dialect. He can be terribly bossy, but we get along. We're both addicted to peanut M&M's, Harry Potter, and video games; he's the only person I know who has made it to a higher level of Tetris than me. And he loves my mom a lot, although they have huge fights at times, and she says she can't bear this short-legged Latin male. But all in all we're pretty happy. In Rome, we live on the Cassia, which is where a lot of foreign families live. We're not really a foreign family—we're a mixed family.

Anyway, after siesta time on Favignana, everyone rode bikes to the beach. I was stuck riding with Ginevra, who lives near me in Rome and who was showing off her temporary tattoos and boasting about what a great gymnast she is. I could see Mom up ahead, pedaling quickly past Federico, who was riding with Ginevra's father, Uncle Massimo. The beach had pumice stones instead of sand, and the water was like dark green glass, and though the sun was boiling, the sea was like ice. Ginevra and I swam anyway, while the grownups spread out straw mats and lay down. There were millions of hermit crabs on the rocks, and we got the idea of collecting them and putting them into two big plastic mineral water bottles. Mom said they'd never survive, but Ginevra and I thought that if we just kept filling the bottles with seawater they'd be fine, and we could even take some home and keep them in an aquarium. Federico went snorkeling along the rocks and came back shivering, with about fifty sea urchins in a bucket. Somebody took out a knife and a lemon, and pretty soon all the stepcousins and aunts and uncles were opening them up and eating them raw. Yech—you couldn't get me to touch them: spiny on the outside and red and slimy on the inside. Mom ate one, but you could tell it was just out of politeness. She's not a beach person. She sat in the sun with her hat and long-sleeved shirt, chatting with Aunt Saveria and Aunt Gabriella and the other ladies who had taken off their bikini tops and lay there covered with gold jewelry and oil, cooking themselves, as she calls it. Beside them she looked so pale and different that I felt a little embarrassed for her. She says that most of what Italians call beauty is simple vulgarity, but I always like the way Italian ladies look at the beach: brown and glittering in the sun like Egyptian queens.

Before sunset we walked along the rocks to see a cave that was famous for having amethyst light inside; when we got there, Federico and the other men fooled around, shouting to make echoes, and jumping in the water. And on the way back, Fede told Ginevra and me a story about a young man in Sicily who'd spent a summer on a wild seacoast like this, and had met a mermaid and fallen in love with her. The story was by Tomasi di Lampedusa, a famous Sicilian writer, and had an ending that Fede couldn't remember exactly—a sad ending, he thought, or perhaps it was that the story was never finished. The writer probably got stuck, Ginevra whispered to me, because how do you describe sex with a mermaid?

That night we all ate dinner at a long table in a room full of oil paintings of fat naked women, fruit, and jumping tuna fish. The *primo* was spaghetti Sicilian style, with fresh sardines. I didn't think it tasted like anything but fish, but everybody else seemed to think it was fantastic. "The real taste of Sicily," Federico kept saying. "The taste of all my summers at the seaside when I was a dirty-minded little boy dreaming of little girls' bottoms." He gave some to my mother, insisted on her eating lots, and she kept protesting, and he said to her, wiggling his eyebrows, *"Ma è un afrodisiaco,"* and she looked at him and laughed, the unhappy kind of laugh she has when she's feeling sorry for herself and mad at the rest of the world. "Why have you been ignoring me?" he asked her in English, lowering his voice. "You've been ignoring *me*," she answered. "All day, just playing cards and hanging out with the men as if this were some kind of village." For a minute I was afraid they were going to have one of their awful arguments, but Fede just turned down the corners of his mouth and said: "I'm not asking you to live here—just to observe and to be a bit patient and to try to understand things from a different point of view." "You know me," said Mom. "I'm a great understander."

The next day was the *Mattanza*, and we had to get up early to go out with the fishermen. It was dark and cold when Mom and Aunt Gabriella came and woke me and Ginevra, and though I put on jeans and a windbreaker my legs went numb as we bicycled out to the harbor. There we left the bikes and walked inside a stone building as big as a cathedral with huge arched doorways that opened right out onto the water, and ceilings so high they were invisible in the darkness. Federico told me that the building was a *tonnara*, a place where they bring the freshly caught tuna to be chopped up and probably also put into cans. About a hundred years ago this was the main business on this island—these big echoing places that looked like churches were all full of fishermen and fish. The islanders caught thousands of tuna, but left many to breed so that every year there were more and so there was, he said, a good understanding between men and the sea. But now there were too many big ships fishing with ultrasound and nets that took everything, and the tuna were dying out, and it was possible that this was one of the last old-style *mattanze*.

We waited at the dock for a while in the cold morning air while the sky got lighter, and the grown-ups drank coffee from a little bar

that was open, and Ginevra and I drank hot milk with a little coffee. And we all gobbled down giant sugar-covered pastries called
bombolone. Then we climbed into four open boats attached to each
other by a thick rope. We were in the next to the last boat, Mom and
Federico and I, and Ginevra with Uncle Massimo and Aunt Gabriella. And they towed us out into the middle of the bay, where we got
out of our boat and into another, a big flat one that had been set up
to form part of a square with other flat boats. Federico pointed out
to Mom and me the nets under the boats that were also laid out in
a square. Uncle Massimo told us that this was called *la camera della
morte*—the death chamber. We were all talking in low voices, even
Ginevra, because it was eerie waiting out there in the middle of the
water with the island like a dark streak behind us and everybody's
face the color of cardboard in the gray dawn light. I leaned back
against Mom, who had on a thick wool sweater, and she gave me a
squeeze. "Talk about *camera della morte*," she whispered. "We all
look like corpses!" She hugged me tighter and added: "I don't know
what we're doing here, sweetheart, but we chose to come, so if you
can't take it, close your eyes."

The sky turned pink, and two boatloads of fishermen showed
up. They looked like pirates: tanned brown as shoe leather, and
one with a black ponytail down to his waist and tattoos on the sides
of his neck, and another with peroxide blond hair frizzing out of a
striped wool cap and a big gold ring in each ear. Federico said that
the blond guy was the *rais*: the head of all the fishermen, and that
by tradition the men had to obey his every command. All the day
before, they'd been tracking the movements of a big school of tuna,
and now the fish were about to swim into their trap. The fishermen
shouted back and forth in a language that didn't even sound like
Italian, and Mom told me it was Favignana dialect, with a lot of Ar-

abic words in it. They all began to pull on yellow waterproof jackets and pants, and then they moved to the edges of two big flat boats and stood in two lines facing each other over the water.

We all waited, and I felt my stomach clenching with suspense. As we waited the sun came up and a lot of other boats, full of families from the island, and other visitors, and even a television crew from Germany, joined us. After sunrise everyone, weirdly, began behaving like they were at a party. The grown-ups drank wine from paper cups, and we all ate sandwiches they call *pane condito* down in Sicily because they put oil and vinegar on the bread before adding tomato and prosciutto and cheese. Everyone laughed and talked and shouted jokes to the fishermen. The *rais* turned around to answer once or twice, laughing so that you could see all his big white teeth, but the rest of the men just stood like statues, staring out over the water. In the middle of the fishermen stood a small Japanese man in a warm-up suit. Federico said a Japanese company had bought the whole catch, and that in twenty-four hours the tuna would be sushi in Tokyo.

All of a sudden the tuna arrived. We saw one huge silver body inside of the square and then another and another, and then it seemed that there was hardly enough room for water; there were just dozens of silver bodies bigger than any fish I'd ever seen, churning around and around, and the fishermen began to pull on the ropes of the net. They pulled all together, and as they pulled they began to sing in strange words that Federico told me were Arabic. They sang and they pulled the net further and further up until we could see the fish clearly. And the tuna began to move faster and faster until you could feel how panicky they were. The water looked like it was boiling. Just then Mom asked if I'd like to go to another boat further back so I didn't have to watch, because they were going to kill the fish. I said I'd stay where I was.

What the fishermen did was take long poles with spikes on the end and stab them into the tuna and then with a quick, almost mechanical movement, hoist them flopping and struggling out of the water. It was hard to believe that single men could be strong enough to lift such giant fish. The tuna were covered with blood, and the water began to fill with blood until it turned dark red, the color of wine. I thought how strange it must look from an airplane: the water red and boiling in that square between boats, but the sea around a normal color. As they pulled out more and more fish, the fishermen kept on singing, and their voices sounded sad and monotonous. The air smelled of fish and seawater and something raw and wild that must have been blood. People in the crowd were quiet, and a lady in black glasses from the German TV crew told Ginevra and me in English that they were filming this for people back in Germany so they would understand how cruel it was. The Japanese man stood with his back very straight and his arms crossed, his eyes following every movement of the fishermen. Mom gripped my shoulder, and I looked back and saw that her cheeks looked shiny with tears and that Federico had put his arm around her.

They caught three hundred sixty-seven tuna. The number passed in whispers through the crowd. When the last fish was pulled out of the water, the *rais* made a signal and the fishermen began to sing a song that sounded like a prayer. It was a prayer, Federico told me: They were thanking God, or Allah, for a good catch. That was the way they had done it for a thousand years. The big silver heaps of fish didn't move anymore except for a few flips of the tail, and the blood slowly dissolved into the water. The party feeling had dissolved, too, and as they towed our boats back to the dock of the *tonnara*, people sat and thought their own thoughts. Though it felt as if a whole day had passed, it was only ten o'clock in the morning.

Ginevra leaned against her father and slept with her mouth open. I didn't feel sad, just dead tired and hollow inside; I put my head in Mom's lap, and she stroked my hair and we sat in silence. The only thing Mom said during the boat ride was "I want to go home."

Next day we said good-bye to Ginevra and everyone else, left Favignana on the ferry, and drove for five hours until we got to Palermo. Palermo was darker and more confusing than even the oldest darkest parts of Rome, and felt dangerous: a maze of little streets like tunnels, crowded with cars and trash and people strolling in and out of shadows. Old buildings were covered with stone carvings—shells, nymphs—all crusted with ancient grime that turned them into monsters. Mom and I started teasing Federico about having a secret life as a Mafia don, and instead of doing his Godfather imitation, he said in quite a serious voice that people here lived with the Mafia as a fact of life, like the weather. Mom said that it couldn't be that drastic, that this wasn't the Middle Ages, but Fede just clucked his tongue, the way he does when he disagrees. From Palermo we had to catch a plane for home that night, but first we went to visit a prince and princess who were friends of Fede's, and lived above the harbor in a palace made of blackened stone. Fede told us that the building was partly a *tonnara*, like one of those on Favignana. He said that the prince's family had for centuries owned fleets of ships, and that these old noble families had the habit of living above the store. Nowadays they had no more ships, but the prince had smart sons who had made a restaurant and discotheque in the part where they used to butcher the tuna.

So we went through a tall carved doorway and up slippery steps into a garden with palm trees and a stone railing at one end, where you could see the city, and ships on the water below. The garden was dry and wild and full of stacks of boards and huge dusty vases and cats walking among old tools and iron pipes, and one corner was crowded with strange-looking cactus plants that the princess collected. The princess was not very tall and had bright blue eyes, a pointed nose, and gray hair in a braid down her back. She looked stern but friendly as she walked toward us with a cigarette in her hand, and then she grabbed Federico and hugged him and called him an old vagabond, and asked him why it had taken him so long to bring his bride to see her. She had a rough voice almost like a man, and she gave Mom and me big smacking kisses on our cheeks and said we were beautiful girls.

I had a Coke and the grown-ups drank coffee as we sat on creaky red couches in a long room filled with books and Chinese vases as tall as I was. Leaning in a corner beside a television was one of those old-fashioned high bicycles. Federico was tired from driving, and stretched out for a nap while the princess took Mom and me on a tour of the palace. First she showed us a round brick tower that was a gift from an empress of Russia. The empress had been a guest in the palace, and her thank-you present was a Russian tower. After that we walked through dark rooms with marble floors and piled furniture covered with sheets; some rooms had chandeliers and some had ceilings painted with scenes from mythology, and one very big room held nine—I counted them—grand pianos. I tried to play one and it just rattled. We passed through a sort of pantry where in the wall were built dozens of wooden drawers with the Latin names of herbs on them in black Gothic letters: she told us it used to be the pharmacy for the household. Then there was a room full of things from Africa: shields, masks, and even a stuffed shark. But the best was when the princess ducked into a bathroom and came out with a bulgy plastic shopping bag that turned out to have crowns in it: six real crowns or diadems, as Mom called them, made out of real gold set with blood-red stones that were Sicilian coral. They had been bridal crowns for women in the family, and nobody in the world had a collection like that, and it was kept in the bathroom because no thief would think of looking there. The princess set one on my head, and I performed a pirouette and a curtsy for her, and she laughed and told us about a German governess she had when she was my age. This strict governess ruled her life completely, except for an hour a day when she could run wild. She could do anything she liked in that hour—be rude, wet, filthy—and the only rule was not to get killed. I liked this story very much, and the princess, too. You could still see the wilderness twinkling far inside her blue eyes.

Back in the room with the Chinese vases, the prince had arrived and was chatting with Federico. They stood up when we came in, and the prince kissed the air over my mother's hand and mine too, and looked at Mom and then said to Fede that he didn't deserve his good fortune. The prince was tall and had straight gray hair down to his shoulders. He wore khaki pants and a pair of old sneakers, and was tanned as dark as the fishermen on Favignana. Federico had told Mom in the car that the prince was seventy years old and that he stayed young through wickedness; that he was a famous *viveur* who led the princess quite a life. I thought that he looked not wicked but kind and that, gray hair or not, he and the princess were the most exciting people I had ever met. He sat down and took my mother's hand between both of his and said in a soft voice that she was a work of art, and that if she didn't mind he would talk to Federico but look at her. The grown-ups all laughed at that, the princess more than anyone, and I noticed how straight her spine was as she sat on the red couch, like a queen on a chessboard.

I wandered around looking at some old model planes on the bookshelves while the grown-ups drank whiskey and Federico and the prince talked about their fishing adventures together in Kenya long ago. Then they all started gossiping about people they knew, and I tried to make myself invisible so I could listen. In fact they forgot about me for a while and began to tell stories about young wives playing tricks on old husbands, about husbands fooling around in Africa with beautiful African girls, about a new medicine made in Cuba from sugarcane that knocked the spots off Viagra, and about a woman who had such huge breast implants that she couldn't go deep sea diving. They went on talking, and I heard the princess say to my mother: "It's only fair to explain to you, my dear, that I have a very particular kind of marriage. I have to take care of both my husband and his *fidanʒate*—his girlfriends. Otherwise he makes a muddle of things."

"It seems perfectly reasonable to me," said Mom. "But it's delicate work."

"There are diplomats in my family," said the princess. "And a couple of saints." She smiled, and both women glanced at me. Then the princess called me over and slipped her arm around my waist and told me that if I promised to visit her at Christmas she'd stuff me with *cassata*, a celestial pudding that looked like a white mountain, and only ever tasted good in Palermo.

On the way to the airport, Mom said: "That marvelous woman. Why does she put up with it? Why does she stay?"

"What woman?" I asked, though I knew she was talking about the princess.

Then Federico, who was smoking a cigarette and driving very fast in and out of traffic, said: "She stays because he is marvelous, too. And she's actually quite happy. If you think otherwise, you've missed the point."

"And what point is that?" asked Mom coldly.

"The point of everything you saw this weekend."

Mom said, in a still colder voice, that she hadn't known that this was supposed to be an educational tour, but that even a benighted foreigner like herself could grasp that the main theme over the last two days had been simple inhumanity. Imagine, she said, singing hymns while you slaughtered tuna. Or being a wife who felt it was her duty to help out a husband's outrageous affairs. She grabbed up her hair and clipped it tightly the way she does when she gets mad, and I thought they were finally going to have the fight that had been brewing since we arrived in Sicily. But Federico, who can lose his temper over incredibly small things, for some reason didn't seem to mind at all. He laughed and threw his cigarette out of the window, and said that Mom was melodramatic like all Americans, and one day when she grew up she might realize that Sicilians understood the real nature of the world better than anybody else. And why, he added in a plaintive tone, hadn't he chosen to marry a good Sicilian woman?

"Well, why didn't you?" asked Mom, settling back in her seat. Strangely enough, she didn't seem at all angry anymore.

At the airport I made a depressing discovery: the plastic bottle full of hermit crabs I'd collected on Favignana was a plastic bottle full of dead hermit crabs. Of course my mother and Federico had been telling me that for two days, but I'd ignored them. Now it was clear, because the crabs really stank. I didn't want to show the bottle to Mom, because I knew what she'd say, but I showed it to Fede and he whispered: "Shall I throw it out?" "Yeah," I said, so he strolled away when Mom wasn't looking and stashed the bottle in a trash bin. I felt gloomy until he went off to the souvenir shop and came back with a bag of marzipan fruit; then I cheered up as I bit into a pomegranate and tasted the familiar sickening flavor of sweet

almonds. Mom grabbed a piece of marzipan too—a prickly pear—
and as she did, Federico shot me a wink. We were in the plane by
then, racing through the night away from Palermo over the Strait of
Messina toward Rome and the known world, and as I leaned against
my reflection in the window and imagined the dark sea below, it
seemed like great luck to be flying home with a mouth full of sugar.

Winter Barley

Night; a house in northern Scotland. When October gales blow in off the Atlantic, one thinks of sodden sheep huddled downwind and of oil cowboys on bucking North Sea rigs. Even a large, solid house like this one feels temporary tonight, like a hand cupped around a match. Flourishes of hail, like bird shot against the windows; a wuthering in the chimneys, the sound of an army of giants charging over the hilltops in the dark.

In the kitchen a man and a woman sit eating a pig's foot. Edo and Elizabeth. Together their years add up to ninety, of which his make up two-thirds. Edo slightly astonished Elizabeth by working out this schoolboy arithmetic when they first met, six months ago. He loves acrostics and brainteasers, which he solves with the fanatical absorption common to sportsmen and soldiers—men used to long, mute waits between bursts of violence. Edo has been both mercenary and white hunter in the course of an unquiet life passed mainly between Italy and Africa, between privilege and catastrophe. He is a prince, one of a swarm exiled from an Eastern European kingdom now extinct, and this house, his last, is a repository of fragments from ceremonial lives and the web of cousinships that link him to most of the history of Europe.

The house is full of things that seem to need as much care as children: pieces of Boulle and Caffiéri scattered among the Scottish furniture bought at auction, a big IBM computer programmed to trace wildfowl migrations worldwide, gold flatware knobby with crests, an array of setters with pernickety stomachs in the dog run outside, red Venetian goblets that for washing require the same intense concentration one might use in restoring a Caravaggio. In the afternoons Edo likes to sit down with a glass—a supermarket glass—of vermouth and watch reruns of *Fame* magically sucked from the wild Scottish air by the satellite dish down the hill. With typical thoroughness he has memorized the names and dispositions of the characters from Manhattan's High School of Performing Arts and has his favorites: the curly-haired musical genius, the beautiful dance instructor he calls *la mulâtresse*. The television stands in a thicket of silver frames that hold photographs of men who all resemble Edward VII, and women with the oddly anonymous look of royalty. Often they pose with guns and bearers on swards blanketed with dead animals, and their expressions, like Edo's, are invariably mild.

To Elizabeth, Edo's kitchen looks unfairly like a men's club: brown, cavernous, furnished with tattered armchairs, steel restaurant appliances, charts of herbs, dogs in corners, Brobdingnagian pots for feeding hungry grouse shooters, and green baize curtains, which, as they eat tonight, swell and collapse slowly with the breath of the storm. The pig's foot is glutinous and spicy, cooked with lentils, the way Romans do it at Christmastime. Edo cooked it, as he cooks everything. When Elizabeth visits, he doesn't let her touch things in the kitchen—even the washing up is done in a ritual fashion by the housekeeper, a thin Scottish vestal.

"These lentils are seven years old," he announces, taking another helping.

"Aren't you embarrassed to be so stingy?"

Dried legumes never go bad, he tells her, and it's a vulgar trait to disdain stinginess. His mother fed her children on rice and coffee during the war, even though they crossed some borders wearing vests so weighted with hidden gold pieces that he and his sisters walked with bent knees. Edo grew up with bad teeth and an incurable hunger, like the man in the fairy tale who could eat a mountain of bread. He has a weakness for trimmings and innards, the food of the poor.

Elizabeth knows she adopts an expression of intense comprehension whenever Edo reminisces; it pinches her features, as if they were strung on tightening wires. Still, she doesn't want to be one of those young women befuddled by lives lived before their own. She grew up in Dover, Massachusetts, went to Yale, and hopes that one day she'll believe in more than she does now. At the same time she has a curiously Latin temperament—not the tempestuous but the fatalistic kind—for someone with solid layers of Dana and Hallowell ancestors behind her. This trait helps her at work; she is a vice president at an American bank in Rome. Tonight under a long pleated skirt she is wearing, instead of the racy Italian underwear she puts on at home, a pair of conventual white underpants and white cotton stockings held up with the kind of elastic garters her grandmother's Irish housemaid might have worn. Edo has been direct, and as impersonal as someone ticking off a laundry list, about what excites him. She is excited by the attitude in itself: an austere erotic vocabulary far removed from the reckless sentiment splashed around by the men she knows in Rome, Boston, and Manhattan.

Elizabeth discovered early on that the world of finance, far from moving like clockwork, is full of impulse and self-indulgence, which extend into private life. When she met Edo she had just come out of a bad two years with a married former client from Milan, full of scenes and abrupt cascades of roses, and a cellular phone trilling at all hours. In contrast, this romance is orderly. She supposes it is an idyll when she thinks about it, which, strangely, is almost never; it flourishes within precise limits of ambition, like a minor work of art. The past he sets before her in anecdotes—for he is a habitual raconteur, though rarely a tedious one—keeps the boundaries clear.

Africa; dust-colored Tanzania. Edo is telling her how his mother once got angry on safari, blasted a rifle at one of the bearers, missed, and hit a small rhinoceros. Under a thatch of eyebrows Edo's hooded blue eyes glow with a gentle indifference, as if to him the story means nothing; the fact is that he couldn't live without invoking these memories, which instead of fading or requiring interpretation have grown more vivid and have come to provide a kind of textual commentary on the present. His hair is white, and he has a totemic Edwardian mustache. His cheeks are eroded from years of shooting in all weathers on all continents. It's the face of a crusty old earl in a children's book, of Lear, and he is appropriately autocratic, crafty, capricious, sentimental.

He watches Elizabeth and thinks that her enthusiasm for the gluey pig's foot and the rhino story both grow out of a snobbish American need to scrabble about for tradition. Americans are romantics, he thinks—"romantic" for him is the equivalent of "middle-class"—and she is no exception, even if she does come from a good family. Accustomed to judging livestock and listening to harebrained genetic theories at gatherings of his relatives, he looks at her bone structure with the eye of an expert. She is beautiful.

Her posture has the uncomplicated air of repose which in Europe indicates a wellborn young girl. But there is an unexpected quality in her—something active, resentful, uncertain, desirous. He likes that. He likes her in white stockings.

She says something in a low voice. "Speak up!" he says, cupping his ear like a deaf old man. He is in fact a bit deaf, from years of gunpowder exploding beside his ear. He often claims it turned his hair prematurely white and permanently wilted his penis, but only the first is true. "You're a gerontophile," he tells her.

She'd said something about storms on Penobscot Bay. The rattling windows here remind her of the late August gales that passed over Vinalhaven, making her grandmother's summer house as isolated from the world outside as a package wrapped in gray fabric. She recalls the crystalline days that came after a storm, when from the end of the dock she and her cousins, tanned Berber color and feverish with crushes, did therapeutic cannonballs into the frigid water. She sees her grandmother in long sleeves and straw hat, for her lupus, dashing down a green path to the boathouse with a hammer in her hand: storm damage. In the island house, as in Edo's, is a tall clock whose authoritative tick seems to suspend time.

Elizabeth and Edo finish the pig's foot and stack the dishes in the sink. Then they go upstairs and on his anchorite's bed make love with a mutual rapacity that surprises both of them, as it always does. Each one has the feeling that he is stealing something from the other, snatching pleasure with the innocent sense of triumph a child has in grabbing a plaything. Each feels that this is a secret that must be kept from the other, and this double reserve gives them a rare harmony.

Later Edo lies alone, under the heavy linen sheets, his lean body bent in a frugal half crouch evolved from years of sleeping on cots and on bare, cold ground. He sent out the dogs for a last piss beside the kitchen door, and now they sleep, twitching, in front of the embers in his fireplace. He has washed down the sleeping pill with a glass of Calvados that Elizabeth left for him and lies listening to a pop station from Aberdeen and feeling the storm shuddering through the house, through his bones. He imagines Elizabeth already asleep in the bedroom with the Russian engravings, or—hideous American custom—having a bedtime shower. He has never been able to share a bed with a woman, not during his brief marriage, not during love affairs with important and exigent beauties. It gives him a peculiar sense of squalor to think of all the women who protested or grew silent when he asked them to leave or got up and left them. Alone among them, Elizabeth seems to break away with genuine pleasure; her going is a blur of white legs flashing under his dressing gown. Attractive.

After immersion in that smooth body, he feels not tired but oddly tough, preserved. An old salt cod, he says to himself, but for some reason what he envisions instead is a burl on a tree. At Santa Radegonda, a vast country house in Gorizia that nowadays exists only in the heads of a few old people, there was in the children's garden an arbor composed of burled nut trees trained together for centuries. The grotesque, knobby wood, garish with green leaves, inspired hundreds of nursemaids' tales of hobgoblins. Inside were a rustic table and chairs made of the same arthritic wood. The quick and the dead. A miracle of craft in the garden of a house where such miracles were common—and all of them grist for Allied and German bombs. He seems to see that arbor with something inside flashing white, like Elizabeth's legs, but then the Tavor takes hold and he sleeps.

2. REMEMBERING EASTER

The storm has blown itself out into a brilliant blue morning, and Elizabeth lies in bed below an engraving of a cow-eyed Circassian bride and reads the diary of Virginia Woolf. Volume II, 1920–1924. She imagines Bloomsbury denizens with long faces and droopy, artistic clothes making love with the lighthearted anarchy of Trobriand islanders. Through the window she can hear Edo talking in his surprisingly awful English to the gardener about damage to *Cruciferae* in the kitchen plot. Rows of broccoli, brussels sprouts, and a rare black Tuscan cabbage have been flattened. The gardener replies in unintelligible Scots, and Elizabeth laughs aloud. She finds it shocking that she can feel so happy when she is not in love.

They met when she was depressed over the terrible, commonplace way things had ended with her married lover from Milan, with all her friends' warnings coming true one by one like points lighting up on a pinball machine. She had sworn off men—Italians in particular—when a gay friend of hers, Nestor, who spoke Roman dialect but was really some kind of aristocratic mongrel, invited her to Scotland to spend Easter with him and some other friends at the house of a mad old uncle of his. Nestor and the others didn't show up for their meeting at Gatwick, so Elizabeth bought a pair of Argyle socks at the airport shop and took the flight up to Aberdeen on her own. It didn't feel like an adventure, more like stepping into a void. After the tawny opulence of Rome, the obstinate cloud cover through which she caught glimpses of tweed-colored parcels of land far below suggested a mournful Protestant thrift even in scenery. She listened to the Northern British accents around her and recalled

her mother's tales of a legendary sadistic Nanny MacGregor. In her
head ran a rhyme from childhood:

> There was a naughty boy,
> And a naughty boy was he
> He ran away to Scotland,
> Scotland for to see.

Nestor was not in Aberdeen, had left no word, and the mad
uncle was disconcerting: white-haired, thin-legged, with the piti-
less eyes of an old falcon. He was exquisitely unsurprised about her
coming alone, as if it were entirely usual for him to have unknown
young women appear for Easter weekend. Jouncing along with her
in a green Land Rover, he smoked one violent, unfiltered cigarette
after another as she talked to him about Rome, trying to conceal
her embarrassment and her anger at Nestor. Air of a near-polar
purity and chilliness blew in through the window and calmed her,
and she saw in the dusk that the landscape wasn't bundles of tweed
but long, rolling waves of woodland, field, and pasture under a sky
bigger than a Colorado sky, a glassy star-pricked dome that didn't
dwarf the two of them but rather conferred on them an almost ceremonial sense of isolation. No other cars appeared on the road. They
passed small granite villages and plowed fields full of clods the size
of a child's head, and Elizabeth felt the man beside her studying
her without haste, without real curiosity, his cold gaze occasionally
leaving the road and passing over her like a beam from a lighthouse.

Edo was wondering whether his young jackass of a nephew
had for once done him a favor. But he himself had offered no
kindness that merited return, and Nestor was ungenerous, like
the rest of Edo's mother's family. Perhaps the girl's arriving like

this was a practical joke: he remembered the time in Rome when a half-clothed Cinecittà starlet had appeared on his terrace at dawn, sent by his friends but claiming to have been transported there by group telekinesis during a séance. But Elizabeth's irritation, barely lacquered with politeness, was genuine, and lent a most profound resonance to her odd entrance. In the half-light he admired the gallant disposition of her features below her short, fair hair, the way she talked in very good Italian, looking severely out of the window, from time to time throwing her neck to one side in her camel-hair collar, like a young officer impatient with uniforms.

"We're on my land now," he said after forty minutes, and she observed ridges of pleated dark forest and a jumble of blond hills. Down a slope behind a wall of elms was the house—a former grange, two hundred years old, long and low, with wings built on around a courtyard. With windows set deeply below an overhanging slate roof, it looked defensive and determined to endure; on each wing, black support beams of crudely lapped pine gave it the air of an archaic fortification. When Edo opened the Land Rover's door for her and she stepped out onto the gravel, the air struck her lungs with a raw freshness that was almost painful.

"Why do you live here?" Elizabeth had changed from jeans into a soft, rust-colored wool dress that she wore to the bank on days when she felt accommodating and merciful. She stood in front of the fire with one of the red Venetian goblets in her hand, feeling the airiness of the crystal, balancing it like a dandelion globe she was about to blow, watching the firelight reflecting on all the small polished objects in the long, low-ceilinged room so that they sparkled like the lights of a distant city. She knew the answer: gossipy

Nestor had gone on at length about Byzantine inheritance disputes, vengeful ex-wives, and drawn-out tantrums by climacteric princes. However, with Edo standing before her so literally small and slight but at the same time vibrant with authority, so that one noticed his slightness almost apologetically—with him playing host with immaculate discretion, yet offering, subtly, an insistent homage—she felt strangely defenseless. She felt, in fact, that she had to buy time. Already she was deliberately displaying herself, as the fire heated the backs of her legs. Before she let everything go she wanted to understand why suddenly she felt so excited and so lost and so unconcerned about both.

"Why do I live here? To get clear of petty thieves," he said with a smile. "The daily sort, the most sordid kind—family and lovers. When I got fed up with all of them a few years ago, it occurred to me that I didn't have to go off to live in Geneva like some dismal old fool of an exile. Africa was out, because after a certain age one ends up strapped to a gin bottle there. So I came up here among the fog and the gorse. I like the birds in Scotland, and the people are tightfisted and have healthy bowels, like me." He paused, regarding her with the truculent air of a man accustomed to being indulged as an eccentric, and Elizabeth looked back at him calmly. "Are you hungry?" he asked suddenly.

"I'm very hungry. Since breakfast I've only had a horrible scone."

"Horrible scones are only served in this house for tea. I have something ready which I'll heat up for you. No, I don't want any help; I'll bring it to you as you sit here. It will be the most exquisite pleasure for me to wait on you. There is some snipe that a nephew of mine, not Nestor, shot in Sicily last fall."

"What do you think happened to Nestor?" asked Elizabeth. "Could you call him?"

"I'd never call that bad-mannered young pederast. He was offensive enough as an adolescent flirting with soldiers. Now he's turned whimsical."

When Edo went off to the kitchen Elizabeth walked back and forth, glancing at photographs and bonbonnières, touching a key on the computer, looking over the books on cookery and game birds, the race-car magazines, the worn, pinkish volumes of the *Almanach de Gotha*; and she smiled wryly at how her heart was beating. In the kitchen Edo coated the small bodies of the snipe in a syrupy, dark sauce while from her corner the Labrador bitch looked at him be-seechingly. His thought was: How sudden desire makes solitude—not oppressive but unwieldy, and slightly ludicrous. It was a thought that had not come to him in the last few years—not since his last mistress had begun the inevitable transformation into a sardonic and too knowledgeable friend. Randy old billy goat, he said genially to himself, employing the words of that outspoken lady; and with the alertness he used to follow trails or sense changes in weather he noted that his hand was unsteady as he spooned the sauce.

The next day, Good Friday, they drove a hundred miles to Loch Ness and stood in the rain on a scallop of rocky shore. Edo broke off a rain-battered narcissus and handed it to Elizabeth in silence. He was wearing a khaki jacket with the collar turned up, and suddenly she saw him as he must have been forty years earlier: a thin, big-nosed young man with a grandee's posture—an image now closed within the man in front of her, like something in a reliquary.

On the drive back, he asked her abruptly whether she knew who he was, told her that his curious first name (Edo was the third in a procession) had set a prewar fashion for hundreds of babies whose mothers wanted to copy the choice of a princess. It was a rather pathetic thing to say, thought Elizabeth, who from Nestor knew all about him and the family, even down to alliances with various unsavory political regimes. Long beams of sunlight broke through over pastures where lambs jumped and ewes showed patches of red or blue dye on their backs, depending on which ram had covered them; shadows of clouds slid over the highlands in the distance. Edo drove her across a grouse moor and talked about drainage and pesticides and burning off old growth, about geese and partridge and snipe.

Then he said: "I want the two of us to have some kind of love story. Am I too old and deaf?"

"I don't know," said Elizabeth.

"I've quarreled with nearly everyone, I'm solitary and selfish, and I understand dogs better than women. I have been extremely promiscuous, but I have no known disease. That's just to prevent any misunderstanding."

"It doesn't sound very appealing."

"No, but I have a foolish, optimistic feeling that it might appeal to you. The thing I like most is a girl from a good family who dresses vulgarly once in a while. Nothing flashy—just the cook's night out. And schoolgirl underclothes, the kind the nuns made my sisters wear. Do you think you'd be willing to do that for me?"

"I might." Elizabeth felt as if she were about to burst with laughter. Everything seemed overly simple—as it did, she knew, at the beginning of the most harrowing romances. Yet, laughing inside, she felt curiously tender and indulgent toward him and toward herself. Why not? she thought. During the rest of the trip home they traded stories about former lovers with a bumptious ease startling under the circumstances, as if they were already old friends who themselves had gotten over the stage of going to bed. His were all bawdy and funny: making love to a fat Egyptian princess on a bathroom sink, which broke; an actress who cultivated three long, golden hairs on a mole in an intimate place.

The telephone rang before dinner that night, and it was Nestor. He was in France, in some place where there were a lot of people and the line kept dropping; he wanted to know whether Elizabeth had arrived. His uncle swore at him and said that no one—male, female, fish, or fowl—had arrived and that he was spending Easter alone. Then Edo slammed the phone down and looked at Elizabeth. "Now you're out of the world," he told her. "You're invisible and free."

They stood looking out of the sitting-room windows toward the northwest, where a veil of daylight still hung over the Atlantic, and he told her that when seals came ashore on the town beaches people went after them with rifles. He came closer to her, felt desire strike his body like a blow, called himself an old fool, and began to kiss her face. Her hair had a bland fragrance like grain, which called up a buried recollection of a story told him by his first, adored nurse (a Croat with a cast in one eye), about a magic sheaf of wheat that used to turn into a girl, he couldn't remember why or how. Elizabeth remained motionless and experienced for the first time the extraordinary sensation she was to have ever after with Edo: of snatching pleasure and concealing it. "We won't make love tonight," he said to her. "I've already had you in a hundred ways in my mind; I want to know if I can desire you even more. Prolonging anticipation—it's a very selfish taste I have. But without these little devices, I'll be honest with you, things get monotonous too quickly."

Later he told her not to worry, and she said happily, "But I'm not at all worried. In a few months we'll be sick to death of each other."

This arrival at Easter has become currency in Elizabeth's sentimental imagination, but unlike other episodes with other men it doesn't pop up to distract her during work or even very often when she's not working. She had never been anxious about Edo, but she wants to see him often. Though he is never calm, he calms her. When he sends for her and she takes the now familiar flight up to Aberdeen, she feels her life simplified with every moment in the air. It's a feeling like clothes slipping off her body.

She thinks of it this morning as she sits in the sunlight with her knees up under the covers, and she takes possession, a habit of hers, of a phrase from the book she is reading. "So the days pass," she reads, half aloud, "and I ask myself whether one is not hypnotized, as a child by a silver globe, by life, and whether this is living."

3. SPORTSMEN

For the last ten minutes Elizabeth, the old prince, and three young men have been sitting around the table talking about farts. The young men are Nestor and two cousins of his, whom Elizabeth knows slightly from parties in Rome. All three are tall and thin, with German faces and resonant Italian double last names; they wear threadbare American jeans and faded long-sleeved knit shirts. They are here for a few days' shooting, and in the front hall stand their boots—magnificent boots the color of chestnuts, handmade, lace-up, polished and repolished into the wavering luster of old furniture. The front hall itself is worth a description: wide, bare pine boards, a worn brocade armchair, antique decoys, a pair of antlers twenty thousand years old dug from a Hungarian bog, ten green jackets on wall pegs, exhaling scents of waxed canvas and dog.

The three young men worship Edo—since their nursery days he has been a storybook rakehell uncle, wreathed in a cloud of anecdote unusually thick even for their family. They are also very interested in Elizabeth—two of them because she's so good-looking, and Nestor from a piqued curiosity mixed with sincere affection. She has stopped confiding in him since he mischievously threw her together with his uncle at Easter. He owns the condominium next to the one she rents in Via dei Coronari and knows that she has been using a lot of vacation time going up to Scotland; he assumes that the old skinflint is laying out money for the tickets and that they're sleeping together, but he can't understand what they do for each other, what they do with each other. She is not an adventuress (in his world they still talk about adventuresses), and she is clearly not even infatuated. Elizabeth's non-whim, as he is starting to call it, only serves to confirm in Nestor's frivolous mind the impenetrable mystery that is America.

Elizabeth sits among them like a sphinx—something she learned from watching fashionable Italian women. But she feels conflicted, torn between generations. Edo feels a growing annoyance at seeing how her fresh face fits in among the fresh faces of the young men. Her presence makes the gathering effervescent and unstable, and all the men have perversely formed an alliance and are trying with almost touching transparency to shock her.

"It's a sixteenth-century gadget in copper called *la péteuse*," continues Edo in a gleeful, didactic tone. "It consists of a long, flexible metal tube that was used to convey nocturnal flatus out from between the buttocks, under the covers of the seigneurial bed, into a pot of perfumed water where rose petals floated. I own three of them—one in Paris and the other two in Turin. I keep them with the chastity belts."

Everyone is crunching and sucking the tiny bones of larks grilled on skewers, larks that the guests brought in a neat, foil-wrapped parcel straight from Italy, it being illegal to shoot songbirds in Great Britain. They eat them with toasted strips of polenta, also imported. Elizabeth hates small birds but is determined this evening to hold up the female side; she draws the line at the tiny, contorted heads, which make her think of holocausts and Dantean hells. Game, she thinks, is high in the kind of amino acids that foster gout and aggressive behavior.

"The worst case of flatulence I know of," Edo says, "was the Countess Pentz, a lady-in-waiting to my mother. She was a charming woman with nice big breasts, but she was short and ugly, and farted continuously. It was funny at receptions to see everyone pretending not to notice. I believe she used to wear a huge pair of padded bloomers that muffled the noise to a rumble like distant thunder."

They go on to discuss Hitler and meteorism. One of Nestor's cousins, Giangaleazzo, sends Elizabeth a swift glance of inquiry, perhaps of apology. There is something sweet about that look. Edo sees it and glowers. Elizabeth seizes the opportunity to contribute, mentioning—she realizes it's a mistake the minute she does—Chaucer. Blank looks from the men, although only Edo is truly uneducated. Edo says: "The middle classes always quote literature. It makes them feel secure."

Elizabeth has lived in Rome long enough to be able to throw back a cold-blooded barb of a retort, the kind they don't expect from an American woman. She knows that the young men aren't even surprised by Edo's remark, since it seems to be a family tradition to savage one another like a pack of wolf cubs. But she is looking at the row of restaurant knives and cleavers stuck in back of the long, oiled kitchen counter, and she is imagining the birds heaped in the freezer—small, gnarled bodies the color of cypress bark. She decides that she would like not simply to kill Edo but to gut him swiftly and surgically, the way she has watched him so many times draw a grouse.

When they have finished the larks and the young men are eating Kit Kat bars and drinking whiskey, they complete the fraternal atmosphere by launching into a *canzone goliarda*, a bawdy student song. This one has nearly twenty verses and is about a monk who confesses women on a stormy night and the various obscene penances he has them perform:

Con questa pioggia, questo vento,
Chi è chi bussa a mio convento?

Between verses Edo looks at her without remorse. He's thinking, She's tough, she holds up—which is one of his highest compliments. "You look like a wild animal when you get angry," he tells her, and she hates herself for the way her heart leaps. Just before midnight she lies in bed wondering whether he will come down to her. She will not go to him; she wants him to come to her room so she can treat him badly. She lies there feeling vengeful and willfully passive, imagining herself a Victorian servant girl waiting for the master to descend like Jove; at any minute she expects the doorknob to turn. But he doesn't come, and she falls asleep with the light on. At breakfast the next morning he greets her with great tenderness and tells her that he sat up till dawn with Nestor, discussing fishing rights on a family property in Spain.

4. HALLOWEEN

Bent double, Edo and Elizabeth creep through a stand of spindly larch and bilberry toward the pond where the wild geese are settling for the night. It is after four on a cold, clear afternoon, with the sun already behind the hills and a concentrated essence of leaf meal and wet earth rising headily at their footsteps—an elixir of autumn. Edo moves silently ahead of Elizabeth, never breaking a twig. His white head is drawn down into the collar of his green jacket, and his body is relaxed and intent, the way he has held it stalking game over the last fifty years in Yugoslavia, Tanzania, Persia.

Even before they could see the pond, when they were still in the Land Rover, chivying stolid Hertfordshire cows, and then on foot working open a gate that the tenant farmer had secured sloppily with a clothesline and a piece of iron bedstead—even then the air reverberated with the voices and wingbeats of the geese. The sound created a live force around the two of them, as if invisible spirits were bustling by in the wind. Now, from the corner of the grove, Edo and Elizabeth spy on two or three hundred geese in a crowd as thick and raucous as bathers on a city beach: preening, socializing, some pulling at sedges in the water of the murky little pond, others arriving from the sky in unraveling skeins, calling, wheeling, landing. Sometimes during the great fall and spring migrations, over two thousand at a time stop at Edo's pond.

He brought them here himself, using his encyclopedic knowledge of waterfowl to create a landscape he knew would attract them. He selected the unprepossessing, scrubby countryside after observation of topography and migratory patterns, and enlarged the weedy pond to fit an exact mental image of the shape and disposition needed to work together in a kind of sorcery to pull the lovely winged transients, pair by pair, out of the sky. After three years, the visiting geese have become a county curiosity. Local crofters have lodged repeated complaints. Edo doesn't shoot the geese; he watches them. This passion for the nobler game birds is the purest, most durable emotion he has known in his life; it was the same when he used to lie in wait for hours in order to kill them. Now he's had enough shooting, but the passion remains.

He grips Elizabeth's arm as he points out a pair of greylags in the garrulous crowd on the water. His hand on her arm is like stone, and Elizabeth, who loves going to watch the geese, nevertheless finds something brittle and old-maidish in the fixity of his interest. Crouching beside him, she experiences an arid sense of hopelessness, of jealousy—she isn't sure of what. Casting about, she thinks of his ex-lovers who sometimes call or visit—European women near his own age who seem to have absorbed some terrible erotic truth that they express in throaty laughter and an inhuman poise in the smoking of cigarettes and in the crossing of their still beautiful legs. They are possessive of Edo, and they make her feel raw as a nursery child brought out on display. But she knows they aren't the real reason that she feels cold around the heart.

"You're not interested in getting married, are you?" He says it abruptly, once they have returned to the Land Rover. He says it in French, his language for problems, reasoning, and resolution. He hears his own terror and looks irritably away from her. It is six months since they met.

"No, I'm not," replies Elizabeth. She is embarrassed by the fatuous promptness with which the words bound out, like a grade-school recitation. Yet she hadn't prepared them. She hadn't prepared anything. They are bouncing across stubble, and to the west, where the evening light is stronger, a few green patches shine with weird intensity among the autumn browns: barley fields planted this month to be harvested in January or February. On the horizon, below a small, spiky gray cloud, a bright planet regards them equably. Without another word, Edo stops the motor and reaches over to unzip her jacket and unbutton her shirt. With the same rapt, careful movements he used in approaching the geese, he bends his head and kisses her breasts. Then he straightens up and looks at her and a strange thing happens: each understands that they've both been stealing pleasure. For a second they are standing face-to-face in a glass corridor; they see everything. It's a minor miracle that is over before they can realize that it is the most they will have together. Instantly afterward, there is only the sense of a bright presence already departed, and the two of them faltering near the edge of an indefinable danger. As Elizabeth buttons her shirt and Edo turns the ignition key, they are already engaged in small, expert movements of denial and retreat. The jeep pulls out onto the darkening road, and neither finds a further word to say.

A tumult of wind and dogs greets them as they pull up ten minutes later to the house. Dervishes of leaves spin on the gravel beside the rented Suzuki that Nestor and his cousins used to get to that day's shoot, near Guthrie. Both Elizabeth and Edo stare in surprise at the kitchen windows, where there is an unusual glow. It looks like something on fire, and for an instant Edo has the sensation of disaster—a conflagration not of his house, nothing so real, but a mirage of a burning city, a sign transplanted from a dream.

"What have they gotten up to, the young jackasses?" he says, climbing hurriedly out of the jeep. But Elizabeth sees quite clearly what Nestor and his cousins have done and, with an odd sense of relief, starts to giggle. They've carved four pumpkins with horrible faces, put candles inside, and lined them up on the windowsills. She interprets it as a message to her, since yesterday she and Gianga-leazzo, who went to Brown, had been talking about Halloween in

New England. "It's Halloween," she says, in a voice pitched a shade too high. She feels a sudden defensive solidarity with the jumble of young men in the kitchen, who are drinking Guinness and snuffing like hungry retrievers under the lids of the saucepans.

"Jackasses," repeats Edo, who at the best of times defines as gross presumption any practical joke he hasn't thought up himself. In this mood, his superstitious mind is shaken, and he can't cast off that disastrous first vision. He hurries inside, telling her to follow him.

Instead, Elizabeth lets the door close and lingers outside, looking at the glowing vegetable faces and feeling the cold wind shove her hair back from her forehead. She wills herself not to think of Edo. Instead she thinks of a Halloween in Dover when she was eight or nine and stood for a long time on the doorstep of her own house after her brothers and everyone else had gone inside. The two big elms leaned over the moon, and the jack-o'-lantern in the front window had a thick dribble of wax depending from its grin, and she had had to pee badly, but she had kept standing there, feeling the urine pressing down in her bladder, clutching a cold hand between her legs where the black cheesecloth of her witch costume bunched together. She'd stood there feeling excitement and terror at the small, dark world she had created around herself simply by holding back. It's an erotic memory that she has always felt vaguely ashamed of, but at the moment it seems curiously appropriate, a pleasure she'd enjoyed without guessing its nature.

Edo opens the kitchen door and calls her, and she comes toward him across the gravel. For a moment before he can see her clearly, he has the idea that there is a difference in the way she is moving, that her face may hold an expression that will change everything. Once, thirty years ago, in Persia, he and his brother Prospero saw a ball of dust coming toward them over the desert, a ball of dust that pulled up in front of them and turned into a Rolls-Royce, with a body made, impossibly, of wicker, and, inside, two young Persian noblemen, their friends, laughing, with falcons on their wrists. He and his brother and the gunbearers had stood there as if in front of something conjured up by djinns. He watches Elizabeth come with the same stilling of the senses as he had that afternoon in the desert. When she gets closer, though, the dust, as it were, settles, and his wavering perspective returns to normal, there on the doorstep of his last, his favorite house, in the cold October night. He thinks of the unspoken bargain she has kept so magnificently for a woman of her age, for any woman, and he says to himself, Very well. He has studied nature too long to denigrate necessity. Then why the word thudding inside him, first like an appeal, then a pronouncement: "Never, never, never"? Never, then.

Laughter comes from behind him. His nephews to summon him have launched into the ribald student song from the other night. When Elizabeth reaches him, he doesn't look anymore but takes her arm firmly, draws her inside, and shuts the door.

The Prior's Room

This was the East of the ancient navigators, so old, so mysterious, resplendent and somber, living and unchanged, full of danger and promise.

What next? I thought. Now, this is something like. This is great.

—Joseph Conrad, "Youth"

Anna Meehan, an American girl seated at lunch with a French father and son, is basking in this common but blissful discovery: what happens sometimes, when you disobey your mother, is that the world turns inside out. She hasn't specifically disobeyed—her mother, still asleep across the Atlantic in Rose Tree, Pennsylvania, never forbade her to take off from her summer language program with five minutes' notice to join a Parisian boy she's barely met at an Alpine resort—yet she knows that every parent on the planet would be opposed to the idea, including the Swiss surrogates who patrol her dormitory at the Cours d'Été of the University of Lausanne.

Anna is a recent high school graduate with honors, bound in September for a college with a renowned department of Romance languages. She is also the youngest of three pretty sisters, each of whom displays a different striking conjunction of the traits of their mother's part-Filipino family and their father's Irish-and-Polish clan. So pretty is Anna and so ingenuous does she seem that her Rosales grandparents shied away from giving her a post-graduation summer in Paris and, instead, sent her to polish her French in tamer surroundings. She's been bored silly in Switzerland, and now that she has kicked over the traces she wonders what took her so long. It was shockingly easy: she accepted a telephone invitation, and now she sits on the other side of the French border, the cynosure of a table glittering with crystal and heavy silver, with a galaxy of waiters hovering and a pair of well-dressed foreign men offering her highly detailed compliments as if they were choice hors d'oeuvres. Revelation has followed revelation: her freckles, for instance, which her hosts say they find seductive. Who would have guessed that the commonplace inscription in brown spots over the bridge of her nose could be subtitled as the gorgeously sibilant, the rich and strange *taches de rousseur? Taches*, she knows, means "stains"—a vague flavor of Lady Macbeth that only makes the translation more delectable.

Another revelation is the restaurant around her: a three-star shrine on the shores of the Lac d'Annecy. It is about one o'clock on a Saturday afternoon at the end of August, and outside the panoramic windows a merciless late-summer sun illuminates the double blue of lake and sky around the bare peaks and pastures of the Savoy region; by contrast, the smoky air in the paneled, upholstered dining room filled with vacationing Europeans is like a bouillon of civilization, a concentrated essence. She will recall it, much later in her life, as Paradise—a standard by which sensual well-being will be measured forever afterward, stamped indelibly in her heart as she sips a house cocktail called Le Lac, a blue curaçao confection that through some casual triumph of artifice exactly reproduces the dominant color of the scene outside.

Anna is no bumpkin: she and her sisters have been dragged thriftily around the capitals of Europe by their parents, a pair of academics who have always displayed the proper American reverence for garlic and old stones, and occasionally even sprung for a fancy meal. And she recognizes the setting from the half-dozen films that have formed part of the prolonged and expensive process of establishing in her soul a small outpost of French culture. She recalls one film in particular: a summer resort, cherry trees, bored men, beautiful neurasthenic women, a tantalizing hint of obsession. Now, suddenly, it is as if she had stepped into the film, as if all those years of conjugating irregular verbs within the excellent Rose Tree Media School District had been preparation for this moment—yes, this very moment, as she holds her blue drink and lifts her eighteen-year-old face to the older Frenchman, whose experienced eye and extravagant praise suggest a wealthy amateur horticulturalist admiring a prize bloom.

Only her clothes, Anna knows, are wrong. She is wearing a pair of heavy tights she uses for ballet, a denim skirt, a tank top, and a pair of sensible Bass sandals that her mother insisted she buy at Campus Corner before she left home. It is the late nineteen seventies, and the other girls and women in the restaurant are all exquisitely dressed in sweeping flowered skirts or elegant tight pants, and sandals or even summer boots with towering heels. When she got out of the taxi this morning, there was a perceptible wince on the part of father and son as they caught sight of her outfit. They are both wearing immaculate jeans and sports jackets, with pale cashmere sweaters thrown over their shoulders. The older man, whose name is Olivier, is at the age that to Anna is simply how old parents and teachers are. He is small and paunchy but strangely emphatic, with a round flat face, a pointed nose, bright green-brown eyes, and wispy colorless hair cut in a precise fringe across his forehead. The son, nineteen years old and much taller, is called Étienne, and he is flat-faced like his father but with a protruding Adam's apple and blue eyes and a sheeplike tangle of fair curls that she found unattractive when they first met, a few weeks ago, on the flight from Newark to Geneva. At the back of the plane, near the toilets, they talked for twenty minutes in unoccupied seats, and then, after they had exchanged phone numbers, he annoyed her by trying to kiss her, an attempt she thwarted with an expert but not unfriendly shove.

She forgot all about him in the bustle of arrival, of settling into the program in Lausanne: the criminally dull classes in a Calvinist-gray building; the hikes straight out of Scout camp, punctuated with hearty choruses of "Chevaliers de la Table Ronde"; the cook-outs with veal sausages from Migros supermarket; the excursions to Ouchy and the Château de Chillon; the dawning realization that she was still just an American in a mass of Americans, and that Europe was somewhere else. Until this morning, when her roommate Sarah, from Pittsfield, Massachusetts, yelled to her that she had a call, and she held the smooth, heavy receiver and found that it was not her parents or her jealous boyfriend. Instead, it was a voice speaking French, and sounding far more attractive than it had on the plane. Hello, hello, the boy said. We are near you—my father and I. We are at the most beautiful place for the weekend, just across the mountains. Will you join us? Please!

Anna giggled into the phone—her French acquiring a sudden fluency that had eluded her in her classes—that she had no way of getting there, whereupon he said, quite matter-of-factly, Well, take a taxi. He meant, she realized, take a taxi over the mountains and across the border into France.

And after that began a sustained act of nerve. A string of decisions in which Anna was more absolutely alone than she had ever been—even in the spring semester of her junior year, when she used to tell all those lies about dentist visits so that she could spend long afternoons in the back of Mark Florio's van. Saying nothing to her roommates, she brushed her hair until it shone, washed her face, and tossed a pair of underpants, her birth-control pills, her passport, and all the money she had into an Indian shoulder bag printed with elephants. Then she left the dreary dormitory, with its cramped steel balconies and scanty fringe of pines, and walked down to the train station, where in the lineup of taxis she located a driver who didn't look as if he would rape and abandon her in the middle of the Alps. Instinctively, she knew what to do. She gave the directions in a tone that she hoped sounded like that of someone used to casual international taxi trips of an hour or two, and kept her spine straight and her chin up in the backseat, as the taxi wound up and down high passes and through tunnels, and the landscape became more desolate and glorious. She tried not to imagine what would happen if the French boy didn't pay the fare that was mounting so alarmingly on the meter; if it were all a practical joke and the taxi driver never found the small lakeside village and hotel whose names she'd scribbled on a piece of paper; what her mother—tiny and fragile but nicknamed the Enforcer by her daughters—would say, crackling furiously over long-distance lines, when she found out that Anna had squandered three weeks' worth of traveler's checks on a taxi ride. As they raced past vineyards and geranium-bedecked villages, Anna sat mentally counting the cash she had and wondering whether the driver would take her watch and Eurail pass and the diamond-stud earrings she had been given for graduation.

Then, suddenly, it was over: the taxi pulled up in front of a hotel, in a cobblestoned courtyard with an old well and clipped golden trees, the lake a jewel in the background, so different from Lake Geneva. And the tall blond boy was there, eagerly opening the car door, and the small father wafted the driver and her terror away with a fistful of francs. She had arrived where she was meant to be, where she had been heading all her life. And though they winced at her clothes, they were immediately complimentary. Ravishing, the father said, clapping his son on the back as if they had settled a bet. Very American, as you said, but with something more. He made a rectangle with the fingers and thumbs of both hands and peered through it as if through a camera. A very definite something, he added.

Now, at lunch, they even praise Anna for her good appetite, as if eating were somehow a rare talent. Eating course after extra-ordinary course with flavors intensified by their incantatory names: *feuillantine d'escargots à l'achillée et pimprenelle; rissoles de poires aux fruits secs et sabayon*. And wines: Chignin-Bergeron, Mondeuse. And coffee, and a plate of little squashy pastries that she wants to snatch and stuff into her elephant bag. She devours them and the chocolate truffles that follow, taking fewer than she'd like, forcing herself for the sake of decency to pause between each one. She tries an old liqueur from a bottle with spidery writing on the label, and it gives her throat a hot glazed feeling as she listens to the father talk about politics. There has been an election, an important one, and he has had something to do with it. It doesn't interest Anna, but it gives resonance to the cloud of language around her, gives her the sense that she has stepped into a realm where high deeds are performed by grave men in dark ambassadorial suits, and the fates of nations decided.

When the father sees her straining to look attentive, he immediately stops talking about politics and switches back to compliments. How small her wrists are; how instinctively well she chose her food; what a wonderful university she will attend next fall—yes, he knows the name; who does not?—how remarkable that she speaks French with such ease and can even recognize a reference to Mallarmé: *le vierge, le vivace et le bel aujourd'hui*. The son says little, staring at both his father and Anna. Occasionally he shows off by speaking in stilted nasal English. The father asks about Anna's family and laughs as she describes her sisters: Barb the saint, who is playing the guitar on a Catholic youth tour this summer; Becca the slut, with her secret tattoo, whose boyfriends always end up going after Anna. Described in French they sound somehow fascinating, not boring or sleazy at all. Three beautiful sisters, the father laughs. Like something out of the Brothers Grimm.

The restaurant is a short walk from the hotel, and they stroll back in the dazzling sunlight as speedboats drone far out on the water. The hotel is a low ivy-covered building that wraps around the courtyard where the taxi arrived. It has small arched windows set deep in stone, and palm trees in pots, and an air of fitting the spot where it sits between the village and the lake promenade as a diamond fits the setting of a ring. It is called the Clos Saint Barthélemy and was once, the father says, a Benedictine abbey, built by the monks expelled from Geneva during the Reformation. Anna pays little attention to this, because as they walk the son is squeezing her hand. She feels tipsy and reckless, her head swelled like a balloon by all the homage. She is drawn to this boy, whom she had judged dull and strange-looking earlier, but who now seems like one of the lords of the earth.

It is unclear what is going to happen. Three in the afternoon after an epic meal: obviously time for a rest. They talk of this in the hotel lobby, another oasis of polished wood and mandarin-faced servitors. The father—Anna has begun to call him Olivier, though she continues to address him with a formal *vous*—proposes with some hesitancy that she spend the rest of the day and the night there at the lake, and that the next day he and his son will make a detour from their drive to Paris and take her back to Lausanne. The hesitancy, she realizes, in one of her few accurate feats of perception all day, is because Olivier is suddenly faced with an ironclad obligation: he must treat her as the proper young girl he has, despite all her efforts, understood her to be. An image she wants to toss aside completely. From a very early age, for all her angelic looks, Anna has on occasion displayed a calm, almost casual inclination to step far outside the usual limits, a trait that has alarmed her sisters—even Becca the slut—and boyfriends alike. It's at work now: at this point she would agree to anything, from more wine and compliments to stripping naked and celebrating a Black Mass.

Of course, she says impatiently, she will stay. At this the son, with his sheep's face and curls, puts his arm around her and kisses her cheek with a ceremonious air, as if she were a cherished young bride. And the father spreads his arms in a delicate sketch of an embrace that includes them both, and says, in a magnanimous paternal tone, So, children. You would like a room; *cela saute aux yeux*. You can have the special one I reserved. It is such a rarity that it even has a name—La Chambre du Prieur—and I do hope you will appreciate it. He asks for Anna's passport and goes to the desk to reserve

another room for himself and inform them that mademoiselle will
be staying.

In the elevator, Anna kisses the son, Étienne. It's not as glorious
a kiss as it should be: his lips and tongue feel oddly wooden. But
none of that matters when he leads her down a hall to a door with a
gold handle—the key swings from a fat silk tassel—which opens to
reveal a wonderful room, a room that is like a chapel, a cave whose
walls and ceilings are covered with a swarm of painted figures.
Amber, red, blue, green, both somber and resplendent. Frescoes of
saints and angels and Biblical throngs, curling vines and dim gilded
fruit running in and out of the hollows of a coffered ceiling. Deep
red rugs, a bed with a velvet canopy and cover, old paneling shining with wax. This is the room where the prior—a rather sybaritic
prior—ran the affairs of the old abbey hundreds of years ago. The
sumptuous apparition takes Anna by surprise, and for a second she
is unable to speak. It is the first time that she has been in a room of
such splendor without a museum rope to keep her from touching
things. This is the first time, actually, that she has even been in a
hotel room not paid for by her parents. But she quickly rises to the
occasion, as she has been doing all day. She feels, in fact, that she
was born to rise to such occasions.

She and Étienne stand by the window; they kiss, they kiss more,
and then they undress clumsily and make love in haste, yanking
back the velvet cover on the bed and flinging themselves on heavy
linen sheets knobby with embroidery. Anna doesn't enjoy it much,
except as an appropriate element of the intoxication of the day, the
frantic sense of life converging at the place where she is. She liked
the pastries at lunch more. She thinks briefly about her boyfriend
and the other boys back home, about wilder times in places that
were sometimes awful and uncomfortable. But one thing she en-

joys: how beautiful the two of them are, naked, in the beautiful room, how they complete it. The French boy has hairless pink skin more delicate than her own. After each orgasm his chest remains mottled for a long time with a bright-red flush. His penis is pink and large, though it seems somehow childish to her, a novelty because it is uncircumcised. In bed, he gives up the stilted English he is so proud of and talks to her in French. Away from his father, he is more commanding: he comments knowledgeably on her body and its loveliness, with finicky precision spreads her open, makes her display herself to him.

They exchange life stories. She tells him about the taunts she and her sisters endured growing up in a mixed-race family in the suburbs. He tells her about the taunts he endured as a boy, in a provincial town in the Ile-de-France, because his parents had never married. Curiously enough, these confidences don't make them feel closer; instead, they thicken the peculiar mist between them that might be called "glamour"—the opacity that makes them more attractive to each other. He tells her how his father, who left the provinces and got rich doing something with newspapers and politicians, took him off to Paris at age seventeen to be an apprentice at *Le Figaro*. He brags about the trips he takes to Dakar and Marrakech, and describes an extravagant and disorderly bachelor life in Paris. Eventually, he tells her that he loves her. She trembles and embraces him tightly at this, not because she is moved but because she wants to shake off the tepidness of her own response, to quash a tiny commonsensical voice in the back of her mind which remarks that he must be slightly feebleminded to blurt it out like that. In a tone whose decisiveness, although she does not know it, exactly resembles that of her mother, the Enforcer, Anna says that she loves him, too. In French, which makes it sound so different, so much more important.

They fall asleep and wake up and then sleep again, and after a while it is like being bound and gagged in silk. She is aware only of a series of isolated flashes: his rough curly head, the sound of a horn from the lake, the mineral water they gulp down, the soreness between her legs when she splashes awkwardly in the bidet, how in the deepening light the figures in the frescoes seem to lean out of the walls.

At six o'clock, Étienne says that they should go and join his father. They dress, and he says, You know, I'd like to buy you some nicer underwear. Like French girls wear. White, blue, with lace. He doesn't let her put on her clumsy skirt and tights. He says, Here, wear my jeans. I have another pair with me. Now you look gorgeous. Like a French girl. She lets him zip the jeans up, as if he were a lady's maid. They are heavy denim, completely different from American jeans, and they hang loosely but handsomely on her slender hips. By the way, he says as he opens his bag, My father is a misogynist—do you know what that is? He dislikes women, but he really seems to admire you. Not like most of the girls I introduce to him. Isn't that lucky?

Anna is studying herself within the tessellated gilt frame of a mirror. Complete, as if in an old portrait, she sees a girl in French jeans, her long hair in place, her *taches de rousseur*, her mascara-smudged eyes, and she doesn't answer, because he doesn't seem to expect a reply.

Then they go downstairs and through the lobby, feeling the hotel staff and the well-dressed loiterers watching, observing with approval because the two of them are young and handsome and have clearly been in bed all afternoon. Anna thinks back to an Elizabethan poem she studied in A.P. English the previous fall, in which the poet describes the circles within circles of creation: Heaven, nature, the newly discovered continents, all of civilization revolving around a pair of lovers on a bed. This was what the painted bedroom, the famous restaurant, the omniscient faces of the concierge and the maître d', the mountains and the lake were created for—as a setting for the small naked object that she and this boy make when they are joined together.

Étienne is behaving like a proper boyfriend now; he wears a stunned expression of bliss while he strolls with his arm tight around her. The sun is beginning to set as they enter the village and pass into a small square where they find his father sitting in a café. Beside him, smiling, is a swarthy young man in a khaki military uniform, who seems hardly older than Étienne. Both the young man and Olivier are drinking glasses of something cloudy, and they are chatting so merrily and confidingly as Anna and Étienne arrive that Anna supposes the soldier must be a family friend, encountered by chance. But no—Olivier introduces him as Paul, and says that he met him a half hour ago, when Paul's platoon band gave a Saturday-afternoon concert. Paul played the trombone. And I could see he was a very promising young man, Olivier says, in a teasing voice. Paul the soldier turns red at this. He looks as if he might be part Turkish or Algerian, with a melon-shaped head on which his shaved hair makes a bluish shadow, round olive cheeks, jug ears, and a pair of melting brown eyes with bizarrely long eyelashes.

Anna and Étienne sit down at the table and order two more of the cloudy drinks. It is Anna's first Pernod: with the ghostly licorice taste in her mouth she feels as if she were living in the pages of her sixth-grade French textbook, where Monsieur LeBrun meets Monsieur LeBlanc *pour l'apéritif.* Étienne acts satisfyingly infatuated, and keeps staring at her, playing with her hands, praising the way she looks in his jeans. The lake is red in the glow from behind the mountains, and elegant people are walking by and sitting around them. Anna spots a tall woman with gold hair piled in a rigid construction of knobs on the back of her head, and a pink suit trimmed in white leather. The woman is intensely beautiful in an adult way that Anna has never seen back home, and Anna announces that she wants to look like that when she's older.

You will if you want to, Olivier says. But you have to be at least forty, and you have to know certain things, to be beautiful like that. His eyes cross Anna's and offer a momentary bland challenge, which for the first time that day gives her the sensation of danger.

The atmosphere has shifted now that the soldier is there. Anna did not expect to step into Paradise when she took the taxi across the mountains, but she quickly got used to it. These people were complete strangers, but they offered her instant worship. Greedily, she expected it to continue. But the focus has changed, and not because of Étienne but because of his father. As at lunch, Olivier sits at the table offering a constant stream of sophisticated compliments—but they are all for the round-faced, jug-eared, red-cheeked soldier. Paul, it seems, is a handsome boy, an extraordinary boy, an intelligent boy, even a brilliant boy. All this is observed in the older man's cool voice, as he smokes cigarette after cigarette. He pauses once to eye his son and Anna benevolently. Ah, one can tell that the children had a very good time this afternoon. There is that slight flush, that delicate, weary bloom. Did you like La Chambre du Prieur, my dears?

All through dinner, which they eat at the hotel—in another grand restaurant, filled with rich weekenders and foie gras and syrupy golden light—it is the same thing, the almost suffocating string of compliments directed at the soldier, who continues to blush and duck his head. Anna knows from books and films that men make love to other men, but this is more like a complicated game whose rules she doesn't understand. Words like "innuendo" drift through her mind, though the older man is quite straightforward about what he is doing. She studies Olivier, who seems ageless in his jeans and soft sweater and jacket; the skin of his face full and radiant, his nose as pointed as Pinocchio's, his moss-green eyes somehow sad and querulous, even when his voice is at its most caressing. The flattery intensifies, becomes almost Baroque, and it is as if the older man were amusing himself at the expense of the three young people sitting around him, even though he keeps his gaze fixed, with precise intent, on the soldier. As for his son, Étienne, he has fallen by the wayside: he continues to talk charmingly to Anna both in English and in French, to gaze at her, to caress her knees under the table, but at the same time she can feel a careful blankness in his manner, a deliberate unseeing aimed in his father's direction. Anna orders curried soup and guinea hen cooked with wild mushrooms; she eats caramelized pineapple and drinks verbena tea. For this last she is praised by father and son—We think a girl who drinks a tisane after dinner is very refined—but it is clear that no clever thing she does will make her the star of the show again.

She and Étienne excuse themselves finally, but Olivier says jovially that he thinks he'll stay downstairs in the bar to chat with his new soldier friend. He rises and gives his son and Anna a warm kiss on each cheek, and Anna for an instant has an urge to slap his face. Only much later in her life will she ask herself whether she had expected him to make love to her, too. Right now she feels toward Olivier the kind of furious disappointment that up to this moment she has felt only when very angry at her parents. As for the interloping soldier, Paul, she can't even look at him; he might give her a familiar smirk or a wink of complicity, and that would be unbearable.

Upstairs, in the Prior's Room, the curtains have been drawn and the bed turned down for the night. And once more between the linen sheets she and Étienne hold each other like fretful children. Anna feels stuffed and queasy from all the eating and drinking, and sore from making love too much. Also, she is suddenly sick of Étienne, of his blond smell that is infantile and a little off, like week-old milk, of the fact that he is the only reason she has for being here in this magnificent room. She can't see her watch, but she knows it is too early or too late to leave. The windows are shuttered tight in the European way, the way they do it back at her dormitory. She is a prisoner here for the night, in a luxury cell. She thinks with nostalgia of her roommates in Lausanne, who have no doubt spent the weekend visiting the public pool, sipping bad beer in the tourist bars down at Ouchy, dancing with South Americans at the horrible student discothèque, Le Treizième Siècle. She is having the adventure that all those daydreaming American girls long for, and it has consumed her, left behind only this small point of alien consciousness, alight in a vigil amid the mountains, the past, the Old Country.

It is probable that Ètienne feels sick of her, too. They have made love in every possible position. He has described to her what hard work it was, back in Paris, introducing his ex-girlfriend to oral sex; confided that he thinks he got a Spanish girl pregnant on a vacation in the Balearics, and that he has to perform a ritual act of masturbation every night before going to sleep. With the air of passing on great chunks of wisdom, he has even entrusted to her several crackpot theories about America—that the wrong side won the Civil War, for one—and he has praised bad American movies and horrendous rock and roll that nobody Anna knows would be caught dead listening to. And Anna, instead of bursting out laughing and telling him that he is full of shit, as she would have done with any boy back home, has listened with solemn attention.

Now they lie in a halfhearted embrace, neither sleeping nor talking, until Étienne moves his legs restlessly and complains of a stomachache. It was the fish, perhaps, he opines, in a way that Anna doesn't yet know is very Gallic. My father has something for an upset stomach. I should go and ask him. I'll just pull on some clothes. Étienne sits up in bed, his pink muscular shoulders looking as new as those of a plastic doll against the lamplight. He swings his legs out of the bed. But then he pauses and looks for an instant back over his shoulder at Anna. There is no expression at all in his round blue eyes. *Non, je ne vais pas*, he says. I won't go. I'd wake him. He wouldn't mind, of course, but—He breaks off, and Anna can clearly picture the melon-shaped head of Paul the soldier, with his smudge of shaved hair and preposterous eyelashes. The steadfast tin soldier, she thinks for some reason, and for a moment she feels sorry for Étienne. He slowly gets back into bed, and there is nothing for the two of them to do but make love again, which they do without any pretense of tenderness until Anna feels scraped raw. Afterward, though, she sleeps so soundly that even a summer storm over the lake barely disturbs her.

Sunday morning they awaken late, and then eat a huge breakfast, naked, at the window overlooking the lake, which lies flat under a newly washed sky as church bells resound from the mountain villages. Things are wonderful again. Étienne shows Anna how to sip her chocolate through a lump of sugar, and she piles her bread with a half-inch layer of butter that has an elusively fresh taste, like pastures, a taste she can't get enough of. She just has to gobble it and gobble it. She thinks it is the best breakfast she has ever had, and the taste is sharpened by regret because they have to dress and go. Étienne makes her a present of the jeans, and she privately vows not to wash them for the rest of the summer. Then they leave the room and go down to meet Olivier, who is sitting alone reading *Les Nouvelles Littéraires*. He is impeccably brushed and shaved and cheerful, dressed this morning in moleskin trousers and yet another handsome sweater. *Et voici les enfants*, he says, with a real look of pleasure at the sight of them. Fresh from your honeymoon. There is no sign and no mention made of Paul. Anna, smiling forgiveness at Olivier, can almost believe that the soldier was only a ghost, perhaps a figure from the Prior's Room who had stepped out of a painting in the night and vanished at sunrise.

They get into the car, a large shining sedan delivered reverently to them by the hotel attendant. And swaddled in the scent of leather they head over the mountains toward Lausanne and her student life. She and Étienne sit in the backseat—Olivier makes a half-serious complaint about having to play chauffeur—and kiss. All at once, she feels madly in love. Below them, the Lac d'Annecy is getting smaller. Étienne quotes yet another terrible American rock song and begs her—as his father's head twitches skeptically in the driver's seat—to come and live with him in Paris once she has finished her summer course. Though she knows that it won't happen, this proposal puts the cap on Anna's satisfaction: she imagines a garret in twilight, a glittering net of boulevards, and a lover at her side who is not exactly Étienne but just as French. And with this new image in her mind she strains her neck to look back at the lake for the last time for approximately twenty years.

After that time passes, she'll come back to Clos Saint Barthélemy and even sleep in the Prior's Room. She will come back with a European husband—one might almost call him the product of this earlier visit: a kind, conservative man who is still enough in love with her to sulk when she tells him that she actually spent a night here once before. She will come back fully educated, well employed and well dressed—if not as well as the woman in pink—familiar with the regional wines and cuisine, the *goût de terroir*. She'll be able to distinguish between the different gradations of prosperous Frenchmen and Germans and Italians, and will understand what red-cheeked soldiers and young American girls mean to them. And as a mother herself she'll give a private shudder at the chance she took so many years before, throwing her lot in so unquestioningly with that curious father and son. The singular pair she never heard from again, who for all their crotchets turned out to be generous and benevolent gatekeepers to the world that has become hers.

And only at night, when the shutters are closed—the hangings in the Chambre de Prieur have been changed from ocher to leaf-green, the frescoes expertly restored, the bathroom remodeled, and a minibar added—will she admit to herself how dreadfully dull the room is now. She'll glance at the painted saints around her and remember—not for long, because otherwise it becomes depressing—how she once had a body so perfect that they leaned out of the walls to look at it. And how she lay under the decorated beams with legs and mouth open to take in the foreignness and the mystery, her appetite the measure of her ignorance; alive in the glory, possible only then, of being hungry, hungry, hungry.

For inspiration and moral support, I would like to thank Amanda Urban, Lee Boudreaux, Courtney Hodell, Dan Menaker, Alice Quinn, Bill Buford, Hilton Als, Helen Garner, Elinor Schiele, Catharine Lencíone, Susie Ropolo, Laura Anderson, Sherry Davis, Sarah Parsons, Kit Parsons, Michael Chisholm, Nancy Wilson and many others of the Baldwin School, Mabel Rooks Taylor, Lucy Rooks Hall, Mabel Lee Revaleon, and the rest of the Lee-Jacob-Bartolomeo-Taylor clan.

About the Author

Andrea Lee is also the author of the novels *Red Island House*, *Lost Hearts in Italy*, and *Sarah Phillips*, and the National Book Award–nominated memoir *Russian Journal*. A former staff writer for *The New Yorker*, she has written for the *New York Times Magazine*, *Vogue*, *W*, and the *New York Times Book Review*. Born in Philadelphia, she received her bachelor's and master's degrees from Harvard University and lives in Turin, Italy.